DARK TERRITORY

Center Point
Large Print

Also by Terrence McCauley and available from Center Point Large Print:

Where the Bullets Fly

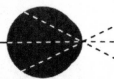

This Large Print Book carries the Seal of Approval of N.A.V.H.

Dark Territory

A Sheriff Aaron Mackey Western

Terrence McCauley

Center Point Large Print
Thorndike, Maine

This Center Point Large Print edition
is published in the year 2019 by arrangement with
Kensington Publishing Corp.

The text of this Large Print edition is unabridged.
In other aspects, this book may vary
from the original edition.
Printed in the United States of America
on permanent paper.
Set in 16-point Times New Roman type.

ISBN: 978-1-64358-234-4

Library of Congress Cataloging-in-Publication Data

Names: McCauley, Terrence, author.
Title: Dark territory : a Sheriff Aaron Mackey western /
    Terrence McCauley.
Description: Center Point Large Print edition. | Thorndike, Maine :
    Center Point Large Print, 2019.
Identifiers: LCCN 2019012164 | ISBN 9781643582344 (hardcover :
    alk. paper)
Subjects: LCSH: Large type books. | GSAFD: Western stories.
Classification: LCC PS3613.C356894 D37 2019 | DDC 813/.6—dc23
LC record available at https://lccn.loc.gov/2019012164

Chapter 1

Dover Station, Montana, late fall of 1888

Sheriff Aaron Mackey and Deputy Billy Sunday came running when they heard the shotgun blast from Tent City.

Mackey was not surprised to find one of the Bollard twins blocking the end of the alley between the new Municipal Building under construction and the old bakery on Second Street.

Since the man was facing the other way, Mackey could not tell which Bollard twin it was, not that it mattered. Both buffalo skinners were as big as they were mean, with the same bald head and long greasy black hair that hung practically to their shoulders.

Whichever twin this was, he was holding a smoking double-barreled shotgun at the end of the narrow alley. He was most likely drunk, too, given the way he was swaying.

The crowd that had gathered booed when the sheriff ran toward him and slammed the butt of his Winchester into the back of the bigger man's skull. Bollard timbered forward into the dense mud of Second Street. Mackey yanked the shotgun from beneath the fallen man and handed it to Billy.

His deputy opened the shotgun. "Both barrels are spent." He cast the shotgun aside. "I'll cover you from here."

The sheriff stepped over one Bollard twin to confront the other on Second Street; the heart of what had become known as Tent City. He almost gagged at the stench of over-boiled meat and drying laundry filling the cold air as he pushed through the bedraggled crowd that had gathered to watch the spectacle.

The rapid growth of Dover Station thanks to investment from the Dover Station Company had attracted too many people looking for work and not enough places to live, hence the creation of Tent City. Many who lived there had plenty of money in the bank, but nowhere to spend it except the saloons and joy houses. Such squalor tended to breed a misery of its own devising, and Tent City was no exception. They never had much occasion to cheer and made the most of it when they did.

They were cheering now.

Mackey saw the other Bollard brother was putting on quite a show, standing over a man bleeding from the kind of chest wound only a shotgun blast could make. Surprisingly, the victim was not dead yet and was doing his best to squirm free from the giant looming over him with a skinning knife.

Mackey, tall and lean, turned sideways to make

himself harder to hit if Bollard pulled a gun. It also made it easier for Mackey to draw and fire the Peacemaker holstered next to his buckle if it came to that. But the sheriff made a point of keeping the barrel of the Winchester down. No sense in forcing Bollard to act and make a bad situation worse.

"Drop the knife and step away from the man, Bollard," Mackey called out. "Right now."

The crowd booed, and the big man held his ground. "Not on your life, sheriff. Not after what he done. Stabbin' my brother? Sneakin' around, stealin' other people's goods? T'aint right and you damn well knows it."

Mackey kept his eyes on Bollard when he heard Doc Ridley yelling from the boardwalk across the thoroughfare. "That man is still alive. I might be able to save him, Aaron. Get that animal away from him!"

Bollard pointed his knife at the acting mayor of Dover Station. "Don't go calling me no animal, you little bastard. Check on my brother's wounds if'n you want to be useful."

Then he pointed the knife at Mackey. "And you had no call to buffalo my brother like you done. Tom's already hurtin' and was well within his rights to shoot this son of a bitch I got right here."

The crowd of Tent City grumbled in support. Keeping his eyes on Bollard, Mackey spoke over his shoulder to his deputy. "Check on Tom for me."

"Already did," the black man whispered. "Given the amount of blood pooling into the mud around his belly, I'd say he was gutted. Can't tell for certain, but I think he's dead. Slamming that rifle butt into him probably didn't help much, though."

The sheriff was glad Billy had kept his voice down. The crowd might riot of they knew Tom was already dead and the situation would quickly spin out of control.

Despite Mackey and Billy's best efforts, the law had a tenuous grip on Tent City. A riot would make him lose control of the ragtag settlement forever. He had no intention of allowing that to happen.

"I told you to do something, Bollard." Mackey raised the Winchester and placed the butt of the rifle on his right hip, careful not to aim it at him. "I won't tell you again."

"And I ain't heeled like you," Bollard yelled. "Toss yer guns and we'll talk."

"That's not going to happen." Mackey switched the Winchester to his left hand, once more keeping it aimed down at the mud. But his hand was on his buckle, near the Peacemaker holstered at his belly. "Now we're even. Drop the knife like I told you."

But Bollard refused. "Not good enough. I seen

what you can do with a pistol and that cross-belly draw you got. You and that Negro ya brung with ya."

Emboldened by a cheer from the crowd, Bollard said, "Both of you toss all yer guns and we can parlay." He grabbed a handful of the dying man's hair and yanked up his head to the delight of the crowd. "Or, so help me, I take me the scalp I intend on gettin'."

Doc Ridley jostled to keep his place in the bustling crowd. "Aaron, there's no time for this!"

Mackey agreed.

In one fluid motion, he drew his Peacemaker and fired. The shot slammed into the center of Bollard's chest and sent the big man tumbling backward into his makeshift tent, snapping the post as he fell. He was quickly buried by the scraps of tarp and rags and animal hides he had used to make his home.

Mackey aimed the pistol at the crowd of men barring Doc Ridley's way. Every one of them froze. "Step aside and let him through."

The crowd reluctantly separated enough to let the doctor stumble into the street with his black medical bag at his side. The smallish man forgot about his own dignity as he ran as quickly as he could manage through the dense mud of Second Street to tend to the victim.

No one stepped forward to help him, including Mackey or Billy. The two lawmen eyed the crowd steadily. The Tent City residents were an unfamiliar bunch and in a damned restless mood. Mackey knew they were unhappy that the sheriff had disrupted their show. And given how badly Mackey and Billy were outnumbered, the best they could do was watch the doctor's back while he tried to save the shotgun victim's life.

Mackey kept an eye on the crowd as Ridley ducked under the collapsed tent and knelt beside his patient. He and the town doctor had never gotten along until recently. Ridley was a pious, religious man who had helped settle Dover Station after the War Between the States. Ridley often objected to Mackey's strict enforcement of the law, claiming his methods were against God's law. Doc Ridley had often told him, "Just because it's legal doesn't mean it's right."

But after Darabont's siege on the town, the two men had attained an unspoken respect for each other. He was the town's acting mayor until a new one could be elected the following month. But Ridley had never been a politician. He was a believer in humanity and in his own skill at easing the suffering of his patients. That was what he was trying to do now as he knelt in the mud, struggling to save the life of a stranger.

Mackey could see by the way the proud doctor's shoulders sagged that the struggle had ended.

Ridley slowly stood, looked over at Mackey

10

and shook his head. "He's gone. The blast took out half of his throat. I'm surprised he managed to hold on for as long as he did. He must have been a very strong man. Young, too."

He glared at the people looking at him from their tents and their spots along the boardwalk. "Like most of you. Young and in a bad way, fighting against the world. It isn't bad enough that you have to live like this, do you have to kill each other, too?" His voice rose to a shrill. "I hope you bastards are happy. You certainly got your show, didn't you?"

Mackey called out to the crowd. "Anybody know the stranger's name?"

A man in the crowd said. "I see three dead men, Sheriff." The man was tall and skinny with a misshapen hat, a scraggly gray beard, and clothes that were little more than rags. "Three hard working men ground to dust in the machinery of this place. The gears of greed have been oiled today by the blood of the workers."

A murmur went through the crowd, and the man continued. "We must make sure their deaths were not in vain."

Another murmur went through the crowd. It was clear they knew him, but Mackey had never seen him before. "Step forward. I want to talk to you."

But the gaunt man did not step forward. "And what if I don't, sheriff? Will you shoot me, too?

I think you've done enough of the Dover Station Company's bidding for one day, don't you?"

The man stepped back and the crowd shifted to block Mackey's view of him. The sheriff decided not to push the matter.

The quicker they got out of there, the better. He gestured toward six young men standing near Doc Ridley. "Go fetch a flatbed, load up the bodies, and take them over to Cy Wallach's place for preparation for burial. And make sure you bring the wagon back where it belongs after you're done."

The six men looked at each other and laughed, embarrassed by the sudden attention and unsure of what to do.

But Mackey didn't laugh. He hadn't holstered his Peacemaker yet, either. "You boys just saw what happens when people defy me."

The six men bolted like scared horses. Mackey tucked the pistol back into his holster and shifted the Winchester to his right hand. "Go with them, Doc. Make sure they don't forget what they're supposed to be doing."

Ridley looked down at the dead young man, whose worn shoes were sticking out from beneath the ruined tent. "What are any of us supposed to be doing, Aaron?" He looked at the half-built buildings and the tents and shacks of Second Street. "This used to be a fine place to live. Now look at it. Being torn down and rebuilt, only to be made worse than it was before. People living like pigs in the mud and squalor? Workers dropping from exhaustion? Is this what progress is supposed to look like?"

First, a bunch of nonsense from a mouthy stranger, now poor Doc Ridley was getting in on the act. Mackey had no intention of discussing weighty subjects in the middle of Tent City. The longer they stood among the mob, the more likely they were to become targets.

"There'll be plenty of time for questions later, Doc. Right now, we have to clear these bodies off the street, and I'd appreciate your help doing it."

As Doc Ridley reluctantly followed the six men, Mackey turned his attention to the Bollard twin he had hit.

Billy had managed to roll the big man onto his back, despite the thickness of the mud. There was a large gash at the man's belly.

"Looks like I was right," Billy said. "Bollard, too. His brother wasn't staggering because he was drunk. He caught a bad one in the belly before he blasted that man."

"Didn't give him the right to scalp anyone," Mackey said, "but at least we know why it happened."

Mackey felt all the eyes of Tent City on him and decided this was no time to leave. It was dangerous to turn away from a mob, especially

13

when it was watching your every move. He had to say something.

"I know none of you wants to be living like this, but it's the best any of us can do until more houses get built. A lot of people want me to break up this place and send you up to the old mining camps and logging camps Darabont burned out when he attacked the town. Since the company hasn't rebuilt them yet, I don't want to do that."

He made a point of looking as many of them in the eye as he could. "But I won't have a choice if things around here get out of hand. You've all got a hard time of it here. I know that. But don't make it worse by stealing and killing each other. Don't make me come back." He looked at the collapsed tent that partially hid the two corpses. He pointed at the dead man in the mud at his feet. "You won't like it if I do."

Mackey stood alone as he watched the grumbling crowd slowly ebb away, ducking back into their tents or shacks or moving elsewhere. He made a point of stepping up onto the boardwalk and walking back toward the jailhouse. When the crowd had thinned out enough, he looked down at the dead man at his feet.

"Big son of a bitch, wasn't he?" Billy observed.

Talking about it would not make him any smaller. "You grab one arm, and I'll grab the other. Drag him over to the others. Might as well let Doc Ridley and his new friends make one trip of it."

With their rifles in one hand and one of Bollard's arms in the other, the men grunted under the weight of the corpse.

Billy said, "Can't believe we lost both Bollard boys in a single morning. The world may never recover."

Mackey struggled to keep hold of his rifle as they dragged Bollard's deadweight through the mud. "I'm sure they've got brothers. Bastards usually do."

When they had finally dropped the corpse next to his brother, Mackey noticed ten or so stragglers scattered around the boardwalks and the alleys along Second Street. He recognized the look in their eyes. They might not have been sporting feathers, but they were vultures just the same.

Billy had noticed them, too. "How long after we leave before they strip these bodies? Tent, too?"

"Fifteen seconds after we turn our backs," Mackey said. "At most."

Mackey and Billy raised their rifles as a group of men came barreling toward him. Mackey thought an angry mob from Tent City had come to avenge the death of the Bollard brothers. The riot was finally starting.

But they quickly lowered their weapons when they recognized the men as some of the ironworkers who were building the Municipal Building.

Mackey called out to them. "What's going on?"

Another man said, "You'd better come quick, sheriff. Jed Eddows is fixing to hang Foreman Ross right now before God and everyone!"

Billy trailed behind Mackey as they ran. "So much for a quiet morning in Dover Station."

Chapter 2

A stiff wind blew up Front Street as Sheriff Mackey gauged the situation.

It was not good.

Three stories above, framed against the gray sky of a coming storm, Mackey saw the wiry Jed Eddows had not only bound and gagged the portly foreman Jay Ross. He was also holding him at the edge of the scaffold by the back of the foreman's pants.

Eddows had cinched a noose around Ross's neck, and the sheriff had no doubt the other end had been secured to one of the many iron beams of the building. Mackey hoped Eddows was stronger than he looked, or Ross would be dead before they had a chance to talk.

The wind took most of what Eddows shouted down at him, but Mackey caught the gist of it. "You stay right where you are, sheriff. And that buck you have for a deputy best stay on the porch where he belongs. Either of you take one step toward this building, and I swear to God my oppressor will hang!"

Mackey squinted to make sure this was really Jed Eddows talking. He had always considered Eddows to be a quiet, forgettable man who came and went from his job at the Municipal Building construction site without incident or notice. He had never spent time in jail for being drunk or disorderly. In fact, Mackey only knew his name from hearing it called out so often during the summer while Mackey and Billy sat on the jailhouse porch, watching the future of the town rise across the street.

But judging from the amount of blood he could see on the foreman's shirt and the swelling about his head and face, Mackey now knew that a quiet fury had been building inside Eddows for some time. He had given his foreman one hell of a beating before trussing him up and bringing him outside to hang.

There would be plenty of time to find out why this had happened. Right now, he had to find a way to keep a skinny man from allowing a fat man to hang from the biggest construction site in the territory.

From behind him, Mackey heard Billy call out, "I'm not going near you, Eddows. I'm just going to speak to the sheriff about how to keep anyone from getting too close to you. I won't go an inch past him, I promise."

Eddows stammered before saying, "You try anything, black boy, and Ross hangs. Understand?"

Billy stopped a few paces behind the sheriff. "Let me shoot this son of a bitch, Aaron. I can take his head off with the Sharps, even in this wind."

18

Mackey had to hold on to his hat by the brim to keep it on his head. He had no doubt Billy could hit him, especially with that buffalo gun he carried. Billy Sunday had been the best shot in the outfit when they had served together in the cavalry, and his skills had only improved in the years since.

But there was a time for gunplay and a time for other things. "Can't shoot him. Look at the way he set it up. If we shoot Eddows, he lets go of the foreman's belt and Ross hangs. He's also got Ross too far out over the edge so we can't try to wing him and knock him back inside."

Mackey looked over the setup again in the hopes that he had missed something, but he had not. "Looks like Eddows is a more complicated man than we thought."

"Then what are we going to do?" Billy asked. "We can't just stand here and watch like everyone else."

Mackey looked out at the crowds beginning to gather on the boardwalks. Whether it was Tent City squatters over on Second Street or old-line Dover Station townsfolk on Front Street, everyone enjoyed a spectacle.

"I think we can talk him down," Mackey said. "If Eddows wanted to kill Ross, he could've shot him or just thrown him off the building. He didn't. He's doing this because he wants an audience. He has something to say. Let's give him the chance. Maybe the more he talks, the longer Ross lives." He grabbed his hat again before it blew off his head. "Besides, there isn't much we can do about it anyway."

Billy held on to his hat, too. "Might not be able to stop him anyway if the wind stays like this. And when Grant finds out what's going on down here, he's liable to turn this into a goddamned circus."

Mackey knew the general manager of the Dover Station Company was not one to shy away from public events. He knew Grant would be here the moment he heard of it. If Eddows hated his foreman, it stood to reason he probably hated Grant even more.

Mackey did not want that to happen. Three men had just died less than a block away. But, then again, Mackey knew he rarely got what he wanted, especially when it came to James Grant.

To Billy, he said, "Hang back by the jailhouse with the Sharps. If we have to, you hit Eddows and I'll take Ross. In the meantime, watch the crowd and steer Grant clear of this place until we know what Eddows wants."

Billy slowly took a few steps back toward the porch. "I will. I'm right here if you need me."

The number of spectators cramming the boardwalks around the site had nearly doubled in the short amount of time Mackey had been speaking with Billy. The horror of the townspeople was only rivaled by their curiosity about what would happen next.

The cluster of workers at the base of the building had begun jockeying for position for the best view.

With the storm kicking up and Grant on his way, Mackey decided it was time to get Eddows talking. "All right, Jed. You've got your audience, and you've got my attention. No one's coming near you, and Billy and me are in plain sight. How about you pull Mr. Ross back from the ledge and tell us what's on your mind?"

"No way," Eddows shouted back. "I know what that black bastard of yours can do with that Sharps of his. I swear to God, I see him so much as look in my direction, Ross swings, understand?"

"No one's aiming anything at you and no one's going to, either, as long as you don't do anything stupid. You've obviously got something on your mind, so might as well say it." He motioned to the crowd that now jammed every available space on the boardwalk. "You've got plenty of people here willing to listen."

Eddows looked away. He still held on to the foreman's belt but clearly hadn't expected the chance to say anything.

One of the workers clustered at the base of the building yelled to Mackey, "Just shoot the son of a bitch and get it over with."

"Yeah," another called out. "Blow his damned head off and let us get back to work. This nonsense is costing us money."

Still another yelled, "There's ten men in Tent City who'd take Jed's place, and the company's got other foremen they can send to run the job."

Mackey ignored them. He didn't think Eddows had heard them because of the wind, but the man had been quiet too long to suit him. "Come on, Jed. Speak up and let's talk this through."

Eddows looked confused, as if he had only just realized what he had done. But his grip on Ross's belt never faltered, and the foreman was still pitched dangerously at the edge of the scaffold.

"It wasn't any one thing that done it, I guess," Eddows yelled. "It was a whole bunch of things balled up into a knot. Him yelling at me, screaming all the time. Threatening to fire me or throw me off the goddamned building because I wasn't working fast enough or because I'd made a mistake. You know how long I've been working here?"

"Not exactly, but it's about four months near as I can figure." He decided it would be a good idea to add, "Billy and I remember sitting in front of the jailhouse seeing you go to work. Saw you here every single day, rain or shine. Heard good things about you."

"That's a lie!" Eddows screamed. "The only

22

time you heard my name was when this cruel son of a bitch screamed at me over something I'd done or hadn't done yet. Nothing I do is ever good enough for him. He's an oppressor. He feeds off my labor and does none of his own. He needs to be stopped."

He pushed Ross closer to the edge of the scaffold. The foreman screamed and so did many of the spectators, as much out of excitement as fear.

Mackey kept his rifle aimed at the ground. The wind was still too strong.

Eddows laughed as he eased Ross back a bit from the edge. "This is the quietest I've heard him since I started working for him. For once, he ain't yelling at me about staying on his goddamned schedule so he can make his goddamned bonus. None of us get any bonuses, sheriff. Only him. That sound fair to you?"

"No, it doesn't. I didn't know about that. I can talk to Jim Grant about that if you want."

But Eddows had not heard him. "You know how many houses I framed for him? Ten in three weeks. Ten! A lot of us did. He worked us like dogs and whipped us worse, but we got it done, didn't we, boys?"

Some of the workers cheered up to him. Most hurled curses at him.

Eddows went on. "And now he's working us even harder to get this damned building open in a month. This place look like it'll be done in a month to you, sheriff?"

One of the ironworkers called out, "It would be if you weren't pulling this shit now, you crazy bastard."

Mackey had to yell over the ensuing argument to get Eddows's attention. "I know you're tired, son. A lot of people have been working real hard to change this town, and we appreciate it, even if Ross doesn't. You remember seeing me and Billy on the porch all those mornings, don't you? So you know I'm not just saying that."

The sheriff couldn't be sure, but he thought Eddows pulled Ross a little farther away from the ledge.

Mercifully, the wind had died down, so Mackey didn't have to yell as loud when he said, "I know you've had a bad time of it. A lot of people have, so how about I make a deal with you? Take that noose off Ross's head and pull him back inside, and I promise I'll talk to Jim Grant about easing up their schedule some. I know my head could stand a little less banging and I'm sure yours could, too. A bump in wages and a slower pace. Sound fair?"

"Sounds like a bunch of bullshit, if you ask me," Eddows yelled. "I know all about you, Mackey. You're just as bad as the cruel bastard I've got strung up right here. I saw you riding around with Mr. Rice after Darabont hit us. His

24

company owns you like it owns everything else in this damned town. There ain't no way I live after what I've done. Hell, even I know that, and I'm an idiot." He pushed Ross to the edge and the foreman screamed again. "Ain't that right, Mr. Ross? Ain't that one of them pet names you've got for me?"

Mackey gripped the Winchester at his side a little tighter. If he let Ross fall, Mackey would have no choice but to shoot Eddows. And he'd have to do it fast before the wind picked up again.

He had to give it one last try. "I don't think you're stupid, Jeb. I just think you're tired and scared and need some rest. And there's no reason to kill you over what you've done so far. Who cares if you hurt Mr. Ross? Hell, I can't think of a soldier or a workingman who hasn't dreamed of hurting his boss at one time or another. I know I have."

Eddows's face grew scarlet as he yelled, "I want him dead! I want my oppressor dead! I want fair pay for fair work and I want to be treated like a human being!"

Despite his rage, Mackey could see Eddows changing somehow. He could not tell if that was good or bad, but he knew he had been given the chance to end this.

"But you're not a killer," the sheriff continued. "If you were, you would've done it by now. You're doing this because you want to be heard

25

and you want help. I'm offering all of that to you right now. All you've got to do is pull him back inside and end this peacefully."

Eddows surprised him by stepping back and pulling Ross with him. The foreman was now practically standing on the scaffold, though the tips of his feet were still over the side. Ross would still hang if Eddows let go.

But he was safer than he had been since the entire mess began, so Mackey kept pushing. "That's a good start, Jeb."

"It's not going to end too well for me if I end up in jail," Eddows yelled back.

"I'm sure he won't press charges against you," Mackey lied. He didn't know Ross at all, except that he worked on the Municipal Building. But there was a time for the truth and a time to lie, and this was no time for the truth. "You've got everything you want, Eddows. You'll have accomplished something for you and your friends. All you've got to do is pull him back inside and take that noose off his neck."

"That true?" Eddows nudged Ross closer to the edge again. "That true about what he said about you not pressing charges? I want to hear you say it."

"Of course!" Ross screamed. "I-I was wrong to say those horrible things to you, Jeb, and I'm sorry. Things will get better, I promise. Just don't let me hang. Please. I've got a family to feed. Please."

"Family?" Eddows's rage seemed to spill over as he yanked his boss all the way in from the ledge so that they were practically standing next to each other. "You don't think I have a family? What about my wife and my kids? You think I take the strap from you all day every day because I like it? You think I let you treat me like a dog just because I think that's all I am? You talk about *your* family, you miserable . . ."

Mackey saw Eddows shift his weight.

His anger had finally won the battle.

He was going to throw Ross off the scaffold.

Billy had seen it, too, because both lawmen raised their rifles and fired at their chosen targets at exactly the same time.

The impact of the fifty-caliber slug from Billy's Sharps threw young Eddows back into the building.

Mackey's shot struck Ross high in the right shoulder and sent the bound man spinning before he fell back and out of view. The amount of slack on the rope still hanging over the edge of the scaffold told him that the foreman had not been hanged.

Mackey joined the flow of ironworkers and townspeople running into the building. He yelled back to Billy, "You stay here and try to keep everyone back. I'll go check on Ross."

• • •

Mackey raced into the building, but found the way clogged with carpenters and ironworkers scrambling to get back into the building. He yelled for them to clear the way, but it was no use.

By the time the sheriff forced his way through the crowd and up to the third floor, he saw the workers cheer as they cut loose the last of the foreman's bindings.

A small group had gathered around the spot where Eddows's body had landed. Billy's fifty-caliber round had made a massive hole in the left side of his chest, probably killing him on impact. They might not have seen what a gun designed to kill buffalo could do to a human body before, but Mackey had. It was never pretty.

Mackey quickly made his way over to Ross and found one of the workers had already rigged a tourniquet for the foreman's right arm from some of the rope that had previously bound him.

The wounded man smiled up at Mackey. His nose had been broken and a couple of teeth had been chipped, but he looked happy. "That was some damned fine shooting, sheriff. I owe you and your deputy my life. Which one got me?"

"That was me," Mackey admitted. "I tried to wing you, but . . ."

"No need to apologize. I thought that crazy son of a bitch was going to kill me for sure."

"Just be grateful you're still alive." To the worker who had tied the tourniquet, he asked, "How bad is it?"

"You hit him through and through," the man told him. "Nicked the bone some, but I saw worse on the trail out here. Me and the boys will get him to Doc Ridley right quick, don't you worry."

Mackey stepped aside as six men scrambled forward with a wooden plank to carry Ross down to the street. Eddows had screamed that he hated Ross, but enough of the other workers seemed fond enough of the man to make sure he got medical attention.

That told Mackey something about Ross. But it didn't say much about the man who had threatened to hang him. What had driven Eddows to the edge of murder? And to do it so publicly? And what of his talk about oppressors and fair wages? Eddows had sounded like the mysterious stranger at the shooting at Tent City. Mackey knew there were malcontents in any outfit who enjoyed complaining, but to try to kill a leader was something else.

As he stood aside, waiting for the men carrying Ross to pass, he realized he had never seen Dover Station from such a height, at least, not this close.

From up there, all of the other original buildings looked smaller than he had expected. Even the jailhouse looked tiny by comparison.

It was one of the few stone structures in town,

built by a former sheriff who had been a mason. He wanted a building that would stand up well enough to fire, should one start in a town where most of the other buildings were wooden. The walls were over a foot thick, and the heavy ironwood door facing Front Street was the only way inside. There were no windows in the cells, only the barred window from where Mackey and Billy could look out on Front Street.

The jailhouse had long been seen as the only permanent building in town until the Dover Station Company began to build the iron and brick monstrosity where Mackey currently stood across the thoroughfare.

From where he stood, Aaron Mackey could see what Dover Station had been. The town he had known as a boy and as a captain returned from the army. He saw the streets and avenues Billy and he had patrolled and the stores whose locks he checked each night. They were the old Dover Station. They were the past.

The Municipal Building and all of the other new construction symbolized what the town was to become. A town he no longer recognized. A town filled with strangers who didn't know him, only of him. He was Sheriff Aaron Mackey, formerly Captain Mackey, the Hero of Adobe Flats. Lately, and over Mackey's objection, James Grant had taken to calling him the Savior of Dover Station. The general manager of the

Dover Station Company saw it as some kind of attraction to draw people to town and make them feel safe, as if news of Frazer Rice's interest in town was not enough of a draw.

From the third floor of the iron building, Mackey wondered if this new town held any attraction for him. He wondered if there would be any place for him in this building after it was finished. He wondered if he even wanted one.

When he heard another commotion down on the street, he rushed to the edge of the scaffold. "Christ," he muttered to himself. "What now?"

He was not surprised to see James Grant on the boardwalk in front of the jailhouse, waving at the cheering crowd. He had Walter Underhill and two other men with rifles standing by him. Brandishing firearms was illegal in town, even for employees of James Grant. Underhill, a former United States Marshal from Texas, had helped repel Darabont's raid of the town six months before, so Mackey often let his indiscretions slide.

None of the townspeople seemed to notice this violation of town law. Everyone cheered Grant like a conquering hero. Given that he represented the company that had made many of them wealthy, Mackey could understand the adulation.

But understanding James Grant proved a much harder task for the sheriff. Grant was older than Mackey by more than a few years, which put him in his mid-forties. His sandy blond hair and full beard had begun to gray in all the right places, making him look more distinguished than old. What he lacked in height, he made up for in powerful build; he was broad shouldered and thick around the chest. He looked more like a laborer than a man who worked in an office all day. Mackey imagined this was part of his appeal with the public. For, Mackey knew, James Grant had not always worked in an office.

He had been a rancher in a neighboring town, and before that had owned a stagecoach station after he had run a telegraph office. Rumors abounded that he had once served as a lawman in some capacity in Nebraska, though the town and the time of his service was a matter of some debate.

But there was no debate that Grant had managed to amass a lot of influence since Mr. Rice's partner, Silas Van Dorn, hired him to manage the operations of the Dover Station Company. The reasons for Grant's hiring were as obscure as his past, and Mackey did not care how he got the job, only that he had it now. Grant had quickly established a reputation for not only setting aggressive construction deadlines, but beating them.

As he watched the ironworkers gently carry Ross down to the street, Mackey began to wonder if Grant's ambition had caused Eddows to snap. He wondered how many other men like Eddows were ready to fall.

In Mackey's experience, ambitious men needed to be watched.

Grant held his hat aloft as he bellowed from the jailhouse boardwalk. "Ladies and gentlemen, I have just learned that Jay Ross is alive and expected to make a full recovery. Let us have three cheers for Jay Ross. Hip-hip. Hooray!"

Underhill and the two riflemen had formed an arc in front of Grant to keep the crowd back as they cheered.

When the echo of the last hurrah died away, Grant pointed up at Mackey on the scaffold. "And three cheers for the brave man who saved that good man's life. The Hero of Adobe Flats! The Savior of Dover Station! Sheriff Aaron Mackey! Hip-hip."

The crowd chanted "hooray" without any prompting from Grant.

Mackey saw Billy taking in the whole scene from the doorway of the jailhouse. The black man smiled up at Mackey, touched the brim of his hat, and went inside to make a fresh pot of coffee.

Grant waited for the crowd to quiet before continuing his speech. "Now, I'm well aware that you good people have been tolerant of all the changes the Dover Station Company has been making here in town. But change isn't easy. It never is. But we're more than halfway through our initial phase of work and that much closer to undoing all of the damage Darabont left in his wake when he attacked this fair town. This morning I received a telegram from Mr. Rice in New York City, wherein he gave me permission to inform you of some wonderful news. Later this week, the Dover Station Mining Company will be reopening the living quarters at the mines, the Dover Station Lumber Company will reopen their living quarters, and the Dover Station Cattle and Land Company will be hiring fifty more cowboys, farmers, and more."

Hats were thrown in the air, and the people clapped and cheered.

Grant spoke over them again, struggling to make his voice heard over the euphoria. "My friends, our work has not finished. Indeed, it is only beginning. But men of vision and generosity like Mr. Rice and his partner, our neighbor Mr. Silas Van Dorn, cannot be relied upon to do everything. We have an election for mayor coming up in a month and we are distressed over the lack of interest among all of you to run for office. We thank Doctor Ridley for filling in as mayor after Brian Mason resigned the office to join the company, but we need the good people of Dover Station to elect a good, strong leader, lest all of our hard work goes for nothing. Look to yourselves and, I implore you, to consider running for this noble office."

Mackey looked over the crowd as one man yelled out, "Grant for Mayor!" A few more people took up the chant and, within seconds, it echoed as if one voice through the narrow streets of town.

Mackey saw a few familiar faces in the sea of people, but most were total strangers. The rapid growth of the town over these past six months had served to change it so much that he hardly recognized it anymore.

Four men had just been killed a block away from each other within twenty or so minutes. But no one he saw seemed to care about that. They were cheering for a man they hardly knew to run for an office no one wanted. Grant waved it off, of course, but he accepted it all the same.

No, Mackey decided, he did not know these people anymore. People he considered outsiders, even though the town did not belong to him.

Mackey ducked back inside and began heading downstairs.

He needed a mug of Billy's coffee more than he needed the adulation of strangers.

Chapter 3

Mackey made his way through backslaps and cheers and pushed toward the jailhouse. One of Grant's new riflemen pushed him back as he tried to mount the steps of the boardwalk.

Walter Underhill shoved his man out of the way. "He's the sheriff, you idiot." The big Texan nodded at Mackey. "Sorry about that, Aaron. He's new and with the crowd and all, he didn't see your star."

Mackey normally would have brained the man for touching him, but he had seen enough blood for one day. And given how Underhill had helped defend the town against Darabont's raiders, the sheriff was more inclined to give him a pass. "It's fine. What are you still doing here? I don't see your boss around."

Underhill thumbed over his shoulder toward the jailhouse. "That's because Mr. Grant is inside waiting for you."

A meeting with Grant was the last thing he wanted just then. "Any idea what he wants to talk about?"

"He didn't tell me, and I wasn't in a position to ask."

Mackey didn't know the big Texan well, but well enough to know he probably was not happy about it. "Guess I'll find out soon enough. By the way, what's with the two extra gun hands? Having you trailing him is one thing, but now he's got three of you."

"When I signed on," Underhill said, "it was to help Mr. Rice. But when he went back to New York, he told me to watch out for Mr. Van Dorn. But seeing as old Silas never leaves the house, Van Dorn told me to ride around with Grant. Mr. Rice is a talker and good company. Grant keeps his own counsel. He knows why he does things but doesn't feel compelled to tell me."

Mackey decided this might be the time to test a theory he had been turning over in his mind. "Maybe he's worried about all those train robberies that have been going on south of here."

"I wouldn't know because he doesn't tell me much," Underhill admitted. "But those robberies have been going on for months now. He only asked me to hire on some new boys a couple of days ago. You should ask him yourself. I told him you wouldn't like it."

"But he keeps his own counsel."

The big Texan looked over the crowd. "I know what you're thinking, Aaron. The money's good and regular. But if you could let me know if he tells you anything, I'd appreciate it."

Mackey clapped the man on the back as he walked up the steps and pushed in the heavy wooden door of the jailhouse.

• • •

He found James Grant standing just inside, with former mayor Brian Mason right beside him. Billy Sunday was at the stove, pouring a mug of coffee.

"Afternoon, Aaron." Grant was holding his gray bowler hat in his hand. "Fine job you did out there today."

"You can say that again, Mr. Grant," Mason added. The ex-politician was a florid-faced man who stood a head shorter than Grant and was much rounder. His considerable girth had only increased since resigning as mayor to take a position at the Dover Station Company. The exact nature of that position had always been a mystery to the sheriff, but he had never been curious enough to find out more.

Mason had been a merchant by trade, but had no discernable skills Mackey thought Van Dorn could use. Like the position of sheriff, Brian had only been elected to the office because no one else had wanted the job.

Mason continued to gas on. "Aaron here's our hometown Hero of Adobe Flats. The Savior of Dover Station. The pride of the town."

Mackey took some cartridges from the rack drawer and fed a new round into the Winchester. "How many times do I have to tell you to quit calling me that? It's the kind of moniker puts a bull's eye on a man's back, and I've got enough problems without worrying about some idiot looking to make a name for himself by gunning me down." He put the Winchester back in the rack and closed the drawer.

Grant demurred. "I can see now is not the time to talk about what happened, sheriff. We can come back at another time."

"Afraid we don't have the luxury of time, Jimmy." Mackey shrugged out of his coat and hung it on the peg next to the rack. "Because Eddows isn't the only excitement we've had this morning. We've got three dead bodies over in Tent City." He looked at Grant. "Squatters on company property, Jim."

Mason gasped. "You mean you've killed four men in one day? I thought I was very clear about curbing your tendencies for excessive violence when I was mayor."

"Didn't hear many complaints about my violent nature when Darabont had the town by the throat."

"That was different."

"Must be comfortable for you to think that it was, but it wasn't." He had no desire to debate past history when it was the present that concerned him most. "There's three dead in Tent City, but I only killed one of them. The other two did each other in."

Grant said, "Many of our workers live in Tent City. Do you know who the men were?"

"Both Bollard boys and some guy no one seems to know." Mackey accepted the mug of hot coffee Billy handed him from the stove and dropped into the chair behind his desk. "One of the Bollards said the third man had robbed from them before things got out of hand. He gutted Bollard, who hit him with both barrels of a shotgun. That's two in case you're keeping score. The remaining Bollard wanted to scalp the man who'd knifed his brother and refused my commands to lower the knife, so I had no choice but to put him down." He looked at Mason. "So technically, I only killed one man today, Brian. Billy over here shot Eddows with the Sharps, so as it stands, we're tied."

From the stove, Billy said, "Let's hope it stays that way."

Mackey had never seen much honest emotion from James Grant since he had come to work for the Dover Station Company, but he sensed the surprise the man was showing was genuine. "Good God. The Bollard boys worked for me hauling material on some of our projects. Only a fool would try to steal from them."

"Tent City," Mason spat. "A den of iniquity, sir. Someone should take a torch and burn them out."

Billy laughed. "I'd like to see you try it. Go anywhere near that place with an open flame, you'll be dead before you get within fifty paces. Those people might not have much, but they're awfully protective of what little they have."

"They're not all bad, Brian," Grant said, admonishing his assistant. "It breaks my heart that so many of our workers are forced to live in such deplorable conditions. We're trying to get the apartment houses built as soon as possible, but there are only so many workers to go around."

Mackey sipped his coffee. "Managed to get the saloons open fast enough."

Grant shrugged. "A saloon's just a barn, really, with a few interior modifications. Proper residences are a far more complicated matter."

"Not to mention saloons make a hell of a lot more money than houses do," Mackey said. "And that's assuming the rent comes in on time, which it rarely does."

Grant gave him the same grin he had shown the crowd only a few minutes before. "You're a brave and dedicated man, Aaron, but building a town isn't as easy as it sounds. It must happen in stages and with great care, not to mention proper order."

Billy said, "So the saloons and whorehouses opening first wasn't an accident, then?"

Clearly sensing defeat, but seeking to avoid a fight, Grant turned to leave. "You've both had a full morning. Please accept our thanks again for saving Mr. Ross and for dealing with poor Eddows." Then, as an afterthought, "And for handling the incident with the Bollard twins, too, of course."

"Not so fast, Jim." Mackey pulled out a sheet of paper and a pencil from the top drawer of his desk. He saw the yellow telegraph envelope he had received earlier that morning, but quickly shut the drawer before Grant saw it. "We need to talk about what happened out there just now."

Grant kept his hand on the door latch. "Why, it's as plain as the noonday sun. You saved a good man from being executed by a lunatic. I'll make sure Mr. Van Dorn hears of this as soon as I get back to the office. I am sure he will want to convey his thanks."

"Afraid it's not that simple. I know what happened. I'm asking you why it happened at all."

"I imagine it's because the young man frayed under the strain of progress."

Mackey looked at Billy. "That's a new phrase we've got to use more in the future. 'Frayed under the strain of progress.' How do you like it?"

"Fancy." Billy poured himself more coffee. "But it doesn't answer your question."

Grant glared at Billy. "Meaning?"

"Meaning the sheriff asked you what made Eddows do all of this fraying you're talking about."

Grant looked to Mason for an answer.

The former mayor said, "We hired him on as a day laborer about four or five months ago. I can't recall exactly when, and I can't recall having any problems with him, either." His double chin wiggled as he caught himself. "Well, that is, until today's unpleasantness, of course."

"Unpleasantness," Mackey repeated. "Another good word. Got to use it next time there's a shooting. Eddows said Ross was a cruel bastard who pushed him and the men too hard. Spouted off about him being an oppressor and how he wasn't making a fair wage. Any idea what he's talking about?"

Grant looked at Mason. "Sounds like more of that Marx business."

"What's that?" Mackey asked.

"Karl Marx, damn him," Grant said. "We've had some rabble-rousers appear in camp riling up the men with talk of forming trade unions and other nonsense. It fills their heads with bigger ideas than they're capable of grasping, and they often act out in rash ways. Not to this extent, of course, but given the inflammatory nature of the rhetoric, I suppose it was bound to happen sometime. We'll make sure we'll keep an eye on it, won't we, Brian?"

Mason was eager to comply. "I'll make inquiries immediately, sir."

Mackey didn't know much about Marx, but he knew a dodge when he heard one. "You pushing those men too hard, Jim? Maybe holding back their pay as an incentive to meet your deadlines?

Those kinds of things tend to make a workingman angry."

Grant's eyes flared for an instant before he remembered himself. It was only a flash, but long enough for Mackey to see it. Despite all of the various jobs Grant had held in his life, he was not fond of being questioned, not even by sheriffs.

The general manager was calm when he said, "I'm sure I don't need to remind you of how much work we've been doing in town these past several months. We can't keep up that pace without holding the men to a strict schedule and high expectations."

Mackey pointed to the cells in the back. "And I'm sure I don't need to make you aware of how many people we've been holding back there for the past several months. Today's the first day I can remember where we didn't have a full house. Drunk and disorderly men, mostly. Your men. Your workers. And not many of them have much money on them when they get hauled in here."

The sheriff leaned forward in his chair. "I'm going to ask you one last time. Are you pushing those men without paying them?"

"Each man is paid a fair wage for a fair day's work." Grant pointed outside. "Take a look at what we're building out there, sheriff. The Municipal Building is the likes of which this territory won't see again for a generation, maybe more. Mr. Rice and Mr. Van Dorn envision it as the foundation upon which the renewal of Dover Station, and perhaps Montana's statehood, will be based. Why, by the time we're done with this phase of construction, we'll have nearly doubled the size of the town. Next year, with the mines and logging and farming and ranching consolidated, we may need an even bigger railroad station than the one we just built. Might even triple the size of the town."

Grant slapped his hat against his leg, bringing a ready smile from Mason. "Yes, sir. Things are changing around here and for the better, too. But success isn't something that's lying on the ground waiting to be picked up. You have to dig for it and dig deep."

Mackey sipped his coffee. "At what cost?"

Grant demurred. "I think Mr. Van Dorn would be embarrassed if I told you the actual amount the company has spent so far."

Mackey set his mug on the desk. "I'm not talking about money. I'm talking about the cost in human lives. What happened out there today was luck, pure and simple. Eddows could've easily killed Ross and probably would have killed him if we weren't there."

"But you were there, sheriff," Grant pointed out, "and performed admirably, given the choices you had."

"We got lucky. The wind died down at just the right time. There's nothing admirable about luck.

And despite all the names you've pinned on me, I don't like killing, especially men who are pushed like mules."

Grant laughed. "A man who has an entire section of the cemetery dedicated to the men he kills and now you claim you don't like killing? What is it they call it? 'Mackey's Garden,' I believe?"

Mackey felt his anger starting to build. "That's the unclaimed part of the cemetery, nothing more." The sheriff leaned forward in his chair. "Eddows didn't just fray. He snapped. He planned out his attack on Ross, even fashioned a noose for him. And none of your workers stopped him."

Grant raised his chin. "I'll look into it, I promise you."

"You'd better," Mackey said. "Because if you don't, Jed Eddows isn't going to be the last man of yours I have to kill. But he's the last one I'll kill without asking you a lot more questions about it."

Grant put on his brown felt Stetson bowler. "Then let's hope that our next meeting is under more pleasant circumstances. I bid you gentlemen a good day."

Mason popped his bowler hat back on his head, too, and opened the door for Grant.

Mackey sat back in his chair. "We're not done."

Grant slowly turned to face him. "I'm getting annoyed, Aaron."

"You're about to feel a whole lot worse. I see you've got gunmen trailing you wherever you go. Why?"

Mason saw an opportunity to make himself useful. "There have been threats against Mr. Grant's life and he took the precaution of hiring some men to protect him. After witnessing the horrible scene across the street, I'm sure you can understand why he took it so seriously."

"So you knew this Eddows business was going to happen?" Billy asked.

Grant closed his eyes like a man losing patience with a child. "Of course not. We would've stopped it long before if we had. Every manager receives threats of some kind from the men who work for him at some time or another, especially in the building trade. It was anonymous grumbling, nothing more. Still, I thought a show of force might help tamp down the rhetoric before it got worse." He looked at Mackey. "You were a cavalryman, sheriff. Surely you can appreciate that notion."

Mackey had no intention of discussing his past just now. He thought of the telegram in the top drawer of his desk. He thought it might be a good time to show it to Grant but decided to see how this played out. "These threats the only reason why you've got gunmen around?"

"I'd say threats on my life are a fairly good reason. Why?"

Mackey skipped it. "Then why didn't you report these threats to me or Billy?"

Grant smiled. "I'm not accustomed to having people hold my hand for me. I'm used to taking care of myself."

"In Dover Station, the sheriff's office takes care of everyone," Billy said. "That includes you. Firearms are illegal in town. That includes your protectors, too. No guns unless they're on horseback and moving through town."

Grant's jaw muscles tightened. "I wasn't aware of the ordinance, but now I am." He looked at Mackey. "I hope you don't mind my saying this, but it seems like the town has grown too big for two men to handle on their own, even for legends such as yourselves. Perhaps you should hire more deputies."

"Be glad to if there was a town government to pay them," Mackey said. "But the town board resigned after Brian took a job with you. Doc Ridley's acting mayor, but he's more interested in medicine than governing."

"What a shame," Grant said. "And with elections coming up in a few weeks' time, and no one has thrown their hat into the ring. A town like Dover Station that has such a future needs a leader now." Grant seemed to remember himself. "Sorry for allowing myself to wander. Are you done with us now, sheriff?"

"For now." Mackey picked up his pencil and

began writing. "I'll send a copy of the reports of both incidents when it's done. I'm sure Mr. Van Dorn will want it for his records and all."

Grant touched the tip of his hat before heading out into the street, immediately engaging a couple on the boardwalk. "Mr. and Mrs. Jennings! So good to see you. Just stopped in to have a word with Sheriff Mackey. It's not every day one gets to speak with a hero, you know? The Savior of Dover Station, they say."

The rest of his words died out as Mason struggled to close the heavy ironwood door behind him.

"Mason might have a different job," Billy observed, "but he's still a weasel."

Mackey set down his pencil. "Don't think he knows any other way to be, but he's harmless. Grant's the one to watch. Van Dorn has given him too much power too soon."

"I don't exactly trust that son of a bitch, either."

"Neither do I." He opened the top drawer of his desk and took out the telegram he had held back from Grant. "And something tells me that Mr. Rice doesn't trust him, either."

"Saw you reading that before the gunshot from Tent City." Billy set down his mug on the desk. "You never got around to telling me what it was. Given your reaction, I figured it was bad news."

"It's news." He pulled the telegram out of the envelope and read the telegram aloud. For the sake of brevity, he decided not to read "STOP" each time it appeared in the telegram.

"It says: *'Seven trains to and from Dover Station have been robbed over the past two months. Three dead. Request your immediate assistance to investigate and halt the robberies. Expect all due authority and pay. Respond at your earliest convenience.'*" He put the telegram back in the envelope. "It's signed by Frazer Rice."

Billy let out a low whistle. "A personal correspondence from the town's benefactor. All the way from New York City, no less."

"Sent directly to me," Mackey noted. "What do you make of it?"

"I've read about the robberies in the paper, but since they happened well south of here, I didn't pay them much mind. Olivette and Chidester stations, I believe."

"You believe right." Mackey set the telegram on the desk. "Out of our jurisdiction, but Mr. Rice wants to make them our responsibility."

Mackey had gotten to know Mr. Rice during and after Darabont's siege. He had grown to like the man despite his wealth. He respected the way the multi-millionaire had helped keep people calm during the siege. He also appreciated his support afterward when Mackey, Billy, and some others rode out to hunt down Darabont and rescue the women he had taken with him. The fact that

Mrs. Katherine Campbell had been one of the captives made Mackey feel even more gratitude toward the man, for Katherine was the love of Mackey's life.

As was Billy's custom, he took a practical approach to the matter. "Mr. Rice might want us to take responsibility, but we've got plenty of responsibility right here at home, Aaron." He inclined his head toward the jail cells in the back. "Today's the first day in two months when we don't have a full house, remember? We can't go off on a separate errand for Mr. Rice right now, at least not for a few days. Tent City's ready to go up in flames at any moment. Our place is here, not on some cattle car hunting down bandits."

"Maybe it's not a separate errand," Mackey said. "Maybe the robberies have something to do with what's been going on around here lately."

"I'm sure it does," Billy said. "It's no secret that Mr. Rice owns the railroad and the Dover Station Company. Dover's a boomtown, so it stands to reason that his trains would be packed with valuable goods and people with money headed to his town. Any robber worth his salt would be a fool not to hit a train like that, and Rice is a fool for not protecting his own property. All I know is that I'm not risking getting shot in Olivette because the Doc there is a drunk, and I have too much pride to die in Chidester. Rice should wire the territorial marshals about this, not us."

Mackey knew Billy was right. Technically, the territorial marshal had authority in a matter like this, but old John Casswell and his deputies were all close to retirement. Having lived this long, none of them would be in any hurry to run down a gang of vicious bandits in the twilight of their careers.

"Casswell's not going to trade a rocking chair for a bullet at this point in his life. This bunch has killed three people already. An old marshal at the end of his string wouldn't mean much to whoever's behind these robberies."

"Fine," Billy said. "Let Rice hire Pinkertons or gunmen to keep an eye on things. God knows he's got the money for it."

"That's my point." Mackey wasn't entirely certain what his point was, but he knew he had one. He could see the outlines of it in the distance, and the more he talked, the closer and clearer the point became. "Rice owns the railroad and the Dover Station Company, yet he didn't send this telegram to Van Dorn or to Grant. He sent it directly to me. Why?"

Billy picked up his mug and sat in a chair by the window. "I don't know and neither do you. The one thing I *do* know is that look you've got on your face. Quit filling in blanks that aren't there, Aaron. That's how you get into trouble. There could be a hundred different reasons why Rice sent that directly to you."

"No one ever sent a telegram by accident," Mackey said. "This is company business and should've gone to Van Dorn or Grant, first, but it didn't. I think he deliberately sent it to me because he doesn't want Van Dorn or Grant involved."

"That's a pretty big stretch, Aaron. Even for you."

"Is it?" It was all beginning to make sense now. "Think about it. I gave Grant every chance to tell me why he needed gunmen. He said it was because of anonymous threats from his workers. He never mentioned anything about the train robberies. It would've been the perfect reason why he needed extra guns around, but he didn't even mention it. It's like he didn't pay the robberies any mind, either, even though they directly affect the company he works for."

"They've slowed down some of the traffic into town, though, which suits me just fine."

Mackey's faith in his own idea weakened. But he knew something was there. Grant hiring gunmen just before two incidents in Tent City and on his own construction site? That was too close to be a coincidence.

He sat back in his chair and looked out the window at the scaffolding of the new Municipal Building across the street. "In any event, I believe Mr. Rice might be a good man to have on our side, especially now."

"Against who?"

"Against that." Mackey nodded toward the Municipal Building. "Every day that damned building moves closer to completion is one day closer you and I get to losing our jobs."

"No way. We're elected, remember? Besides, Mr. Rice is paying for that building and we stand in good with him. No way he'd stand for us being pushed aside."

But Mackey wasn't so sure. "Mr. Rice is a good man, but he's back in New York, and Grant seems to be running the show here with Van Dorn's blessing. It might be Mr. Rice's money, but Grant is deciding on how it gets spent."

Billy shrugged. "Mr. Rice isn't the type who lets much slide by without his notice. He'll put his foot down if he has to."

"If he knows about it," Mackey said. "Besides, a new mayor could pass a law abolishing the office," Mackey reminded him. "With the election coming up in a month, I view that as a damned likely possibility."

"No one's said they're even running yet. Hell, after how we got rid of Darabont, you could run for mayor if you wanted."

But Mackey didn't want the job. "Someone will run. Grant will see to that and he'll own whoever it is. They'll come for our jobs soon after, mark my words. We're not part of the new town, Billy. We're part of the old, and everything Grant does changes that."

"So?" Billy finished the last of his coffee and set his mug on the window ledge. "If they want our jobs, they can have them. If you'll remember, we weren't so sure we were going to stick around after we killed Darabont and brought the women back. We only stayed because Mr. Rice asked us to."

"And because of Katherine," Mackey added. Mrs. Katherine Campbell. One of the women Darabont had taken with him when he had attacked the town. The woman some blamed for killing Mackey's dying marriage. The only woman Aaron Mackey had ever truly loved.

Billy winced. "Shit, Aaron. I wasn't thinking. I'm sorry. She doing any better after her time with Darabont?"

Mackey didn't like dwelling on it. Darabont and his men might have been dead, but the horror they had inflicted on Katie and the other women who had lived was still very much alive.

"She's fine as long as she doesn't try to leave her hotel," Mackey said. "She's made it as far as the porch but won't step foot off the property. Running the place keeps her busy, and the ladies we brought back are glad to work there."

"She could always sell the place and leave if you wanted to take her with us," Billy said. "I've heard Grant is interested in buying the place from her."

Mackey knew that already. The hotel had

always been Katherine's, bought and paid for by her own money. What she decided to do with it was her concern. He would support her either way. "I don't think she'd be able to make it to a wagon, much less handle a ride to another town if we lose our jobs."

Billy looked down at the telegram on Mackey's desk. "I guess we can't do much good for her or anyone if we don't have jobs. Maybe we ought to help out Mr. Rice after all? I hear he's pushing hard for statehood and might get it next year. A good word from him could come in awful handy if changes are coming."

"I like the way you think." Mackey took a new sheet of paper from his desk and began writing a reply to Mr. Rice's telegram.

Billy looked out the window as the noises from the construction site across the street started up again. Foreman or no foreman, the future of Dover Station would not wait. "I swear, Aaron. Where there's money, there's always problems."

Mackey saw no reason to argue with him.

Chapter 4

On his way to the telegraph office, Mackey found his father sitting on the bench in front of the store he owned, the Dover Station General Store.

The sheriff was anxious to get to the telegraph office, but trying to avoid Brendan "Pappy" Mackey was pointless.

In addition to being mayor, Brian Mason had also been Pappy's only competition in town for a decade. Now that Mason had taken a position with the company, he had neither the time nor the inclination to own his own store. He had sold out to Pappy about five months before, making him the only general store owner in town, not to mention one of the biggest in the country.

The elder Mackey could never have been described as a tall man, but what he lacked in height he made up for in size. His broad shoulders, strong back and thick forearms were more worthy of a blacksmith than the shopkeeper he was. He was going on sixty, but still often did the work of three men half his age. His hair and beard had long turned steel gray, making his stern countenance appear even more so, though his eyes belied a vibrant spirit and a wicked tongue.

His father eyeballed him over the bowl of his pipe. "You're looking spry this morning."

His Longford brogue added a bit of music to everything he said. "But that's hardly a surprise, given you've just killed four men before breakfast."

"Your rumor mill's got a busted gear," Mackey said. "I only killed one man today. One of the Bollard bastards. Billy killed Eddows at the Municipal Building. Two others took care of themselves. You can read all about it in the *Record* tomorrow morning."

"Ross is expected to make a full recovery, thanks to you. He's already home and resting with his wife and children at his side."

Mackey was not surprised Pappy knew so much. His father's capacity for gossip was unrivaled. There wasn't a bartender or barber or housewife within a day's ride of Dover Station who heard anything before Pappy got it first. "What's the rumor mill saying about the shootings?"

"Generally supportive of you and Billy," Pappy said. "Think you did a fine thing for the town and saving Ross's miserable hide the way you did. The people know a firm hand is required in a boomtown and Dover Station certainly qualifies as such."

Mackey was a bit surprised he had supporters. "Wasn't always that way. I can remember a time not too long ago when they didn't like the way I did my job."

"Mr. Rice seems to like it well enough," Pappy said, "and what he likes, everyone else likes if they know what's good for them." He waited until a couple of people strolled by before beckoning his son closer. "But not all of the talk of the man has been positive."

Mackey *wasn't* surprised to hear that. The only thing the people of Dover Station loved more than making money was complaining. "What is it?"

"Complaints about your Mr. Grant, mostly." He took the pipe from his mouth and pointed the stem down Front Street toward the Municipal Building. "And about Tent City in particular. The stench from the place hangs over everything, even worse in summer. And with winter coming on, people wonder how safe they'll be. What if the rabble decide to break into homes for firewood, or worse, look for warmer places to sleep? They're wondering why the company is spending so much money on that damned thing instead of places where the workers could live. Brick and iron cost a fortune and take ten times as long to build than a wooden structure that could put a roof over people's heads."

Mackey knew rumors were rarely open-ended and often came with a conclusion. "What do they think is happening?"

"They're wondering if that damned palace won't serve as Grant's personal office, much in the way Van Dorn looms over us from his house upon the hill."

From where he stood, Mackey could also see the building that had now become known as Van Dorn House. It was a sprawling cottage of sharp roof angles intended to keep the rain from pooling and the snow from sticking. Someone had added wooden gingerbread adornments to the eaves and corners in an attempt to soften the severity of the structure, but it was a failed attempt. Every window was black due to the shades being closed and the drapes drawn shut.

A thin wisp of gray smoke rose from the middle of the house's three chimneys. The wraparound porch facing the town had never been used, and Mackey doubted it ever would. Silas Van Dorn was not a man who loved the outdoors.

The placement of the house wasn't an accident. Van Dorn and Grant knew exactly what they were doing when they built that severe monstrosity that lorded over the town. It gave them a perfect view of everything that happened below them. The construction, the activity, who arrived at the station and who left. They didn't even have to walk out their front door to see what was happening. Silas Van Dorn merely had to look up from his books and his ledgers to gaze out the window at all he had wrought.

Mackey decided Pappy's gossip mongering might be useful for a change. "You hear anything about people making threats against Grant's life?"

Pappy's eyes brightened. "No. Who'd want him dead? Everyone's getting rich off him and the company. Workers, shop owners, whorehouses. I can't think of a man or woman who doesn't like him. They don't trust him, myself among them. He's a bit too sweet to be wholesome for my taste, but he's mighty popular at the moment. Why, the people would love Van Dorn even more if he ever left the house."

Mackey had suspected as much. If anyone had threatened Grant's life, even one drunken night over a bottle of cheap whiskey, Pappy would have heard about it. "What about the train robberies?"

"Read about them," Pappy said, "but who gives a tinker's damn about what happens in Olivette or Chidester? Two wind-scoured hovels that God should strike from the face of the earth as far as I'm concerned." Pappy seemed to think about the nature of the question. "Why do you ask? You don't think they'll rob a train here next, do you?"

"Of course not." He was anxious to move on to something else. "What about Marx? Hear anyone talking politics?"

"Marx? No. Who is he? He one of the new-comers thinking about running for mayor? I wouldn't put it past them, you know. We invite these interlopers into our bosom and next thing you know, they're looking to run the place."

"Marx doesn't live here. He's in London, I think."

"Then what the hell does he have to do with life here?"

"That's a good question," Mackey admitted. "If you hear anyone talking about the robberies or workers organizing or Grant, let me or Billy know, will you?"

"Consider it done. Now tell your old father, have you and Mrs. Campbell set a date yet?"

"There's nothing dear or old about you, Pop. You're just nosy."

As he rounded the corner off Front Street and on to Fourth Avenue, Mackey heard someone calling his name. He turned and saw Doc Ridley striding toward him through the muddy thoroughfare. "Wait a moment, sheriff. I would like a word."

Six months before, Mackey would have ignored the doctor and kept walking. He had been one of the sheriff's harshest critics back then, constantly calling his tactics brutal affronts to God. He believed all men were children of God and must be treated accordingly. Mackey tried to point out that God's children had a habit of trying to kill him and needed to be dealt with accordingly. It was a point the doctor refused to accept and the principal reason why Mackey often ignored him instead.

But since the Darabont siege on the town,

the two men had reached something of an understanding. Something south of friendship, but north of contempt.

"I wanted to thank you for your assistance today in Tent City," Ridley said after Mackey helped him climb up to the boardwalk. "Damned dirty business if you ask me. I wish someone could take a torch to that damned place and burn them all out."

"That would be against the law," Mackey said. "Wasn't too long ago when a Christian man such as yourself would never entertain such notions."

"That was before Tent City and that damnable company took this town by the throat. Just look at what they've done to our town, Aaron. We forged a nice quiet place in the wilderness. Now it's a godforsaken den of iniquity. The peace is broken every waking moment by hammering and sawing everywhere you turn, not to mention the foul language of the workers that assault the ears of our womenfolk."

Mackey chose his words carefully. Pappy may have been the biggest gossip in town, but Doc Ridley gave his father a run for his money. Anything Mackey said to him was liable to be spread halfway around town before he got back from the telegraph office. "Progress takes time, Doc. We might have to put up with a little inconvenience now, but in a year, it'll be a distant memory."

"From what I hear, that might not be the only thing around here that'll be a distant memory."

Now he had Mackey's complete attention. "And just what the hell is that supposed to mean?"

"Language, young man," Ridley said. "And I meant no personal threat to you, of course. Not from me, anyway. But from your new employers? I'm not so sure."

"I work for the town, Doc. Not Mr. Rice or anyone else." He remembered the telegram in his pocket but decided the doctor did not need to know about that. "In fact, technically I work for you now that you're the mayor."

"Acting mayor and only for another week, praise the Lord," Ridley said. "I never wanted the position in the first place. But I know someone who does." He leaned in closer and said, "Mr. Grant is rumored to be throwing his hat into the ring."

This was not the first time Mackey had been told of Grant's political aspirations, but it did not make sense. Grant already had a good thing going as the eyes and ears of Silas Van Dorn. He controlled the Dover Station Company without risking a dime of his own money. He would be giving up an awful lot to be mayor of a town he already controlled.

Still, Ridley's gossip was usually more selective than Pappy's, so he could not afford to dismiss it out of hand.

"Grant tell you this himself?"

"A patient told me." Ridley blushed as he said, "Let's just say he tends to talk after their time together and he mentioned it to her."

Mackey enjoyed the pious man's embarrassment. "Why, Doctor Ridley. I thought you'd never treat such women."

"Fallen women are children of God, same as you and me, sir. And, despite her shortcomings, she has never lied to me once."

Mackey didn't doubt it. "I don't think Mr. Rice would stand for him being with the company and the mayor at the same time."

"The way things have been going lately, I wonder how much influence Mr. Rice even has these days. I know he owns the company, but he didn't strike me as the kind of man who would approve of Tent City, do you? Besides, being mayor could give Grant a tremendous amount of power in this town, Aaron. I think he has too much already and I'm not the only one, either."

Mackey chose his next words carefully. If he gave Doc the slightest hint of dissension between him and the company, it would be all over town by nightfall. He did not want to goad Grant more than he already had. "The election's still a couple of weeks away. A lot can change between now and then. Now, if you'll excuse me, I have to see a man about sending off a message."

But Ridley surprised him by grabbing his arm

as the sheriff tried to move away. "Goddamn it, son. You've got two good eyes and a brain in your head. Use them. You've seen what's been happening since Mr. Rice left town. Van Dorn has given Grant too free of a hand. He decides what gets built when and where. He opened the whorehouses and saloons and the gambling parlors before he built places for people to live. Now we've got Tent City on our hands and all of the vice and horror that goes on in squatter settlements. Mark my words, Aaron, that none of this is an accident. All of this is a coordinated effort for some higher purpose that will ultimately serve James Grant, I promise you."

Mackey was used to Doc Ridley yelling at him, even insulting him for shooting someone or beating them badly during an arrest. But the look in the doctor's eyes was something new. Something he had never seen there before.

Fear.

Mackey looked at Ridley's hand on his arm until the doctor slowly removed it. "Forgive me, sheriff. I seem to have forgotten my manners."

The man had gone from rage to mildness so quickly, Mackey felt sorry for him. "Nothing to apologize for, Doc. You've given me a lot to think about. In the meantime, I'd appreciate it if you'd sign the death certificates for the four men over at Wallach's place. I'll need them for my report, especially when I give Van Dorn a copy."

"Why does that scoundrel need a copy?"

"Because all four deaths happened on company property."

"Yes," Doc Ridley said thoughtfully. "I suppose they did. Imagine that. A year ago, I would have blamed you for the deaths. Now, we seem to be on the same side. Funny how things change, isn't it, Aaron?"

"Dover Station gets stranger each and every day, Doc." Mackey decided to get to the telegraph office before his luck with Doc Ridley changed.

The Dover Station telegraph office was located in the railway station at the edge of town. Van Dorn and Grant had introduced plans to double the size of the town on the other side of the tracks, but for now, it was one of the last places where someone could enjoy the pastoral views of the Montana wilderness that hadn't changed since the town's founding.

On a clear day, smoke from the bunkhouse chimneys at the old JT Ranch could be seen wafting up to the sky, the only sign that man inhabited that part of the world. It was a view Mackey had never taken for granted. Not when he was a boy, not on the day he left for West Point and at no time since. He had spent many a troubled hour sitting on the old bench outside the station in the early morning hours, watching the sun rise above the distant peaks as he ordered his mind.

67

He had plenty to think about that day, especially after what Pappy and Doc Ridley had told him about Grant's plans. Both sets of gossip were headed in the same direction but were independent of each other. They bore some contemplation, but not now. The telegram in his pocket was more important.

The station building had been the first structure the Dover Station Company had rebuilt after they announced their intentions for the town. It had once been a plain wooden building with a few benches inside for passengers to wait for the train. The platform had been a warped, wooden affair where one could easily walk to the small corral at the end of the platform, where cattle and horses could be loaded onto the train.

The Dover Station Company had completely transformed it. Since they also owned the railway, they wanted a structure befitting their vision of Dover Station's promise.

The old wooden structure had been replaced by a brick and iron building with spires at its peaks, a modern telegraph office, a waiting room with high vaulted ceilings and a proper corral at the far end where both cattle and horses could be loaded onto trains heading to market in Butte and points elsewhere. A brick wall lined with ivy kept passengers boarding the train from seeing the beasts being loaded or unloaded from the train.

As someone who'd spent most of his life in

Dover Station except for his army career, Mackey felt compelled to hate such an elaborate structure in his hometown. But unlike many of the other lifelong Dover residents, he could not help but appreciate the building.

Mackey found Joe Murphy, the telegrapher, in the stationmaster's office in the middle of eating a ham sandwich. Joe had only been assigned to Dover Station for a few months and always acted nervous whenever he saw Sheriff Aaron Mackey. He had probably heard the stories about Mackey's exploits since the day he arrived in town—most of them exaggerations—and he never knew how to act around the lawman.

That morning was no exception.

Joe dropped the sandwich on his desk and quickly wiped his hands. "Yes, sir. Good morning. What can I do for you?"

Mackey had been uncomfortable with formality since he had left the army. "How many times do I have to tell you not to call me 'sir'? Aaron or 'sheriff' is fine."

"Yes, sir." He pawed at his hands with a towel. "How can I help you?"

Mackey was too tired to correct him again. "I need you to send a telegram for me." He took the envelope from his pocket. "It's a reply to Mr. Rice's telegram from earlier today. I need it to go straight to him, understand? I need it to be confidential. Can you do that?"

Joe paled. "I can try to raise the person who sent it from New York. If they're on the other end of the line ready to receive, I can tap out whatever you like. But it'll still go over the wire, so some of the other stations will most likely get it if they're of a mind to."

Mackey's years in the army had taught him how telegraphs worked. "That's fine. But I want the contents of what I send to be confidential as far as Dover Station goes. Do you understand?"

The look on Joe's face showed he did not, so Mackey put a finer point on it. "If anyone asks you about this telegram, I want you to keep your mouth shut. That goes for Mr. Van Dorn and Mr. Grant. It's official sheriff business strictly between me and Mr. Rice. If you get in trouble for it, I'll accept full responsibility. Do you understand that?"

"Certainly, sir. But Mr. Grant gets a copy of all the telegrams that go in and out of the office. Every station up and down the line sends him copies every week on the train. He wanted it that way since the robberies started." He lifted up a blue telegraph book. "Every message gets written in here before I send it out." He looked around for a moment. "But, seeing as how this is special for Mr. Rice, I suppose I could lose the page with your message if you order me to."

"I'm ordering you to." He took the note out

of the envelope and handed it to Joe. "I also appreciate it."

Joe eagerly took the paper and began writing it in block letters in his telegrapher's book. It read:

MR. RICE: RECEIVED YOUR MESSAGE AND WILL HELP. AWAITING FURTHER INSTRUCTIONS. AARON MACKEY

He watched Murphy tap out a code on the telegraph machine. After a few seconds, he smiled. "They're ready to receive on the other end, sir. I'll begin sending it out right now."

As he watched his message being transformed into a series of electronic dots and dashes, something Murphy had just mentioned began working its way through his mind.

Grant had ordered all railway stations to send him copies of all the telegrams they sent after the train robberies began. That meant Grant must have thought there could be a connection between the telegrams and the robberies. Grant had run a telegraph office a few years ago. If true, he'd be familiar with how the system operated.

But what did telegrams have to do with the robberies?

Mackey was still puzzling over this when Joe startled him by sneezing. He'd used a ruler to tear the page out of the book and covered the sound of the tearing page by faking a sneeze for the benefit of anyone who might be listening.

Joe folded the page and Mackey's message

together and handed them back to the sheriff. "Here you are, sir. Anything else I can do for you today?"

Mackey took both papers and put them in his shirt pocket. "You mentioned Mr. Grant has ordered that copies of all telegrams be sent to him after the robberies."

"Yes, sir. Indeed, I did."

"Where does he keep these copies? In his office up at Van Dorn House?"

"No, sir. There are too many of them to be stored in such a small house. We keep them here in the office."

Interesting. "He ever look at them?"

"Can't say as I've ever seen him do it," Joe admitted. "He's got a key to the place, so I'm sure he has, just not while I'm here. Why?"

Mackey didn't have an answer for that. Yet. But he planned on getting an answer right away.

Chapter 5

The offices of *The Dover Station Record* had been the second building to be redone after the railroad station. It had also been the first business bought by Mr. Van Dorn—at Grant's urging—before the Dover Station Company announced its intentions to expand the town. A new printing press had been brought all the way from Ohio and installed at great cost.

While the press was ordered, a new building was erected. It might not have been as grand a structure as the rail station, but it was a big improvement over the crooked wooden house that had occupied the space. A new stone façade with Greek columns now surrounded the building, complete with the paper's new slogan, *Veritas Vos Liberabit*, carved into the stone beneath the sign reading THE DOVER STATION RECORD. Mackey's passing understanding of Latin told him it meant, "The Truth Shall Set You Free."

Charles Everett Harrington had been the founder of the *Record* who had been kept on by Mr. Rice to run the operation, though Mackey could not understand why. Harrington was an affable newspaperman who always had a full flask in his pocket and a story on his mind. He had more of an affinity for drink and late nights spent telling tall tales in saloons than for the running of a serious newspaper.

But the *Record* building was not the only town institution to enjoy a transformation following the paper's sale to the Dover Station Company. Harrington had ditched his slovenly appearance for a pinstriped suit and tie. He had his hair cut once a week and shaved twice a day. He kept regular hours and oversaw the production of a respectable daily journal of events from all over the territory.

Harrington was the image of the prosperous newspaperman when Mackey found him at his desk, poring over a rough copy of the *Record*'s next edition.

Mackey knocked on the doorframe. "Catch you at a bad time, Charlie?"

Harrington looked up from his paper and immediately brightened. "It's never a bad time for you, Aaron. My door is always open for the Savior of Dover Station."

Mackey winced as he closed the office door and took a seat without waiting for Harrington to ask him in. "Told you to knock off that shit, remember?"

"I know and I have," Harrington said, "but you must allow me a little fun in private. Articles featuring you always sell plenty of copies. Tomorrow's edition promises to be no exception." He lifted the paper on his desk. "Want to read it?"

"No."

Harrington read it to him anyway. "The headline will read, 'Swift Justice Strikes Twice.' " He beamed at Mackey. "Catchy, isn't it?"

"I don't care."

But Harrington was on a roll, and nothing could stop him. "Blood flowed, but justice prevailed in the streets of our fair town yesterday as Sheriff Aaron Mackey brought two villains to heel in spectacular fashion." He looked across his desk to Mackey. "The rest is on hold until you send us your report, which I would imagine is coming directly, eh?"

"You'll get it when it's ready."

"Why wait when you're right here? How about an exclusive interview right now? You can tell me how it happened, straight from the horse's mouth, as it were? It might make me inclined to accept some favorable editorial suggestions from you as my way of showing gratitude."

"Exclusive? Jesus, Charlie. You're the only newspaper in town. Every story you run is an exclusive. And the answer is still no. I've never given you anything early before and I'm not going to start now. It'll be in my report later tonight and you can read it then."

Harrington sagged in his chair. "Well if you didn't come here to feed me an exclusive, what the hell brought you here?"

"I need a favor?"

"A favor?" His bushy eyebrows rose. "You need a favor from me but refuse to grant me one? That's hardly fair, Aaron."

"Life's not fair, Charlie. Now, you get copies of all the papers from the territory, don't you?"

Harrington waggled his hand back and forth. "With varying degrees of regularity, but yes, we do. Why?"

"You remember the train robberies we've been having in the area?"

"Not technically in the area as far as the *Record* is concerned, but farther down the line. We have run stories from other publications about them, but Mr. Van Dorn doesn't want us featuring it."

Mackey caught that. "You mean he told you personally to not run a story?"

"Well, not exactly personally," Harrington admitted, "but through his manager Mr. Grant. A most excellent man, wouldn't you say?"

"Quit trying to sound cultured, Charlie. I knew you when you lived above the North End Livery."

Harrington frowned. "You have a vicious memory, Aaron Mackey. Worse than your father's, and that's saying something."

"Quit showering me with compliments and let me see a copy of each edition of the *Record* that covers the robberies."

"I can have them brought over to you by the end of the day."

Mackey stood up and went to the door. "You can have one of your people show me now or I tear the place apart looking for them. I'll make sure to make a mess when I do."

Harrington scrambled out from behind his desk faster than Mackey thought such a round man could. "Jesus, Aaron. Why do you have to be so flinty all the time? A little humor wouldn't kill you, you know?"

"Don't be so sure."

Harrington opened the door and called one of his clerks into his office and told him the sheriff's request.

"And be quick about it," Harrington called after him as he ran off to accomplish his task. To the sheriff, he said, "Happy now?"

"No. It's been a long day. I'll make a deal with you. If you send one of your people by my office around four, I'll let you read the report so you can have it for your morning edition. That's whether or not you drop off the editions before then. Happy?"

Harrington softened. "Good God. That's as close to an apology as I've ever gotten from you. That wasn't so hard, now was it?"

Mackey eased past his belly on his way out. "Speak for yourself."

Chapter 6

Seeing as how the *Record* building was halfway between the jail and Katie's Place, Mackey decided to split the difference and have lunch with Katherine. Her hotel smelled a lot better than the jail, anyway.

He found Joshua Sandborne cleaning glasses in the hotel bar. Like many people in and around town, he had suffered at the hands of Darabont when the raiders burned down the JT Ranch, along with all of the mining and logging camps. Mackey, Billy, and the small posse they had cobbled together to chase Darabont had found Sandborne wandering along the trail, half dead once Darabont's men got through with him.

The young man had proven to be tougher than he looked. He recovered from his injuries and proved himself admirably when they finally caught Darabont and his men. He and most of the women they had rescued found a home at Katie's Place. The women who could work chose to do so as cooks, bookkeepers, and as maids upstairs.

With his job at the JT Ranch gone, Sandborne filled Old Wilkes's spot as bartender, bouncer, handyman, and pretty much anything else Katherine needed him to be.

"Afternoon, sheriff," Sandborne greeted Mackey when he saw his reflection in the mirror above the bar. "What brings you around so early?"

Mackey could not help but like the young man's enthusiasm. He was only twenty, or so Sandborne claimed, but he had already seen so much of life. A few of the patrons mistook his youth for weakness and found there was more to this thin young man than they first believed.

"Was hoping to join Miss Katherine for lunch. She around?"

"She's in the back, looking over things like she always does this time of day." He set the clean glass among the others and leaned across the bar. "I heard about what happened earlier today down by the jail. You know, if you ever need an extra deputy, I'd be honored to fill in."

Mackey was fond of Sandborne, too fond to get him involved in gunplay. "I'll keep it in mind. In the meantime, I need you to watch over things here and help Miss Katherine whenever you can."

Sandborne assured him he would as Mackey walked into the dining room. He found Katherine visiting each of her guests as they enjoyed lunch. The hotel had a reputation for offering the best food in town and was as popular a destination for locals as it was for travelers.

Despite a life spent facing Apache and Comanche; bandits and bad men, ranchers and drovers, Mackey always felt just a bit nervous whenever he saw her.

Mrs. Katherine Campbell was tall for a woman, though not as tall as him and Billy. She was thin, but not as scrawny as his wife, Mary, had been or hefty as some of Sam Warren's whores at the Tin Horn Saloon. Her hair was light brown, which suited her fair complexion. Lately, a streak of gray had appeared in the middle of her hair, hastened, no doubt, by her experiences as a captive of Darabont. She had not fretted about the gray and neither did Mackey.

Her high cheekbones and bright blue eyes gave her a strong, yet friendly countenance. Peaceful, Mackey thought, though far from innocent. She came from a good Boston bloodline and could trace her heritage as far back as the *Mayflower*.

Their affair had begun in Boston, back when she had been the young wife of a much older major, and Mackey was a lieutenant awaiting his promotion to captaincy. They only had the pleasure of one summer together before his reassignment to the Arizona Territory came through, but those precious weeks had formed the foundation of a love that had lasted ever since.

It was that love that had brought her to Dover Station, in an effort to rekindle their romance following the death of her husband. It was an unrequited romance as Mackey was already married at that time. It was that love that haunted

Mackey when Darabont had taken her and he cursed himself for being too selfish to send her back to her family in Boston.

She was made for carriage rides around Boston Common and hosting parties in her family's town home on Beacon Hill. She had no business being in the harsh Montana wilderness, yet here she was, and he was the reason why. He begged her to return to Boston after he had brought her back from Darabont and his men. Yet, despite all she had endured, she refused to let him take away the life she had chosen for herself. Her life with Aaron Mackey.

She saw him when she looked up as she moved between tables and acquired that special look she reserved only for him. A softening of her face and a certain smile he never saw until they were alone.

A smile that warmed him in a way nothing else ever had and served to drive all thoughts of dead men and Grant's ambitions for the town from his mind.

She inclined her head just enough to signal him to join her in the back room that served as her office. He took off his hat and naturally complied, acknowledging the few greetings he received from the various patrons as he passed their tables.

She joined him in the office a few moments later, quickly closing the door behind her as she rushed into his arms. Her kiss was as tender, yet as intense as their first kiss back in Boston all those years ago. A lifetime ago, really, back when they had each lived different lives.

She broke off the kiss first as she always did, burying her head in his chest as she hugged him tightly. "Sheriff Mackey. How you make me forget myself."

He smiled as he laid his chin atop her head, breathing in the fragrance of her hair. She claimed it was only rose water, but rose water had never had such a calming effect on him before.

He began to feel sleepy as she slowly began to rub his back. "And you, Mrs. Campbell, are pretty distracting in your own right."

She was quiet for a moment. "I heard about what happened today. At Tent City and at the new building they're putting up."

He hoped she hadn't heard yet, but news spread quickly in Dover Station. "How many men did they tell you I killed? Number seems to be somewhere between four and one."

"Oh, I didn't care about that," she said, "just that you were okay. I know you don't take killing lightly."

He caressed her hair. "I know, but it had to be done. For the record, I only killed one man, a Bollard twin. The other bled out from a knife wound to the belly. He shotgunned the man who stabbed him. Billy killed the man at the construction site, not me. Funny, I used to be the one doing all the killing. Must be getting soft in my old age."

She lifted her head from his chest as she pulled his hips closer to her. "Funny. You don't feel soft to me."

He felt himself blush. He had never known what blushing was until she came into his life. "That's your fault."

She laughed and slapped him on the rump. "Good. I'm glad." She began to mindlessly straighten his collar, though it did not need straightening. "I had a visitor today."

In all his life, he had never known anyone else who could say so much simply by changing the tone of their voice. That was why he knew something was bothering her. "Who was it?"

"James Grant stopped by to see me." She must have felt a change in him, for she quickly added, "Now, don't get upset. It was a social call. We met in the parlor before God and everyone."

Mackey had heard rumors from Pappy that Grant had designs on Katherine. And although the sheriff and the widow were not officially a proper couple, their relationship was an open, scandalous secret. Aaron was still technically married to Mary, although she had chosen to abandon him following the siege. She didn't believe his intentions in tracking down Darabont and his captives had been entirely pure. She knew Katherine had been one of the hostages and knew, deep down, it was the main reason why he rode after them. It had not been the entire reason, but enough to cause Mary to leave. She had been naïve about many things, but his feelings for Katherine had never been one of them.

Mackey tried to keep the anger out of his voice. "What did Grant want?"

"Just the usual proposition," she said. "He offered to buy the hotel from me again."

Mackey knew the Dover Station Company had made many generous offers to buy the hotel in the past six months, but Katherine had turned Grant down each time. "And what did you say?"

"What I always say. That it's not for sale at the moment, but he would be the first person I contacted if I decided to change my mind. Only this time, he made an interesting request. He asked if I would consider changing the name of the hotel to The Campbell House. He said "Katie's Place" was a bit too informal and failed to reflect the standards of a town on the rise." She laughed to herself. "I have to admit he has a point. I kind of like the sound of it."

Mackey knew that was part of Grant's charm. He was never totally wrong and had a way of making his ideas seem like your own. "What did you say?"

"I told him I'd think about it, but agreed the idea had merit." That laugh again. "You know, sometimes I think he likes to visit me just for the conversation. I don't think too many people stand up to him."

He kissed her forehead. "I think he's got more on his mind than conversation."

She pressed against him again. "Reminds me of someone else I know."

They kissed again, longer this time, before she gently stopped. "Personally, I think Mackey Manor has a much nicer sound to it."

"Sounds like a jail," the sheriff said, "though the idea of you being Mrs. Mackey makes anything sound a hell of a lot nicer."

He felt her body stiffen as she looked away, and he immediately regretted forgetting himself. "I'm sorry, Kate. I didn't mean to upset you."

"You didn't upset me. It's just that I won't do that to you." She gently took his face in her hands. "You were already married to one impossible woman. I won't let you get tied down to another."

He slowly ran his hands along her arms. "You're nothing like Mary. She made herself miserable and me along with it."

"And how could I offer you anything different? God, Aaron, I haven't even been able to step out of my own hotel since you brought me back. I don't even like going out on the boardwalk." Her eyes began to water. "It's been so long since everything happened. I should be getting better by now, but I'm not. I can't."

He thumbed away the tears from her cheeks. "There was a time when you first came back where you wouldn't leave your room. Then you weren't able to come down the stairs. Now you're able to glide around the dining room like a princess."

She rapped him on the chest. "I'm a Yankee, not a Brit. We left all those trappings behind, thank you very much."

He laughed. "Then how about gliding around like an angel?"

"Now I know you're lying." She hugged him again, even tighter than before. "But I love you for saying so."

He felt her tension melt away into his body. It made him feel good to be able to do that for her. He protected a town, so he should be able to do the same for the woman he loved. "There's no timetable for pain, Kate. The healing will take as long as it takes. And no matter how long it takes, I'll be right here."

Her voice was soft when she asked, "What do you think 'here' will look like, Aaron? The town, I mean. I hear all sorts of things from my guests. Talk of plans Van Dorn and Grant have for the town. I don't think anything will be the same anymore. And I don't know what that means for you."

Mackey didn't know, either. And at that exact moment, he didn't care. "Whatever happens won't matter. It's you and me from now on. And there are plenty of other places we can live."

"If I can ever get up the strength to leave my own hotel."

"You will when you're ready."

She hugged him tighter.

As much as he did not want to think of the outside world, he decided now was the time to discuss Mr. Rice's request. If he did not do it now, he might not mention it at all.

"Mr. Rice has asked me to look into something for him personally. Might be gone for a week or so."

"Do you want to do it?"

"Not particularly," he admitted, "but he's done a lot for this town, and he sounds like he needs me. I feel like I owe it to him to at least try. But I won't go if you're not up to it."

"Is it about the train robberies I've read about in the papers?"

Mackey smiled. He should have known she would have read about them. "Yeah, it is. He wants me to look into it, but something tells me he doesn't want Grant to know about it. He sent the telegram directly to me."

"Then he might not trust Grant any more than you do."

"That's my impression, but I won't know that until I talk to him personally. And I can't ask him that over a telegram. Too many eyes could see it, including Grant's."

Katherine placed her head on his chest and grew quiet, the way she always did when she thought.

"Are you going to tell him your concerns about Grant?"

"If he gives me the chance, sure. Why?"

"Because if you're going to do that, you have to do it the right way."

She never ceased to amaze him. He gently eased her away and asked, "How?"

Katherine smiled. "Because you can't tell a man like Rice anything straight on. He's made his money shooting holes in ideas, then filling them in again his way. You can't just tell him Grant's acting on his own. You'll be implying that Rice doesn't know what's going on in his own company, and he could get defensive. You have to lay out the facts and let Mr. Rice come to his own conclusions. Make it seem like it's his idea. It'll stick better."

Mackey was genuinely impressed. "I never thought of it that way."

"Of course, you didn't. You're used to just giving an order and expecting it to be followed. A woman can't just bark at a man all the time, or she's considered shrill and eventually gets ignored. Hints and influence work better."

Mackey laughed, actually laughed, for the first time since he could remember. "How the hell did you get so smart?"

"The benefit of years spent in polite society in Boston, of course."

He held her tighter. Her words made him feel

better already. "And you're sure you don't mind me leaving town to help Mr. Rice?"

"Nonsense," she said. "I'll be fine. I've got the girls here if I need anything. Jessica has become my right arm and Joshua is just like Wilkes except much younger. He has a way with handling the drunks, too, without them swinging or shooting."

"He's happy to have the job," Mackey said. "Smells a hell of a lot better in here than it does with cattle and horses."

"See? Nothing for you to worry about then." She raised her head off his chest and looked at him. "You're a lawman, Aaron. You've got a job to do, and I have no intention of changing that."

He had not heard her sound this strong in months. He decided she could stand a little teasing. "So I don't have to worry about Mr. Grant moving in while I'm gone?"

"Mr. Grant is many things, but he's not you." She looked into his eyes as she slowly moved her hands up and down his back. "I won't change my mind, but you'll have to make it up to me first."

He realized she was putting all of her weight against him, pushing him toward the back stairs leading up to their bedroom.

And the thought of resisting never entered his mind.

Chapter 7

When he got back to the jail later that afternoon, he found Billy reading the editions of the *Record* that Harrington's clerk had dropped off for him to read.

Without looking up from the paper, Billy asked, "How was Miss Katherine?"

"How did you know I was with her?"

"Been around long enough to recognize that glow when I see it. Besides, when you're not here and you're not on patrol, you're over there. Can't say as I blame you. She getting better?"

"A little better every day. Mentioned Rice's telegram to her. She has no problems being here by herself."

"You're good for her. She's pretty good for you, too. Humanizes you a bit."

Mackey was eager to change the subject. Billy might've been the best friend he'd ever had, but there were just some things he was uncomfortable talking about with anyone. "What are you doing with those papers? Looking at the ads?"

"Reading through the articles about the train robberies," Billy said. "Same reason why you asked for them, I'd expect."

But Mackey was confused. "I thought you said you couldn't read."

He lowered the newspaper. "I can read printed letters, like in newspapers and books, well enough. I'm not good at reading handwriting, though, and I never was much good at being able to write. That clear enough?"

"Was never clear at all," Mackey said. "Now it is. I didn't mean anything by it."

If Billy was angry about the exchange, he got over it fast enough. "What do you think the dates of the robberies will tell us?"

"Not much on their own," he admitted. "But when I replied to Mr. Grant's telegram earlier, Joe Murphy at the telegraph office said James Grant demanded a copy of all telegrams sent across their lines since after the robberies started."

Billy sat further back in his chair. "Now why do you think he'd go and do something like that?"

Mackey took off his coat and hung it on the peg by the door. "I don't know much about railroading, but neither does Grant. He knows something about telegraphs, though. Heard he ran one at some point in his life. Could be there's something interesting in those telegrams he wants to know. Lucky for us, he keeps all the copies down at the telegraph office right here in town."

Billy stood up to free the chair for the sheriff. "And lucky for us that Joe Murphy is scared to death of you."

Mackey sat down and took a pad and pencil from the top drawer of his desk. "Could come in handy. In the meantime, I promised Harrington an early look at the reports of this morning's incidents for his morning edition. I'm already late. After that, I'll read through these articles and put together a list of all the dates and times of which trains were held up. Maybe we'll take a look at all the telegrams sent on those days. See why Grant got so curious about them after the robberies started."

"What do you want me to do while you're doing all of this writing and such?"

He looked at the Regulator clock on the wall. It was still too early for the evening patrol to start, but he decided that night might be a good time to break with tradition. "Might as well run an early patrol. See if you catch anyone off guard. Pay special attention to Tent City while you're out there. If you see anything interesting, the two of us can take a look at it together."

Billy already had his coat on. "Think there might be trouble on account of the shootings today?"

"Not sure," Mackey admitted. "But something stirred them up. Maybe it's this Marx character Grant was talking about. Maybe it's that strange man who disappeared into the crowd after spouting off some nonsense. Keep an eye out for that raggedy bastard and bring him in if you see him."

Billy selected a Winchester from the rack

instead of his Sharps. Given it was going on dark, the buffalo gun's power and distance wouldn't count for much. "I'll send up a shot if I need help."

"And I'll come running if you do."

Billy closed the jailhouse door behind him. He knew he would.

Billy Sunday decided to begin his patrol by walking through the north end of town first before heading cross town toward Tent City. By the deputy's thinking, it was still way too early for anything serious to happen anywhere in town, but it was good to shake things up after a shooting. He could feel a kind of undercurrent in town, but could not understand why. It was not just because of the shootings, but the reasons behind them.

Billy had never heard of Karl Marx before, but doubted a man's words could stir up so much anger in people that they began attacking each other. At least, words in a book couldn't do that, except maybe for the Bible. He had seen officers rally men in battle, but that was different. Book words burned slower in a man's heart, and the events of the past twelve hours were outbursts.

He could tell Aaron felt it, too, but had no better luck describing it than Billy could. And if an educated man like him couldn't put words to it, Billy would not even make an attempt.

As he began his patrol along Front Street, Billy could not help but give credit to James Grant for some of the improvements the company had made to the town. The streetlamps they had installed made patrols a lot less dangerous. Before, he and Aaron had to rely on whatever light bled out from the shops and saloons into the street. The new lamps not only helped him see better, they employed two of the town's drunks as lamplighters. It had given both of the men some purpose and led them to cut down on their drinking. They lit them every evening and turned them down every morning.

The light also encouraged more people to be out on the street at night, even in cold weather like this. In fact, Billy had to sidestep several couples on the boardwalks as he began to make his rounds.

Visitors and the newer people in town saw the deputy badge pinned to the black man's coat and quickly looked away. He knew they had probably never seen a lawman like him before and were not sure what to make of him.

But the people who had lived in Dover Station for a while recognized him and made a point of wishing him a good evening. Some men even tipped their hats as they passed. A few of their wives or lady friends smiled. He heard a couple of them whisper, "That's Deputy Sunday. He helped the sheriff defend the town against the renegades" or words to that effect.

Billy could not think of another place in the world where that might happen. White folks simply did not respond that way to a Negro, especially at night, even if he was wearing a badge.

Aaron had done that for him, though Billy knew the sheriff would never take credit for it. Aaron always got angry whenever Billy tried to thank him for bring him to Dover Station and giving him a home, so Billy avoided the topic as much as possible. But he knew without Mackey's friendship, no one would be tipping their hat or curtseying to him now. Aaron always said that Billy had earned their respect on his own, through the strength of his own actions and character.

But Billy knew it was not that easy. He knew how people were; how they felt deep down about men like him, though they were usually too polite to ever say it until they were pushed to it. He never allowed himself to believe any of them actually liked him, though he imagined some of them probably did. The fact that they put so much effort into simply appearing to accept him was more than he would have expected.

That was the part about Aaron that Billy knew few people ever had the chance to see. They saw him as the Hero of Adobe Flats or by the even more ridiculous name of the Savior of Dover

Station. They saw a sheriff, a tough man who locked men up or put men down who stood against him. They saw him as a killer with his own section in the cemetery someone had taken to calling Mackey's Garden.

They thought of him as nothing more than a figure, the same mistake Aaron's wife, Mary, had made. And just like her, they did not take the time to consider the man behind the story. They did not understand him and ultimately resented him for what he did to protect their town. They could not understand his loyalty to Billy Sunday or Billy Sunday's loyalty to him. To the people of Dover Station, Aaron Mackey was a hero, a savior, a sheriff, and a captain. He was a gunman, a lawman, and a soldier. They never thought about the qualities that made him, above all, just a man. In their defense, Billy knew Aaron never encouraged anyone to get too close.

Not even Mary.

When she finally understood there was no room in his heart after the cavalry had broken it, she took her resentment of her husband and left. Besides, any undamaged parts of his heart had already long since been occupied by Mrs. Katherine Campbell.

Billy thought of all of these things and more as he passed by the newer saloons and shops along his patrol route.

Soldiering, scouting, and now peacekeeping

had long ago taught him how to think of two things at once. One part of his mind thought of how much happier Aaron seemed to be now that he had Katherine at his side. She had been damaged by Darabont, though Billy had never known how or how much. It was not his place to ask and it was not his business. All he knew was that Katherine had needed him since he had brought her and the other captives back to Dover Station. And Aaron Mackey was a man who liked to be needed. Just like the town needed him. Just like the cavalry before it.

The other half of Billy's mind heard the tinny pianos and the forced cackle of whores as prospective clients pawed them among the poker tables while they whispered prices for services rendered in each other's ears. He saw the cold eyes of the riflemen perched in lookout chairs watching the gambling and the feeling going on in the saloon beneath them, ready to blast the first drunk who pulled a knife or a gun from his boot.

Billy moved along the boardwalk, through the light and shadows of his patrol. He had long since become familiar with the shadows and night sounds of Dover Station. Settling sounds like the clink of a dinner plate or a squeak of a mattress or a hushed conversation deep in the darkness. A glance at the shadows could tell him if a door was open or if a curtain was out of place.

That night, Billy found everything in the north end of town as it should be.

He crossed Front Street and made his wide turn back south toward Tent City. He doubted the rest of his patrol would remain as peaceful.

The newer bars and saloons along the north end of Fourth Street ended. Here, the newer construction in town began, with several buildings in various states of construction or demolition. Among this disorder, Tent City thrived.

Not even the streetlamps could hide the dinginess of this part of town. He could smell Tent City before he could see it. The shadows were a little darker there. A little deeper, too. The conversations were raspy whispers carried on the dank night air. No one ever laughed in Tent City, at least not out of any sense of humor. Only pain and suffering thrived there.

The boardwalks were empty, and most of the people of Tent City were already in bed. Those who had jobs, anyway. They worked construction or in shops or in bakeries or did other people's laundry. They didn't venture out at night because those who did were rarely up to any good. The night creatures of Tent City slept during the day, conserving their strength to prey at night.

All the while Billy and Mackey hunted them. Tonight, it was Billy alone.

He caught a sudden hint of movement from one of the newer ramshackle structures that had been cobbled together at the far edge of the encampment. Instinct drove him to duck into the shadows of a building site just off the boardwalk.

There may not have been much light in Tent City, but there was more than enough for Billy to see what was going on.

Billy stayed in the shadows as he watched a man leave one of the shacks. The stranger pulled his coat collar up and his hat lower as he quickly walked north, the same direction Billy had just left. This man did not move the same way most citizens of Tent City moved. Those with enough strength and daring to venture out at night were often tired after a long day of work. They tended to shamble a bit when they walked; hunched from hours at the washbasin or the cookstove in a restaurant. They had just finished hours of hard labor and did not have much to come back to when their day ended.

That was why Billy knew this man did not belong in Tent City. He moved like he had just enjoyed a good meal in a part of town where food was scarce. He moved like he had somewhere to go, whereas the people of Tent City had nowhere to go but work the next morning.

No, Billy knew this man had no business in Tent City and was anxious to leave it.

Billy moved deeper into the shadows as he watched the man walk toward him along the opposite boardwalk. The longer he watched him, the more certain Billy grew of the man's identity.

It was not until he crossed the street and into the light that the deputy could make a positive identification.

This man walked with purpose because he did, indeed, have somewhere to go. He was on his way back home to Van Dorn House.

His name was James Grant.

And he had absolutely no business being in Tent City at this time of night.

Yes, many of his workers lived there, but he could have summoned them to his office or to some other part of town. They would have eagerly gone to meet him, too, as the prospect of a warm meal would have been too tempting to ignore.

What had brought the great man to Tent City? Billy decided to find out.

He waited until Grant had moved farther up the street before stepping out of the shadows. Following Grant would have been pointless. The man was either going back to Van Dorn House where he lived or to a brothel for female companionship and perhaps a game of cards.

Billy did not care about where James Grant was going. He cared more about where he had been.

The deputy moved from the shadows of the construction site and resumed his patrol, keeping his Winchester low at his side. It was not raised high enough to be threatening, but visible enough for people to know he had it. Sometimes, just the sight of a rifle was enough to give a man pause.

The few people who had not buttoned their tent flaps closed against the bitter Montana night paid him little notice as they busied themselves at their small cook fires or, in rarer instances, by reading by candlelight.

Billy was not surprised to see all traces of the Bollard brothers' tent had already been removed, undoubtedly picked clean of all earthly possessions before the hides and material of the tent itself had been repurposed by another family. He imagined the possessions had been scattered long before Cy Wallach and his helpers at the mortuary had even turned the corner toward Front Street. Tent City had a short memory, and sentiment was an expensive luxury they could ill afford.

Billy moved toward the shack James Grant had just visited, carefully making his way through the tents and dugouts hastily constructed among the ruins of the town's past and the buildings representing the town's future. The cloying mud and the stench of foulness were everywhere. He would have rather lived out in the woods on the outskirts of town than in the muck of this place. Yet, for all of its foulness, there was something to be said for safety in numbers.

Billy paused outside the shack Grant had just

left. It was a lopsided structure that had been cobbled together with scraps of tin and wood cast off from the numerous construction sites around town. A tarp had been secured tightly around the top of the structure, serving as a crude, but effective roof.

He stood, quietly listening as he decided if he should knock. He had no cause to bother who was living there. And since the person obviously knew Grant, announcing himself would probably do more harm than good. After all, it was not illegal to be in Tent City. Just damned strange for a man like James Grant to know someone there.

He saw candlelight flickering through the space around the shack's crude door. He listened, trying to separate the snores and the wet coughing and the other sounds of Tent City from what was happening inside that shack. Grant had left alone, and the candle had remained lit, so Billy knew someone must still be in there.

His question was answered for him when the shack door flew open and a man slashed wildly at him with a knife. Billy leapt back as best he could in the mud and rammed his attacker in the face with the butt of his Winchester.

His assailant fell back into the shack, and Billy moved in after him.

The man was lying on the wooden floor between his bed and the wall of the narrow structure.

Billy recognized him as the ragged stranger who had spouted words at Aaron after the Bollard shooting.

"Don't get up," Billy warned him. "I'm the town deputy. Stay where you are and you won't get hurt."

The man said something in a language Billy didn't understand and sprang at him again despite a bloody nose.

Billy hit him again with the rifle butt, catching him in the temple. He stumbled backward and raised the knife again. Billy brought the stock of the Winchester across the man's jaw and watched him collapse onto the bed.

Seeing the man was unconscious, he looked for the knife and realized it must be beneath the man. When he grabbed the man by the shoulder and pulled him up, he found the knife was sticking out of the side of his stomach. Billy imagined he must have stabbed himself by accident when he fell. He checked the man's eyes, but he was already dead.

Billy cursed to himself in the dank air of the shack.

He had not gone there with the intention of killing anyone. He had not gone in there at all. The man had attacked him. Why? Had he thought he was Grant returning to see him? Had he thought he was someone else?

Knowing Aaron would have questions, Billy

left the man on the bed and decided to take a quick look around the shack. From the center of the structure, he could touch all four walls and the ceiling without moving much. The shack had no decoration of any kind. No windows, either. The mattress that served as a bed was thin and the heavy blanket was made of coarse buffalo hide.

But at the foot of the bed was a chest made of dark, heavy wood, the likes of which not many in Tent City possessed. It had a thick heavy lock on it, and given the fine condition of the wood, looked as though it had been enough to discourage anyone from trying to break it.

He looked around the shack for any sign of the keys. Finding none, he patted down the dead man's pockets. He pulled out a single iron key, slipped it into the lock and opened the chest.

Inside, Billy found a map of Montana, with Dover Station circled in heavy pencil. He found train timetables and what appeared to be a train ticket with handwriting on it that eluded him. He also saw several books in the bottom of the chest. He lifted one of them out and saw the letters on the spine, but knew they did not form English words.

He put all of them together and tucked them under his arm. He was careful to relock the trunk and blow out the candle before he took his bundle back to the jailhouse. No reason to run the risk of fire.

When he stepped outside the shack, he was not surprised to find the street was empty. If anyone had heard the ruckus, no one was interested in finding out more about it. Curiosity was a luxury the people of Tent City could ill afford.

Billy only hoped the contents of the mysterious man's trunk would be enough to explain why a man was willing to lose his life to defend them.

Billy put his head down against the wind as he made his way back to the jailhouse. The cold night wind of Montana held more questions than answers for him.

Chapter 8

Mackey looked up from the book and the maps Billy had just deposited on his desk half an hour before. "And you're absolutely certain he was the loony from the street today?"

Billy drank his coffee. "As certain as I can be without asking him. Clothes were little better than rags, even for Tent City. Looked the same, too."

Mackey flipped through the book Billy had given him. It wasn't English, but close. German, from the looks of it.

The name on the train ticket was German also. Ernst Hendrik. The ticket had been issued the previous week from the Great Northwestern Train Railroad. "What the hell is a German doing here in Dover Station? And how does he know James Grant?"

"Don't ask me, boss. I just kill them, remember."

Mackey glared at him. "Knock that shit off. He attacked you. You had no choice but to defend yourself." He gestured at the pile of books and papers on his desk. "Was this all there was in the chest?"

"Nope. There were other books in there, too. The stuff I brought was on top and easier to carry, given I had the Winchester to lug around. I figured we could go back for the rest when you were ready."

Mackey got up from the desk and pulled his coat on. "Best we get over there right now before anyone else does. Bastards are worse than vultures over there."

Billy handed Mackey a rifle as they were heading out the door. "Why do you think Grant was talking to a man with a bunch of German books in his shack?"

"That's not even the biggest question." Mackey locked the jailhouse door and braced himself against the icy wind blowing up Front Street. "What the hell is a man who prizes books so much doing in Tent City in the first place?"

"All sorts of people end up in all sorts of places for all sorts of reasons, Aaron. Maybe this guy just hit a rough patch and came to town looking for a new life."

"Then how did he know Grant? If the man warranted a visit, you'd think Grant would've gotten him better lodgings."

Mackey kept the wind from taking his hat as they walked. "And why was he ready for a fight when you were at his door? You could've been anybody. You could've been Grant coming back to talk to him about something or look for something he thought he had left behind. Being so eager to kill isn't normal, even in Tent City."

The more Mackey thought about it as they walked, the less sense it made to him. He only hoped that seeing the dead body for himself would give him some answers.

There were times, especially when the wind was blowing the wrong way, that Mackey cursed the fact that Tent City was so close. But on a cold night such as this he did not complain.

All the flaps were closed and all of the lights were out in Tent City as the lawmen walked through the squalid huddle of tents and structures of the town's poor. But he knew someone was watching them. Someone was always awake in Tent City, ready to seize on any opportunity where they could gain an advantage over their neighbors.

Billy led him to the shack in question, which looked like it had been built by a drunken blind man in one hell of a hurry. There was nary a straight line in the entire ramshackle structure.

Billy went in first, thumbed a match alive, and lit a candle. Mackey pulled the door behind him. There was barely enough room for the both of them in the building that was hardly wider than a coffin.

The dim candlelight showed the dead man on the bed, exactly as Billy had described. The knife was sticking out of the right side of his belly. The corpse's jaw was at an odd angle that told Mackey it had been broken.

"The trunk with all of the books is at the foot of the bed," Billy said.

Mackey found the wooden trunk and opened the lid. Even in the dim light from the candle, he could see the trunk was completely empty.

"Goddamn it, Aaron," Billy protested, "that case was filled when I left."

The idea that Billy might have been wrong never entered his mind. "Anything else missing here?"

Billy held the candle before him as he looked around. "Nothing else to take even if someone wanted to. Hell, the most valuable thing in the place is that knife sticking out of his belly, and that's still there. I've heard of bodies being picked clean in this part of town, but why the hell would someone take a bunch of books and leave a valuable knife behind?"

Mackey closed the lid on the chest. "Means whatever was in there were more valuable to them than Ernst Hendrik or the knife. I don't know why, but I intend on finding out."

To Billy, he said, "It'd be best if you fetched Cy Wallach and tell him to bring his wagon. I'll feel a whole lot better if the body's under his care than left for the good people of Tent City to pick over. I'll stay here until you two get back."

"That'll raise a ruckus," Billy observed, "especially at this time of night."

"It's not that late, and it needs to be done."

Billy handed the candle to Mackey. "Guess I should've searched the trunk better."

"You did what you could under the circumstances," Mackey told him. "I've got no complaints and neither should you. Now go light a fire under Cy's ass and get him moving. I know how cozy he gets on cold winter nights, but this can't wait until morning."

Billy took his Winchester and went out into the night, leaving Mackey alone in the shack with the body of the man he had just killed.

Mackey moved the candle close and took a better look at the dead man's face. It was the man from the shooting. His hair and beard were long and curly with thick, uneven streaks of black and gray. His clothes were little better than rags and had never been fashionable to begin with. He had a thick build and, in life, had probably been as tall as Mackey and Billy. But in death, things like height didn't matter much. Neither did a man's clothes.

But why did a man like this have such a fancy trunk full of books? And he probably hadn't gotten on a train dressed like that, at least not without making an impression on some people. Mackey would have heard of it.

Mackey moved the candle over the corpse. He took another look at its clothes. What could a jumped-up dandy like Grant have to discuss with a man dressed in rags?

Mackey set the candle on the trunk and began patting down the corpse. A gust of wind buffeted against the shack, making the boards and tin of its construction creak and groan.

He heard something when he ran his hands over the left side of the corpse. A sound not caused by the wind.

When the gust died down, he ran his hand over the same spot again and heard the same sound. A crinkling of paper in the man's jacket.

Mackey grunted as he rolled the big man over onto his back. The man was bottom heavy. There was too much meat on his bones, considering the way he was dressed. It wasn't all muscle, either. In fact, Mackey judged most of it was fat. For a poor man, he hadn't missed many meals.

He patted down the left side of the jacket again for some kind of an inside pocket. He didn't find anything, but heard the same sound as he had before. A rustling sound, like paper. And since there was no sign of a pocket, it meant whatever it was had been sewn into the lining of the coat.

Mackey grabbed hold of the lining and ripped it open. The cheap stitching gave way easily. Inside, he found an envelope. He took it and brought it over to the candle so he could read it better.

The letter was addressed to Ernst Mohr of Chicago, Illinois. Mackey removed the letter from the envelope and saw that it had been written in an elegant hand in a language he did not understand. Some of the words were close to English, just like those he had seen in the book Billy had taken from the shack, but Mackey still could not make sense of it. The letter was unsigned.

He refolded the letter and put it back into the envelope. He looked at the corpse and the Bowie knife sticking out of its belly. Mackey raised the envelope. "Ernst Mohr," he said to the dead man. "This you? Or are you really Ernst Hendrik? Did you write this to someone? Or were you supposed to deliver it? Why'd you have it sewn into your clothes? What's so damned important about it that you kept it separate from the rest of your things?"

He leaned forward and took a closer look at the knife handle jutting out of the man's belly. "And why the hell did you try to kill my deputy? What were you protecting?"

He looked around the shack. There was nothing in it except the trunk and some bedding. He got off the bed and lifted the mattress. Nothing. Nothing looked like it had been sewn into it, either.

He stood up and looked over the sparse scene again. "What were you protecting? And what the hell does any of it have to do with James Grant?"

He turned when he heard a knock at the door as Billy stepped inside. "Cy's bringing his wagon around. Should be here any minute." He hesitated before saying, "Thought I heard you saying something when I walked up here. Kind of like you were talking to yourself."

"I wasn't. I was talking to our dead friend here."

Billy looked at the corpse, then at his friend. "He tell you anything?"

"Yep." Mackey handed him the envelope he had just taken from the lining of the dead man's jacket. "I think he might have."

Chapter 9

The cleanliness of Doctor William Ridley's office would have put many of the kitchens of Dover Station's best restaurants to shame. His medical degrees hung on the wall behind his desk. Cabinets filled with medicine and books lined both sides of the small examining room that also served as his office. Mackey knew he and his wife lived upstairs as they had since the sheriff had been a boy. Otherwise, he never would have known this room was part of where the doctor had lived most of his life.

Nothing in the office showed he was the acting mayor of Dover Station.

Doc Ridley reluctantly looked at the items Mackey had brought him as the sheriff explained how the man died. He thumbed through the book and a letter addressed to an Ernst Mohr. A train ticket for Ernst Hendrik. "Sounds like Tent City is quickly devolving into a bigger cesspool than we had previously thought."

"More than you know," Mackey said. "It's attracting all types of critters, some you even know."

Ridley's eyebrows rose. "That sounds ominous, Aaron."

Mackey hesitated to tell him more, but had

no choice. He was the acting mayor of the town and had a right to know. Mackey had a duty to tell him. "Before I tell you why, I need you to promise this stays between us. It's important, Doc. You can't mention this to anyone, not even your wife."

"Especially my wife."

Mackey could not argue with the doctor on that score. Mrs. Ridley used to keep Mackey's wife Mary informed of the latest gossip about his interactions with Mrs. Campbell. The old battle-ax had been the source of many a sleepless night in the Mackey household, a matter for which he did not hold the doctor responsible.

"Anything you tell me," Doc Ridley went on, "will be held in the strictest confidence."

Mackey figured that was as close as a guarantee as he could hope. "Billy saw James Grant leaving the dead man's tent right before he died."

Doc Ridley bolted forward in his chair. "You mean Grant killed him?"

Mackey tried to avoid looking annoyed. The doctor sometimes had a tendency to become distracted. "No. I already told you Billy killed this Ernst fellow in a struggle. The question is what Grant was doing there in the first place."

Doc Ridley looked at the pile of books on his desk. "Do you think it has anything to do with any of what you've brought here? A map, a train ticket for Dover Station dated last week, a book

115

in German, and a letter in German? What facts do you hope to be able to divine from this?"

"It's not everything," Mackey explained. "Some of his possessions were stolen when Billy came to tell me about what had happened. The trunk was full of books and such when he left, but all of it was gone by the time I got there."

"Do you think it was Grant or someone else?"

"I doubt Grant came back, so it must've been someone else. But not just any thief. A Tent City vulture would've picked his body clean. Shoes, clothes, everything. Whoever our thief was left all of that behind, including a big bowie knife sticking out of his belly.

"The way I see it," Mackey went on, "the best chance we have of figuring out what they took is by reading what we were able to get. Unfortunately, it's in German. I don't read the language, but I was hoping you might, Doc. I know a lot of medical books are written in German, and I thought you might be able to tell us what some of this meant."

Ridley laughed as he set the letter back on his desk. "Latin comes in handy in my profession, my boy, not German. Though you're not far off. A great many medical books are, indeed, written in German. Many consisting of the science of the mind and medicine. But I have never found any use for such knowledge, nor any reason to study

German. I've always been content to wait for the American translations to come out."

Doc Ridley folded his hands across his belly and sat back in his chair. "I'm less concerned about these documents than I am about the man who visited their owner. Is Billy absolutely certain that it was Grant?"

"Never known Billy to be wrong about something like that. If he said he saw Grant, then he did."

"Yes," Ridley allowed. "His eyesight has always been impeccable, even at night. I remember watching him shoot during Darabont's siege. The amount of people he picked off in near-darkness was remarkable." The doctor looked at the sheriff. "I heard Cy return with the body late last night, you know? I took the liberty of examining it before Cy turned in. The man was dead before the knife went into his belly. Blunt force trauma to the side of the head killed him. Probably from Billy's rifle. Don't get defensive, Aaron. I'm sure Billy had no choice, and I'm going to sign the death certificate as a justifiable homicide."

Ridley tapped the book on his desk. "But the man's death doesn't explain his life. It doesn't explain who he was or what he was doing here in Dover Station. Now, since you found a train ticket on him, you might want to ask our friends up in Van Dorn House if he used the train and where he came from. Work your way back to uncovering his identity from there."

"Seeing as how Grant was one of the last people to see this man alive," Mackey said, "I don't think that's a good idea."

"I happen to think it's a splendid idea, actually. Confront the bastard. See how he reacts. His reaction to the news of the man's death could tell you quite a bit. A lack of reaction or a flat-out denial could tell you even more."

Mackey gathered up the material he had placed on the doctor's desk. "I was planning on doing exactly that. But given that you're acting mayor, I didn't want to do it without talking to you about it first. Depending on how it goes, Grant might make a lot of noise. I won't be surprised if he does."

"Meaning you didn't want another man with a knife to your throat, especially given our history." Ridley slowly stood up and came out from around his desk. "You forget I've known you since you were five years old, Aaron. Any conflict between us since your election to sheriff has always been due to my unshakable belief that you were capable of being so much more than a thug with a star. I still believe that. Your actions during Darabont's siege and afterward proved me right."

Mackey took his bundle and placed it under his left arm. Six months later and Darabont's name still came up. "That son of a bitch changed all of us, didn't he?"

"Perhaps we've both mellowed some," Ridley allowed. "Change is good for the soul. It's good for Dover Station, too. I know Mr. Grant and Mr. Van Dorn have big ideas for this place, and I applaud them for it, but I think there was a more humane way of going about it. Tent City is a cancer on this town, and this man's death is a symptom of that disease. I can't think of a reason in the world why Grant would have visited a man like this, but there must be a reason for it. I beg you to be careful if you decide to look into it further. Grant went there in secret and left the same way. He obviously has something to hide and may be prepared to go to great lengths to keep it hidden."

Mackey had never considered himself to be a dumb man, but knew the doctor had a way of speaking that often took a little while to sink in. "You think I should let this death go?"

"That's your decision to make," Ridley said. "I'm not even a very good acting mayor, so I'm hardly in a position to tell you how to do your job. But if I know anything in this life, I know this town very well. I know James Grant and the company have big plans for this wilderness hamlet. This Ernst whatever-his-name-is obviously played some kind of role in Grant's plan. I'm merely pointing out that you may not want to dig too deeply into the dead man's past lest it cause you difficulty in the present." Ridley's eyes narrowed as he drove home his point. "Pick your battles carefully, Captain Mackey. That's what they taught us at the Point, isn't it?"

Mackey felt himself smiling. "I keep forgetting you were at West Point before the war."

"That makes one of us."

The morning had proven to be warmer than Mackey had expected as he walked back to the jailhouse. He could sense a hint of snow in the air, but not until the next day at the earliest. At least the wind had died down, making the colder temperature easier to take.

The lack of wind also made it easier for him to hear James Grant calling his name.

Mackey turned to see Grant standing in front of one of the newer hotels that had opened on Lee Avenue, a gawdy place called The Bedford Arms. From Mackey's recollection, the hotel had been open for more than a month and neither he nor Billy had ever been called to settle a disturbance there. Whoever was in charge seemed to know what they were doing and how to handle their own trouble.

Grant approached him, his red brocade vest and a white shirt making him appear woefully underdressed for the Montana fall. But if he was cold, he hid it well. "Sheriff Mackey, please join me for a moment. There's a matter of great importance I wish to discuss with you."

Mackey kept his bundle under his left arm. He had planned on meeting Grant at some point, but at a time and place of his choosing. Something else he had learned while studying at West Point.

But life did not always give people the luxury of choosing where and when they fought or if they fought at all. "I was on my way back to the jailhouse to finish up some paperwork. I can meet you later if you want."

"Nonsense." Grant beckoned him to come to him. "I have a table inside already where it's nice and warm. I won't take but a moment of your time, I promise."

Mackey may not have liked the man, but he could understand why so many people did. He had a confident charm about him that was easy to like.

Mackey knew he could have refused, but his curiosity got the better of him. He accepted the invitation.

The dining room of The Bedford Arms was an affair of heavy wood, dark red wallpaper, and a roaring fireplace. It was the kind of room where a man could enjoy a good meal and wish for a place to sleep without ever stepping foot outside.

The tables were sparsely populated as it was

that dead time in the day of a restaurant. Too late for breakfast and not quite time for lunch.

Mackey wasn't surprised to see Walter Underhill already sitting at the table where Grant led him. The big man looked uncomfortable in the elegant setting.

Grant said, "I know I don't have to introduce you two, what with you being blood brothers in the Battle of Dover Station and all."

"Good to see you, Aaron." Underhill looked at the bundle under Mackey's left arm. "Looks like you've been doing yourself some reading."

Mackey felt like a schoolboy as he set the dead man's belongings on the table and took a seat. He sat with his arm draped on the chair's armrest. He liked Underhill, even considered him a friend, but the man worked for Grant. Mackey had no illusions about where the man's loyalties ultimately lay. "Makes for some boring reading, given that none of it is in English."

"Which is exactly the reason why I wanted to talk with you." Grant sat next to him on his right. "I understand there was a death in Tent City last night. The result of an altercation between your deputy and one of the unfortunates who call that pit a home."

Mackey shifted his chair to the left, putting a bit more distance between him and Grant. He sat so his hand was less than the length of his thumb from the handle of his Peacemaker.

122

"Deputy Sunday had to kill a man who assaulted him while he was on patrol. The death was as unavoidable as it was unfortunate."

Grant clapped and cheered, drawing every eye in the room. "You bring happy news, sheriff. The happiest I have received in some time." He raised his hand and caught the attention of the waiter. "It's too early for champagne, but bring us another pot of coffee as soon as you can." He waited until the waiter moved away to add, "Are those the contents of the dead man's hovel?"

Mackey placed a hand on them. "They are. But I can't let you see them until I find out who this man is. They're evidence."

"I don't need to read it," Grant said. "I've already read that nonsense several times."

Mackey caught that. "I didn't know you understood German, James."

"I can't read a word of it," Grant admitted. "Have you ever heard it spoken? God-awful language. Harsh as hell. No, I recognize that book because I've already read its English translation. *Das Kapital* by Karl Marx and Frederich Engels. You remember Marx from our conversation in your office yesterday after that business with Eddows. I understand some of the translation lacks the nuance of the original language, but not enough to change my opinion of it. Just a bunch of childish nonsense if you ask me. I'm certainly not surprised you found such rubbish among the possessions of Ernst Mohr."

Grant leaned in closer toward Mackey. "Tell me, did Mohr suffer much before he died? Please tell me he did. I heard your deputy killed him with a knife to the belly. I hope that's true."

Mackey was in no hurry to answer him. Everything was happening too quickly and all of a sudden. One moment, he was walking down Front Street, wondering how he could approach Grant about this, now he was having coffee with Grant, who admitted he knew Mohr. "How did you know this man?"

"Most reluctantly, I can assure you, sheriff," Grant said. "The son of a bitch was an anarchist, sir. A troublemaker and a rabble-rouser who had caused no end of grief for my employers. Since arriving in our fair country ten years ago, Ernst Mohr has organized numerous work stoppages at Mr. Rice's various holdings. He has attempted to organize several groups of workers everywhere between Chicago and Montana. Stevedores, warehouse workers, railroad workers, builders. The list is nearly endless, but it doesn't matter now that the bastard has finally met his end. His death is all that really matters."

Grant winked. "And don't think I forgot about my original question, sheriff. Did he die from a knife in the belly like I've heard? Or did he die slow? If he did, I'll give your deputy a hundred dollars in gold just to hear it for myself."

Underhill said, "As you can guess, Mr. Grant here didn't care much for this Mohr fellow of yours."

Mackey wanted to ask him why he had visited Mohr the night before, but decided to hold that question back for a later time. "Have you met this man before? We could use your help in identifying the body, maybe notifying his family of his passing."

"Not only can I identify the man," Grant said, "but I can also point out a few scars he has received by my own two fists. Mohr and his rabble tried to organize a work action in Butte when I first joined the company as Mr. Van Dorn's assistant. He got the laborers to refuse to unload the boxcars until we discussed fair wages. So, I rounded up a group of bullyboys from a local tavern to help us unload the train ourselves." Grant smirked. "By then, the workers had formed a line around the boxcars and I knew they'd never let us unload them without a fight. The men I had brought with me were more brawlers than workers anyway. We took a few hits, but when the dust settled, the bastards were back at work and Mr. Mohr was in a hospital ward with a fractured skull."

Mackey was surprised by how much information Grant was feeding him. He decided to press his luck. "When was the last time you saw Mohr?"

Grant frowned. "After Eddows spouted off that workers-of-the-world nonsense, I feared Mohr might have come to Dover Station. Yesterday afternoon, I began reviewing the passenger records of train passengers coming and going from town. I noticed an old alias of Mohr's on the list. Ernst Hendrik. I found he was in Tent City among my people like a cancer among healthy cells and told him he had exactly two days to leave town. He had already held one of his meetings here, which only served to get some of the men worked up. Men like Eddows. Mohr's poison spreads quickly among the working class, sheriff. I can't allow the future of this town to be held for ransom every time some hammer monkey thinks he deserves more money for driving a nail into a piece of wood."

That struck Mackey as odd. "You always check the passenger manifests, Jimmy?"

"Damned right I do, especially given the recent spate of robberies on the railroad. I like to find out everything I can about our town, sheriff. I hate Tent City as much as anyone, and if I can curtail people from coming here before we have proper space for them to live, all the better. Inconveniences like train robberies and social unrest caused by men like Mohr can cripple a town on the rise. I have no intention of allowing that to happen here, so I keep an eye on things. As do you, I'm sure."

Mackey was curious. "Why did you go to see Mohr instead of sending Walt, here? That's what you pay him for, isn't it?"

Grant added, "Given my long history with him, I thought it best if I went to see the troublemaker personally. I gave him the cost of a train ticket and told him if he wasn't on the next train out of town, his next conversation would be with Mr. Underhill. I had no idea he'd be having a final word with Billy so soon."

Mackey knew he couldn't pin Mohr's death on Grant, but that didn't mean Grant hadn't played some kind of role in his death. "You two argue? Any punches thrown?"

Grant shook his head. "Men like Mohr are only tough on a stage in a saloon or warehouse surrounded by fellow malcontents. When the odds are less in their favor, their bravado tends to shrink accordingly." Grant held up his hands for inspection. "I didn't lay a finger on him, sheriff, because I didn't have to, not because I didn't want to. And the only thing I threw at him was money. One hundred dollars, to be exact. To encourage him to leave town without further incident. He agreed to do so." That smirk again. "I suppose even socialists have their price."

The waiter brought over the pot of coffee as Mackey stood. "You've given me a lot to think

127

about, Jimmy. I'll need to put it all in my report while it's still fresh in my mind."

"I'm sure you'd prefer Billy's coffee to what they serve here," Grant said. "From what I understand, Billy makes a fine pot."

"That he does." Mackey gathered up his bundle and once again placed it under his left arm, leaving his shooting arm free. "I'd appreciate it if you could find the time to stop by Cy Wallach's place and make a formal identification for the file. Cy can take down your statement and give it to me."

"We'll be glad to, sheriff, as soon as we're finished with our coffee. Do I have your permission to spit in his eye when I see him?"

"Don't see as how it would hurt him any."

Grant surprised him by standing and extending his hand to Mackey. "You've done the people of Dover Plains a great service, sheriff. A greater service than you know. You have my gratitude, and I'm sure the gratitude of the people of this fine town."

Mackey shook his hand and looked at Underhill. The former marshal looked away.

That told him all he needed to know. Something was going on here. Something more than Grant was letting on. He remembered what Pappy had told him the day before. What Ridley had told him as well. Something about the upcoming election. And he decided to play a hunch. "If I didn't know any better, I'd say you sounded like a goddamned politician."

Grant laughed like a politician as he sat back down. "One never knows where life's journey will take them, do they?"

Mackey pressed his hand flat against his coat, hoping it soaked up some of the moisture from Grant's hand. "No, I suppose we don't."

"One more question before you go," Grant said. "You didn't have your deputy following me, now did you, sheriff?"

"Billy was on routine patrol when he saw you leave the place."

"A happy accident, then."

Mackey left before he could be asked any more damned fool questions. *Mohr's death was a happy accident for someone. But for who?*

Chapter 10

Billy Sunday may not have been an educated man, but he had always considered himself to be a clever man. But he was having a hell of a time following Mackey's logic.

"So you think Grant and the Mohr guy were working together?"

Mackey slammed the copy of *Das Kapital* on his desk. "That's exactly what I think."

Billy drank his coffee while everything his friend had spent the last hour telling him sunk in. "I'm sorry, Aaron, but I'm not following you. I'm not arguing with you, just saying I don't understand what you're getting at."

Mackey took another run at it. "Mohr and Grant have a history. Mohr causes trouble. Grant stops him. Mohr spreads his message. Grant looks like a hero. I think Grant either allows or brings Mohr here to stir up unrest in Tent City." He held up the letter addressed to Mohr. "I've got no idea what this says, but I do see the words 'Dover' and 'Montana' in here. Mohr comes here, starts up trouble, Grant looks like a hero, and all is supposed to be well. But Eddows takes it to heart and goes too far. Grant tells him to leave, maybe pays him off, but then you come along, Mohr panics and strikes first."

"And I did Grant's dirty work for him."

"I'm getting tired of telling you to quit blaming yourself for any of it. You had no choice."

Billy didn't entirely agree, but let it go. "Still don't know what he gets from stirring up labor trouble here when he's got so much going on."

"Could be enough to get him the amount of votes he needs to get himself elected mayor," Mackey said. "Word's been spreading about him having higher ambitions for the town. Putting down a rabble-rouser makes perfect sense. He's controlling both sides of the argument and comes out looking like a hero and Mohr walks away the richer for it."

"Didn't find any money on him," Billy said, "even before I left the shack. I mean, he could've hidden it in one of the other books in the trunk, but I don't think so. All he had was that letter he had sewn into his jacket for safekeeping."

Billy finished his mug and got up to pour himself more from the pot. "I've heard a lot of lies and a lot of alibis since I've been on this job with you, Aaron. And I hate to believe Grant, but everything he said makes sense."

Mackey also knew some of the biggest lies were those closest to the truth. "I'm going to do some digging on this Mohr character. Maybe get Harrington to check some of his old newspaper records. If he was as active an agitator as Grant says, his name is bound to have appeared in some article somewhere."

"He should have plenty of time to look into it while we're gone." Billy opened the top drawer of the desk and handed him the envelope from the telegraph office. "Looks like Mr. Rice wants us on the next train out of town tomorrow morning. Said he'll meet up with you in Butte to discuss matters further since he doesn't trust the telegraph lines."

Mackey read the first telegram.

BE ON 0830 TRAIN OUT OF DOVER STATION TOMORROW MORNING. YOUR ASSISTANCE REQUIRED TO GUARD IMPORTANT CARGO. TAKE ALL PRECAUTIONS FOR SAFE PASSAGE.

The second telegram was more direct. It had been sent to every telegraph office along Great Northwestern Railroad:

BEARER OF THIS TELEGRAM HAS FULL SUPPORT OF RICE VAN DORN COMPANY AND ALL OF ITS HOLDINGS. EVERY EMPLOYEE IS EXPECTED TO GIVE BEARER ANY ASSISTANCE ASKED OF THEM. ALL

QUESTIONS REFERRED DIRECTLY
TO RICE HEADQUARTERS NEW
YORK.

Mackey looked up at Billy. "You said you read this?"

"I did."

"I thought you said you don't read telegrams that aren't addressed to you?"

"Normally don't," Billy said, "but since I knew this particular telegram concerned me, I took the liberty of reading it. Because I'm going with you, Aaron. Whether you like it or not, there's no way in hell I'm letting you go up against these people alone."

Mackey had no intention of turning down any help he could get, especially when that help came from Billy. It might leave the town in a bit of a lurch, but they had managed before with Underhill filling in. He worked for Grant, but Mackey still trusted him.

"By what I read in those newspaper accounts," Mackey said, "we're going up against anywhere between five to seven robbers on an open track. They've already killed three men, and we'll need help to bring them down the right way."

"You thinking of the Boudreaux boys?"

"I am. I'm going to need you to ride out and try to get them for us."

The idea of saying no never entered Billy's mind. "What'll you be doing in the meantime?"

"Packing," Mackey said, "and either calling in a favor or asking for one. I'm not sure which yet."

Chapter 11

Mackey found Walter Underhill exactly where he had been told he would be, on the high hill overlooking the remnants of the old JT Ranch. The spread had once been the envy of the Montana territory, a thriving concern that grew beef, bred horses, and sheared wool to the great profit of John Tyler. But after Tyler was killed and his ranch burned out during Darabont's siege, the place had been a shell of what it had once been.

The Dover Station Company was slowly putting the pieces back together, but had already made great strides. The main house had, indeed, been burned down, but the bunkhouses had been replaced and so had the barn, giving the workers and animals a warm place to be now that the cold weather was fast approaching.

Mackey had to admit that Walter Underhill was quite a sight atop his sorrel, looking out over the project he personally oversaw. His long blond curly hair and beard gave him an impressive, formidable look. He had proven himself to be an asset while Darabont laid siege to the town and in the weeks after while Mackey and his men were off chasing down the remnants of the raider and his gang.

"Afternoon, Walter," Mackey said as he pulled Adair to a stop next to him.

"Afternoon, Aaron." He looked out over the land. "What do you think of it?"

"I think it's in trouble. I think something's going on in this town that threatens all of this as much as it makes it possible. I don't know if that makes any sense, but it's how I feel."

Underhill grunted as he shifted in his saddle. "It makes no sense, but I feel exactly the same way. Can't say what it is, though."

"Can't or won't?" Mackey looked at him. "There's a difference."

"Won't," Underhill admitted. "If that diminishes me in your eyes, then that's the way it has to be. But you've got two good eyes of your own. What do they tell you about what's going on around here?"

Mackey knew they were beyond the politeness of posturing. "They tell me that James Grant is up to something and whatever it is will cause no end of trouble for us."

"Sounds like those eyes of yours tell you a lot. Mine tell me the same thing."

Mackey didn't know why he felt relieved that the big man agreed with him, but he did. "Then why the hell do you still work for him?"

Underhill pointed out at the bustling ranch. "For this. I've never been part of something new. Every place I've ever lived has been settled.

Hell, even Texas is fairly tame by now. But this is something new. A man only gets a chance like this once in his life if he's lucky, and I intend on making the most of mine."

Mackey couldn't blame Underhill for wanting to be part of something like this, even if Grant was involved. "No sin in that."

Underhill was not done talking. "I know a lot of people blame Van Dorn and Grant for Tent City. But it won't be there forever, and there'll be plenty of jobs and houses for people once the spring comes. No one could've figured out how many people would've flocked to town once word of Mr. Rice's investment got out. Even you were surprised and you've lived here your whole life."

"I was," Mackey admitted. "I thought there'd be a few people at first, the way there always was in the past, but not this many. Not enough to build themselves a slum, anyway."

"They'll be in houses soon enough," Underhill said. "I've seen the plans, Aaron, and I promise you, Grant will take care of them."

"After he takes care of himself first." Mackey asked. "I know the man, Walter. I know the type."

"Then you know what a man like him can do," Underhill said. "Maybe he's a bit too slick for my liking, but built buildings don't lie. Neither do the new shops and businesses that have opened up. The purses of the people who own them and work in them jingle, Aaron. There's no lying about that. The people love him, and he's a man who likes to be loved. So what if he likes to hear his name chanted? So what if he wants to run for mayor?"

Mackey's stomach dropped. "So it's official?"

"Nothing's official. I don't know if he's running or not. I hear the same rumors you do. But if I knew something one way or the other, I'd admit it. I wouldn't tell you what it was, but I wouldn't lie about being in the dark. You know I'm not a liar, Aaron."

Mackey remembered the day the big man had come to town. He had lied about his reasons for hunting down the Boudreaux brothers, but even that had been something closer to a fib than a lie. He thought if he could bring the brothers back with him to Texas that it could get him his old job back. But things had not worked out that way, and Underhill came clean during Darabont's siege. To the best of Mackey's knowledge, Underhill had never lied to him since, and he had no reason to believe the man was lying now.

"I know you don't lie. I just don't know what side you'll come down on if it comes time to pick sides."

"As long as it's legal and it's what Mr. Grant wants, I'll do what he pays me to do. I may not like it and I may not agree with it, but I don't have any choice. I take his money, I've got to take his orders, too."

Mackey had imagined he was going to say something like that. It was a fair statement from a fair man. He could not ask any more of him than that.

"Well, let's hope it doesn't come down to that."

"Let's hope."

Mackey cleared his throat and said, "I need a favor from you. I need you to watch the town while Billy and I are out of town on business."

"Both of you? Never heard of both of you needing to go at the same time before."

"Never had a request like this before."

Underhill let out a long, deep breath as he looked out over the ranch. "This a town matter or another matter?"

"Related to the town is all I can say," Mackey told him. "Wish I could share more than that, but I can't."

"A request that big must come from someone pretty high up. Someone like Mr. Rice."

"Like I said, I'm not at liberty to say."

"But if it came from Mr. Rice, Mr. Grant or Mr. Van Dorn should've heard about it," Underhill went on. "If they don't know about it, then maybe Mr. Rice sent it directly to you for a reason."

"Wish I could say more on the subject," Mackey said, "but I can't. I'm sure you understand."

Again, Underhill watched the livestock mill

about their respective fields. "I don't know what I understand anymore. I understood things when Mr. Rice was here. He's a plainspoken man. Tough and fair, but you always know what angle he's got on any given situation. I learned a lot from him. Wish he could've stayed on. I would've liked to have learned more."

"And what about since he left?"

"Feels different somehow," Underhill said. "Everything he promised is happening, but it feels wrong. Like two things are happening at once. It feels like I'm helping something to fail when all I'm trying to do is help it live." He leaned over the side of his horse and let fly with a brown stream of tobacco. "I don't know if that makes any sense. Never been much of a hand at words."

"Makes sense to me," Mackey admitted. "Maybe this business Billy and me are going on will help bring clarity to all of that mud. So, can I tell the mayor you'll fill in for us while we're gone?"

"Does Doc Ridley know why you're leaving?"

"No. And neither does James Grant or Silas Van Dorn. And if they ask, I won't tell them, either."

Underhill turned and looked at him for the first time since Mackey rode to him. "If I asked, would you tell me? Just me?"

"Can't do that, Walter. It's not my secret to tell."

"Figured you'd say something like that." He went back to looking out over the range. "You go about your business, Aaron. I'll watch the town for you. Whether it's a month or a year, I'll be here. Just do whatever you have to do as quickly as possible. I have a feeling things are changing and not for the better. For any of us."

Sandborne helped Mackey load his bedroll and provisions onto Adair. The Arabian was a spirited animal, and Sandborne was one of the few humans she tolerated. The other was Billy.

"It's amazing that you can put all this stuff on her and don't need to tether her to a post," Sandborne said. "She just lets you saddle her without any bother at all."

Mackey patted the mare's neck. "Adair's always been different. Guess I never treated her like other horses because I've never had to."

"Still don't know what you need all this stuff for, sheriff. I mean, you're going to be on the train the whole time, aren't you?"

Normally, Mackey did not encourage questions or second-guessing from anyone. But he knew Joshua Sandborne was not just anyone. Mackey and the others had found the boy wandering the burnt-out wreckage of the JT Ranch where he had worked. Despite a bad head injury, he had refused to ride back to town to the doctor. Instead, he healed on the trail and helped him defeat Darabont and his men.

No, Mackey tolerated Sandborne's prodding because he knew the boy was neither questioning his judgment nor arguing with him. He was a green kid with a curiosity about how and why certain things were done. Given how the young man had been raised among cowpunchers and livestock, Mackey allowed the boy a certain amount of latitude when it came to asking questions.

"You don't plan just for what's supposed to happen, Joshua. You plan for what might happen. Carrying a bedroll and a night's worth of provisions won't hurt Adair any. She'll be unsaddled in the boxcar with the other horses most of the time anyway. I just feel better having something and not needing it than needing it and not having it."

"I never heard that one before," the young man admitted. "Think I might use that in the future."

"Got something you can use in the meantime." Mackey reached into his pocket and pulled out a tin star. "Raise your right hand."

Sandborne's eyes lit up at the sight of authority in the sheriff's hand. "Is that for me?"

The boy's solemnity drove out any words or oaths Mackey had devised for the ceremony from his mind. "Just swear you'll do whatever Underhill tells you while I'm gone, but you'll protect Mrs. Campbell and her guests most of all. Understand?"

The boy cleared his throat and raised his right hand even higher. "I swear it before God and anyone."

"Good. Now put your goddamned hand down. You look like Stonewall Jackson."

Mackey pinned the star on Sandborne's vest and gave the boy a slight tap on the chin. "Make sure you keep it visible at all times when you're not working for Mrs. Campbell, understand? Anyone comes in here bothering her while I'm gone, you see to it she's protected. Don't worry about getting in trouble. That star makes it legal."

"I won't let you down, sheriff." Sandborne surprised Mackey by welling up. "Never had this kind of responsibility before in my life."

"Good. Now head back inside and see what the ladies need you to do."

Mackey noticed Katherine standing inside the doorway of the hotel and wondered just how long she had been there. "Guess you saw our swearing-in ceremony just now."

"Such formality is usually reserved for royalty," she teased from the safety of the hotel. "I'm honored to have been a witness to history."

"Sarcasm." Mackey grinned as he pulled himself up into the saddle. "That's what that is."

"Is it sarcasm to wish I could talk you out of going? Or would that just be selfish?"

"The feeling would be mutual," Mackey admitted. "Going's not my idea. You know that. Want to say good-bye?"

She smiled as she took another step back into the hotel. Today, even the porch was too much for her, and he didn't force the issue. "We already said good-bye this morning, Aaron. Twice."

He looked around to see if anyone had been within earshot. "Katie! Jesus!"

She looked out at him from behind the half-closed door. He wished she would step out onto the porch. She always looked beautiful in the daylight. He only hoped one day soon she would be ready for that big step.

"Come back as soon as you can, sheriff. I'll look forward to welcoming you home with equal enthusiasm."

She quietly shut the front door of the hotel, leaving him speechless.

He snapped out of it when he heard a man clear his throat behind him. He turned to see Billy and Underhill grinning at him from horseback.

Underhill spoke first. "Never saw that shade of red on you, Aaron. Looks good on you."

Mackey noticed the deputy badge pinned to his coat. He looked at Billy. "That one of yours?"

"Had it from the last time you left," Underhill said. "What'd you swear that Sandborne boy in for anyway? Hope you're not expecting there to be that much trouble while you're gone because

I sure as hell ain't. And that boy won't be much good if there is."

"I'm not expecting anything out of the ordinary." Mackey brought Adair about and began riding toward the station at an easy pace. Billy and Underhill fell in beside him. "That's why I deputized him. And I wouldn't go running down Sandborne. He's a hell of a lot tougher than he looks. He's eager and honest and I think he might make a decent lawman someday."

"Handles himself pretty well in a gunfight, too," Billy added. "Something to be said for that."

"I'll swing by and have a talk with him after I drop you two undesirables off at the train," Underhill said. "As long as he stays out of my way and doesn't start believing he's Wyatt Earp, we should be fine."

"Told him to mostly protect the hotel unless you need him for something extra," Mackey explained. "That might put him cross with your boss, but the kid's got to learn sometime."

Underhill brought up the big sorrel short. "Just what the hell is that supposed to mean?"

Mackey reined in Adair. "Means your boss has been paying visits to Mrs. Campbell while I'm not there. First it was to buy the hotel. Next it was to ask her to change the name. But I think he's got other things on his mind. I don't want him encouraged by my absence to bother her anymore."

Underhill didn't look happy. "First I'm hearing about any interest Mr. Grant's had in the hotel or Mrs. Campbell. But now that I'm aware of it, I'll keep an eye on it. He's got no call to be bothering that woman. She's been through enough."

The three men resumed their ride toward the station. Billy was the first to break the uneasy silence that had settled over them. "Didn't peg you for the type to bite the hand that feeds you, Walter."

"And I hope you didn't peg me for the type who sits idle and allows a widow to be bothered by an opportunist. I've got no illusions about exactly who and what James Grant is, boys. If I can make a few bucks by helping him out while the town prospers, so be it. But wages don't buy a man. They sure as hell don't buy me."

Mackey and Billy traded looks. Mackey said, "Didn't think it did, Walter. But it's a relief to hear you say it."

"Just make sure you don't cross him unjustly," Underhill added. "I know you don't like him, but that doesn't give you cause to harass him or block his way. That badge doesn't give you the right, either. I'll stick with him if I have to, even if it's against you. I'd hate like hell for that to happen."

And as was his custom, Billy said what Mackey was thinking. "So would we, Walter. So would we."

The three men rode the rest of the way to the station in silence.

Chapter 12

Mackey was surprised that Mr. Rice had arranged for he and Billy to share one of the company's private railcars. It had a separate sleeping berth for each man, with shared sitting and dining areas. The bar was well stocked with liquor and a humidor full of fine cigars.

"Hell," Billy said when the head conductor brought them aboard after they had stowed their mounts in the boxcar. "This is nicer than some hotels I've stayed in."

As ornate as the car was, Mackey was not happy. "Hard to travel unnoticed in a setup like this."

"Mr. Rice's orders, sheriff," Kennard, the head conductor, told them. He had wisps of gray hair poking out from beneath his cap and was about fifty pounds overweight. The sheriff wondered how well he was able to move his bulk through the narrow passageways and aisles of the train, but since he was the head conductor, he must manage somehow. "He wanted to make sure you and your man here traveled in comfort, so we were ordered to hook up this car in Chicago." He rose on his tiptoes as he said, "Orders came from headquarters in New York City. Came direct, too."

But Mackey was still thinking of something Kennard had said earlier. "Mr. Sunday is not my man. He is the deputy sheriff of Dover Station and is here at the request of Mr. Rice. That means he is to be afforded every consideration and accommodation you would make for me. Conversely, any insult or slight of him is the same as insulting or slighting me. Do I strike you as a man who suffers insults and slights lightly, Mr. Kennard?"

The head conductor clearly was not accustomed to being spoken to in such a dismissive manner. "No, sir. You do not. I meant no offense either to you or Deputy Sunday here."

"Good. Thanks for showing us in. We'll make ourselves comfortable and let you know if we need anything further."

But Kennard did not leave right away. "I'm afraid there's something else, sheriff. Two things, actually." He took a letter from his coat pocket and handed it to him. "This is a letter for you that came straight from the hand of Mr. Rice himself. It has been sealed in wax by his own crest."

Mackey flicked the wax over the flap of the envelope to see if it had been broken. It hadn't. "And the second thing?"

"A Mr. Lagrange of the Pinkerton Detective Agency is waiting to see you. Like you, he is also here on orders directly from Mr. Rice."

Mackey wondered why Rice would have a Pinkerton man on board *and* two lawmen? Maybe the note would tell him more. "Tell Mr. Lagrange

I'll see him as soon as we pull away from the station. Until then, I want privacy." Mackey turned his attention to the envelope. "That will be all, Kennard."

The head conductor thanked him and quietly closed the car door behind him.

Out of the corner of his eye, he could see Billy smiling at him and said, "Not one word, deputy."

"Damn," Billy said anyway. "Watching you light that West Point candle is a thing of beauty. Standing straight, shoulders back and giving orders. Makes me feel like we're back in uniform. Feel like I should salute or something."

Mackey glanced around the car. He couldn't swear to it, but he was pretty sure the wall sconces were made of gold. "If we were still in uniform, we'd be back with the horses. Not in fancy digs like this."

"Still nice to see you dress down that fat man the way you did."

"How about you pull out some of those newspaper articles and the telegrams we got from Murphy's office. I'd like to compare that list of robberies with the telegrams before we talk to that Pinkerton man."

Billy opened a bag and immediately began pulling out papers and laying them on the desk. "Why do you think Mr. Rice put another lawman on this train if we're here? That make any sense to you?"

"Robbing these trains doesn't make any sense to me," Mackey said. "With the amount of troops Rice's trains move throughout the territory, it's a miracle they haven't attacked a troop train yet. Gotten themselves all shot to hell."

Billy stopped unpacking telegrams from the bag. "Or maybe it's not such a miracle after all. Maybe they've been tipped off?"

It was a thought that had been gnawing at Mackey since Rice contacted him about the train robberies, but had not fully formed in his mind until Billy said it. Tent City and Grant and the shootings had crowded thoughts of the train robberies from his mind, but now that he was in the train car, it made sense.

Mackey spoke his mind. "How could the robbers have been lucky enough to only hit trains that were not carrying troops? They would have needed help to be sure."

And he was fairly certain that help was in the bags of telegrams. "Pull out all of the telegrams that were sent on the days a train was robbed. I think we might find something there."

While Billy sorted through the telegrams, Mackey ran his finger under the flap of the sealed envelope and read Mr. Rice's typewritten note.

I am glad to be finally be able to communicate with you directly without fear of compromise via the telegraph operators.

Thank you for agreeing to help me stop or at least deter the people who have been attacking my trains. So far, all I have are the dead bodies of three good men and no idea of whoever is behind it. I have asked the Pinkerton Detective Agency to send a man with you. As of the writing of this note, I do not know the man's identity, but it is my experience that Pinkerton men are most capable. If you find him useful, use him. If he proves to be a hindrance to your efforts, feel free to ignore him.

I have let it be known that your train is carrying a considerable amount of money in the safe in the mail car. This is purely fiction, but I hope it will somehow lure the bandits out of hiding and into attacking the train. It is my hope that finding and stopping these murderers will go a long way toward securing the customers of the Great Northwestern Railway, but may also help Dover Station continue to experience the rapid growth it currently enjoys.

To that end, I have various concerns about how matters are being handled in town, particularly my partner's decision to hand over many of the managing responsibilities to James Grant. I imagine you share many of these same concerns as well and hope to discuss them with you personally in Butte in a few days.

Until then, I wish you good fortune and safety in your quest to bring these bandits to justice.

It was signed with Mr. Rice's rough, deliberate signature.

Mackey put the note back in the envelope and slipped it into his pocket.

Billy was already sorting out the telegrams. "What did Mr. Rice have to say?"

"Want to read it? It's typewritten."

"I'm busy," Billy said. "If I'd wanted to read it for myself, I would've asked. All I asked was what it said."

"Said we can ignore the Pinkerton if we want. Also said he wants to meet me in Butte when this is all over. I think he wants to talk about what's going on back home."

"I'd imagine he trusts Grant just as much as you do," Billy observed as he continued to organize the telegrams. "Like I said, got a good feeling from the man."

Mackey heard Kennard's voice boom, "All aboard!" as the train's brakes released and it began rolling south toward its fate, taking Sheriff Aaron Mackey and Deputy Billy Sunday along with it.

Chapter 13

Mackey did not like Robert Lagrange from the moment he stepped into the rail car.

His gray suit and shined shoes were city attire, and his matching bowler hat had never seen a prairie wind. His moustaches and chin whiskers were perfectly groomed and waxed. He bore the confident air of a man better suited for a boardroom than horseback.

Mackey did not resent this man because of these things. He had seen enough of the world to know that not everyone was meant to live in Montana. Some men were meant for city living and city jobs. He saw nothing wrong with that.

But Mackey saw a city man like Robert Lagrange as a liability in a situation in the wilderness and did not share Mr. Rice's faith in the abilities of the famed Pinkerton Detective Agency.

Lagrange looked out the window as the sun rose higher in the gray Montana sky. "It's a lovely part of the world you have here, Sheriff Mackey. Just lovely. Nothing like this back home, I'm afraid."

Mackey glanced out the window, too. "That's God's doing, not mine. Where's home?"

"New York City," Lagrange said. "Manhattan, to be precise."

"And before then?"

Lagrange looked at Mackey. "You interviewing me for a job, sheriff? I'm already gainfully employed by the Pinkerton Detective Agency, as I'm sure Mr. Rice has already explained in his note to you."

"How'd you know about that?"

"The letter to you?" Lagrange asked. "I imagine Mr. Rice mentioned it to my supervisor, who told me about it. You're the suspicious type, aren't you, sheriff?"

From behind his stack of telegrams on the desk, Billy said, "Haven't lived this long by being trusting of strangers."

"Or gullible," Mackey added. "We're on this train to stop the people who have been attacking this railroad for the past couple of months. It takes a certain kind of man to do that kind of job. The kind that aren't often found in cities, not even in New York."

"You asked me where I lived," Lagrange said. "Never said I was from Manhattan. Come to think of it, I don't think I told you where I'm from or what I've done before becoming a Pinkerton. I don't think I will, either, because it's none of your damned business."

Billy looked up from his telegrams.

Mackey kept his eyes on Lagrange, who did not break the sheriff's glare. "I've got a letter in my pocket giving me full authority over everyone

155

and everything on the railroad between Dover Station and Butte. You've got exactly one minute to convince me how you can help me to that end before I lock you in the boxcar with the horses for the rest of this trip."

"Well then, I suppose I should get cracking, shouldn't I?" Lagrange surprised him by standing up and heading to the humidor at the bar. "I always find that fine tobacco helps me think, don't you? Would you like a cigar, sheriff? Or perhaps Deputy Sunday would like one?" He looked at Billy. "May I call you Billy? I know you're used to cigarettes, but a good cigar can be even more enjoyable, I assure you."

Billy sat back in his chair, forgetting for a moment about the telegrams. "How the hell did you know that I smoke?"

"The tips of your fingers are stained from the tobacco," Lagrange observed. "Same for your teeth. I'd say you're a coffee drinker, too, given the tan hue of the staining." He threw up both hands in mock surrender. "I hope you don't take my observations as criticisms, sir. I enjoy my cigars and coffee as much as the next man."

"Nice trick," Mackey said. "Now you've got forty seconds."

Lagrange smiled. "Serves me right for trying to be hospitable when business is at hand." He looked over at the deputy. "You never answered my question, sir. May I call you Billy?"

about him, either. He's never even called in sick in all that time."

"Could someone else have sent the telegrams?" Billy asked.

"Certainly," Lagrange admitted, "except Chidester Station doesn't have an assistant stationmaster. It would have to either be him or someone else who knows how to work a telegraph machine. And, as I'm sure you gentlemen know, Chidester isn't exactly a cosmopolitan town. We only keep the station open because the pork farmers in the area would raise hell if we made it more difficult for them to bring their product to market."

"Nice quiet little town," Billy said. "Makes a hell of an easy place to tip off robbers about which trains to hit."

"That was our thinking, too, Billy. The times all match. Funny, though. Not all of the misspelled telegrams resulted in a robbery."

Mackey finished the thought for him. "But every robbery had a misspelled telegram, didn't it?"

"You'd make a pretty good Pinkerton yourself, Sheriff Mackey." He gestured at the humidor. "Sure you don't want that cigar?"

"Are you sure it's just Agee who's involved? Why not the station manager from Olivette?"

"We considered it, but no misspellings or irregularities of any kind out of Olivette, only

159

from Chidester. That's why we're going to focus our efforts on Agee when we get to Chidester. We think someone's listening in on the telegraph lines, but we don't know where. We've asked our crews to be on the lookout for a listening post, but it could be anywhere on any pole. In the past three months Agee has sent out fifteen misspelled telegrams. Only ten have resulted in robberies. Whoever is listening in isn't listening in all the time, but when they are, they always strike thanks to Agee's tipoff."

Mackey had no problem admitting he was impressed by Lagrange's tactics. He had not been impressed by the city man at first, but he had no choice but to admire his sense of deduction. "Does Agee know you're coming?"

"No. My name appears on the passenger list, but as I've never worked in this region before, there's no reason to suspect that Agee or his associates know I'm a detective. Your presence on the train is unavoidable, of course, given that Mr. Rice sent you telegrams. However, we believe your presence will only serve to draw out the robbers. After all, who could pass up the chance to be the man who killed the Hero of Adobe Flats or the Savior of Dover Station?" Lagrange puffed on his cigar. "They've sung campfire songs about men who have accomplished less than that."

But Mackey did not care about legends. His

own or anyone else's. "What about Agee's accomplices? Any idea who they are?"

"Other than the accounts you've read in the papers, none. I don't know who they are or where they live. They always hit the train at different parts of the line. Sometimes it's between Chidester and Olivette. Most of the time, it's areas south of Olivette, somewhere before they get near Butte. I had hoped the locations would be regular, but alas, they're random. No pattern at all."

Billy set aside the telegrams and seemed happy to be able to do so. "Looks like we'll have to get this Agee fellow to tell us who he's working with."

"Yet another reason why I'm on this trip," Lagrange said. "I'm not a bad investigator, but I'm an even better interrogator."

"No thanks," Mackey said. "Billy and I have experience in this kind of thing ourselves. Besides, one look at you and Agee's going to know something's off the second you start asking him questions. Billy and I don't know him, but he knows us. He probably figures it was only a matter of time before the railroad sent someone digging around about the robberies, but he won't figure a couple of locals like us could figure it out."

"But you would have," Lagrange said, "by dinner. I'm quite sure of that."

"I don't need your goddamned compliments, Lagrange. I know I'm not stupid and neither is Billy here. But Agee might not think that way. We're known more for our guns than our brains. Might be able to use that to our advantage, especially before he sends out that next telegram before we leave Chidester Station."

If Mackey was expecting a fight from the Pinkerton man, he was bitterly disappointed. "Feel free to proceed as you wish, gentlemen. You'll have no difficulty from me. Though, if I might make a suggestion, I would bring the incriminating telegrams with you. It might come in handy in persuading Agee that you're on to him. Evidence tends to make a man more compliant than merely the threat of violence."

Mackey stood taller again and, as Billy said earlier, lit the West Point candle again. "You mocking us, boy?"

"Merely sharing my experience, gentlemen. No offense meant, I assure you." Lagrange poured himself a brandy and, this time, did not offer any of it to the sheriff or his deputy. He sat down in the sofa and flicked his cigar in the crystal ashtray at his elbow. "Now, tell me of how I can be of service."

Chapter 14

In the cluttered stationmaster's office at Chidester Station, Mackey sipped coffee while Tom Agee sang Mackey's praises. Billy kept watch outside.

"It sure is an honor to have a man of your reputation paying me a visit," the telegrapher said. "I've read all about those things you done up there at Dover Station. How you saved the town, then hunted down the men what attacked your town? Saved them womenfolk and brought them back safe?" He sat a little straighter in his wooden swivel chair. "Yes, sir, I am humbled to have a man of your caliber, your courage, in my office, especially at a time like this."

Mackey decided it was time to interrupt his tribute. "At a time like what?"

"Why, at time when our fine railroad is being attacked damned near once a week. My missus and the boys down at Hurley's think I'm a fool for keeping this job, what with all the danger on the railroad these days. It's just a job, they tell me. It's not worth risking losing your life to a bunch of bandits who steal from innocent people who've done nothing wrong except buy a train ticket."

Agee paused to flatten his shirt. "But I don't pay them no never mind, sheriff. No sir, I tell them I've got a duty to fulfill. And the customers of the Greater Northwestern Pacific Railroad deserve nothing less."

Mackey stifled a yawn.

Outside, Billy Sunday smiled.

The sheriff looked around the office for a place to set down his mug. Every drawer and surface in the tiny office was crammed with papers and ticket receipts and ledgers of various sizes. The place smelled of wet paper and stale coffee. It looked more like a bird's nest than any railroad office he had ever seen. He could practically eat off the floor of Joe Murphy's office back in Dover Station. Maybe that was thanks to the head of the railroad living in town. Maybe it was just Joe Murphy's nature.

If the condition of an office said something about the man occupying it, then Mackey knew quite a bit about Agee already.

Mackey pushed aside a ledger on the desk at his hip and set down his mug. "While I appreciate the compliments, don't let me keep you from your duties. This train's carrying important cargo. We don't want the railroad to lose track of it, now do we? Send out your telegram, and we'll talk after."

"Yes, sir. Getting right on it." Agee spun himself back to the telegraph and began tapping out one electronic signal after another. It was a flat, rhythmic sound that Mackey had forgotten about since his days in the cavalry. In moments like these, he regretted never taking the time to learn how to use Morse code.

But in the past day or so, Robert Lagrange of the Pinkerton Detective Agency had spent a considerable amount of time teaching Mackey and Billy about how the system worked and how messages were sent.

He had learned enough to have an idea of the kind of message Agee was sending now. And the intentional mistakes he was making, which weren't mistakes at all. They were coded messages to the robbers who may or may not be listening.

When Agee finished his telegram, he turned his chair away from the machine, flexing his hand. "All done, sheriff. I know that might look easy, but it takes a hell of a lot more concentration than you might think."

"I don't think it looks easy at all," Mackey said. "If anything, it looks like it would be easy to make a mistake. Like in spelling and such."

Agee laughed too easily. "Yes, sir. Well, we telegraphers have been known to misspell a word from time to time. It's the nature of the business, I suppose."

"But you're a good speller based on what I can see." The telegraph man's smile faded as Mackey pulled several yellow slips of paper from the inside of his coat. "Been looking at your work, at Mr. Rice's request, of course." He held up several sheets. "Your spelling seems to be mighty consistent, except when it's not, of course."

"Care to explain that, Mr. Agee?" Billy asked from the ticket window.

Agee glanced at Billy before whispering to the sheriff. "I'd be honored if you and me could speak privately. Gentleman to gentleman. I'm sure you understand."

"I'm afraid I don't understand," Mackey said. "You implying that Deputy Sunday isn't a gentleman?"

"Never met one of his kind who was." He spared a glance up at Billy. "Present company excluded of course, seeing as how I don't know you."

Agee flinched as Mackey pitched forward and leaned on the arms of the man's wooden chair. His face was only a few inches away from Agee's face, and the sheriff could smell the sweat off the man, despite the cool night. The kind of sweat that came from nervousness, not heat. "You might not have meant offense, boy, but offense has been taken. By my deputy and by me. We're a team, understand? He's my partner and slighting him is the same as slighting me. You're not slighting me, are you, boy?"

Agee's thin lips quivered as he swallowed hard. "No, sir. I'm not slighting you. I respect you. But I ain't scared of you, neither."

Mackey's eyes narrowed. He had expected to

have to put in a considerable amount more effort than this to get Agee to talk. "You do something you need to be scared about, Agee?"

The stationmaster's voice shook as he said, "You're not a subtle man, sheriff. The second you pulled out them telegram copies, I knew what you was here for. Kind of a relief, to be honest, knowing the whole thing is over. Takes quite a burden off my shoulders, let me tell you."

Mackey shook the chair, jolting Agee in it. "Why that's the best idea Billy and I have heard all day. The sooner you tell us what you're talking about, the better off we'll all be."

"You're here about them telegrams I sent with those misspellings," Agee said. "Truth be told, I'm kinda surprised it took you people so long to catch on. Wish you'd caught on sooner and brought all of this to an end before so many people got hurt."

Mackey inched closer to Agee's face. "You're doing a lot of talking, but you're not saying a whole lot. You've got a confession to make, best get to it."

Agee looked around the office; anywhere so long as he didn't have to look at the sheriff's menacing glare. "They didn't give me any choice, damn it."

"Now we're getting somewhere. Who didn't give you a choice. Someone threaten you?"

"Of course, they did," Agee said. "I ain't

167

exactly a brave man, sheriff. Not like you. When a man sticks a gun in my face or threatens my family, I do what he tells me."

"That what happened here?" Mackey pushed. "Who threatened you?"

Agee began to shake now, and the sheriff realized the truth was just over the horizon. There was no need to keep pushing the man for something that would come naturally.

He backed away from Agee and handed him his coffee cup. "Drink this and tell me what happened. Don't hold anything back. You're already in a hell of a lot of trouble as it is."

Agee's hand began to shake, and he set the mug on top of a ledger on his desk. "I see the faces of those dead men every time I close my eyes. The engineer, the conductor, and that poor man who was just protecting his wife." Agee raised a crooked finger to where Billy was standing. "He stood right there before the robbery, smoking a cigar and chatting about the weather. Even gave me one, too."

Mackey had no patience for his guilt. "Tell me how it started and when."

Agee's face grew wet with tears and sweat. His hands shook, and his mouth quivered from fear and regret. "Three months ago, I woke up to use the privy. I was in there tending to business when a man kicked in the door and stuck a gun in my face."

Crude, Mackey thought, but effective. "What did he look like?"

"I was still half asleep and hardly in a position to be assertive, given my circumstances. But I can tell he was tall and big. He had a kerchief tied around his face so I couldn't see his face too well. He told me that, from now on, I worked for him. Not the railroad, but for him. He said he wanted me to tip him off to the best trains to rob. I told him I don't know that all the time and never know it until the train is in the station. That's when he came up with the idea about the misspellings. Double letters at the ends of various words in the train arrival or departure telegrams if the train had anything worth stealing."

"That your idea," Mackey asked, "or the gunman's idea?"

"His idea," Agee said. "I told him I didn't know how to make sure he got the message, but he said that wasn't my concern."

"Must've tapped into it somewhere along the line," Billy said. "Somewhere south of here is my guess."

"They never told me that kind of detail," Agee said. "Hell, they didn't tell me anything, except that I'd get fifty dollars a month just for sending the messages like we agreed on. I never knew which trains they'd hit and I didn't want to know, either. And for the last three months, on the first of every month, I wake up to find a bag with fifty dollars in gold in my privy."

"Did they tell you what would happen if you didn't go along with their plan?" Mackey asked.

"Said if I talked to anyone they'd know it. Said if I tried to trick them or lie to them that they'd burn the whole town down, just like that Darabont feller had done up in Dover Station. I know Darabont didn't do all that, but I understood what he was trying to say. I got the impression he would at least kill me and my wife without the slightest hesitation. Didn't give me no room for doubt on that score, sir."

"You ever see anyone after they visited you in your privy?" Billy asked.

"Nope and I don't want to see them, neither. I couldn't tell you who they were, and that's the God's honest truth. Never saw anyone before or since that day."

"And what about that telegraph you just sent out now?" Mackey asked. "About this train here. You tip off the robbers that this is a train they should hit?"

"And risk putting your lives in mortal danger?" Agee shook his head. "No, sir. I wouldn't dream of such a thing. I'm guilty of a great many things, but not that. My actions have hurt enough people already and . . ."

"That's a lie, sheriff." Robert Lagrange, who had been waiting outside the office just out of view, stepped inside with a notepad. "I wrote down exactly what this lying bastard tapped out, and it was not a benevolent message." He handed Mackey the notepad. "Take a look for yourself."

Mackey took the pad and read what Lagrange had written.

Train abbout to departt Chidester Station STOP Should arive at Olivete ten mins behind schedule STOP Agee STOP

Mackey held the pad up for Agee to read. "You lied again, didn't you?"

The stationmaster made a foolish attempt to run between Mackey and Lagrange. Both men stopped him and shoved him back toward the chair. They had shoved him too hard and sent him sprawling on the floor. Ledgers and papers from the desk fell like snow all around him.

"Why did you lie?" Mackey asked. "Did you think we wouldn't find out? Did you think they'd hit the train and we'd be killed?"

"Yeah," Agee yelled, "that's exactly what I thought. Because I can't take the risk that you'll be able to handle this bunch. What the hell makes you so sure you can stop them? Did you really fall for all of that nonsense I shoveled earlier about you being a hero and all?" That crooked finger pointed again, this time at Mackey. "I know all about you, sheriff. The Hero of Adobe

Flats my ass. You ran down thirty Apache bucks who were more scared of you than you were of them."

Billy attempted to enter the office to shut his mouth, but one look from Mackey kept him at bay.

Besides, Agee was not done yet. "And that nonsense about you being the Savior of Dover Station? Damned foolishness if you ask me. You couldn't even drive off a band of lunatics and lost half your town when you tried. And instead of staying home and making sure your town was safe, you abandoned them to chase down some whores Darabont had taken with him. And what did you get for it? A town that hates you and a wife that left you for it."

He spat on the floor. "The Savior of Dover Station? The Coward of the County is more like it if you ask me."

Conductor Kennard appeared in the ticket window. "Sheriff, we're about ready to get moving." He showed his pocket watch before snapping it closed. "After all, we've got a schedule to keep. Yes, sir. The Great Pacific Northwestern Railroad is the most dependable railroad in this part of the country."

He noticed the three men standing over Agee, who was still on the floor. "Mr. Agee. What are you doing down there?"

Lagrange said, "He's looking for the truth. Get

back on the train, Mr. Kennard. We'll be along in a bit. But if you leave before we get back on board, we will be very cross indeed."

Kennard looked like he wanted to ask more, but given the dispositions of the men in the office, decided against it and returned to the train.

Mackey snatched Agee by the collar and threw him back into the chair. "You said you believed the men would kill you if you didn't cooperate. Was that true?"

Agee shut his eyes and quickly nodded his head. "It was true. I swear to God, they would have killed me if I had given them the slightest cause."

Mackey drew his Peacemaker and pressed the barrel against the stationmaster's forehead. "And what about me, Mr. Agee? Think I'm capable of killing you?"

It was clear by the spreading stain on Agee's trousers that he did, in fact, believe Sheriff Mackey was capable of such an act.

But Mackey needed more. "You have to say it."

"Yes, damn you. I believe you'll kill me. But I don't think you'll kill the men out on the trail. They've killed three men for looking at them crooked. They'll be ready for the likes of you."

Mackey pulled the barrel away from Agee's forehead and holstered the Peacemaker. "For the first time all day, I believe you're telling the truth. So here's what you're going to do.

When we pull out of the station, you're going to send your normal telegraph with the normal misspellings you'd have for any train the robbers should hit. Don't try to over-sell it and don't call out for help, either. If you do, I'll find out about it, and if they don't kill me, I'll come back here and kill you. Do you understand?"

"I understand," Agee sneered. "I understand you're not a coward. You're just out of your goddamned mind."

To Lagrange, Mackey said, "Make sure he sends out that telegram like he should. If he lies, shoot him."

Lagrange produced a .38 revolver from beneath his coat. "With pleasure. And if he sends it without incident?"

"Bring him on board and lock him in the boxcar with the horses," Mackey said. "Can't risk him sending out any telegrams to his friends once we leave the station."

"It will be my pleasure." Lagrange put the .38 against Agee's ear. "We're going to write down what I want you to say first, then you're going to transmit it. Any changes or mistakes, and you'll disappoint me." He jammed the barrel into Agee's neck until the man screamed. "And I don't like being disappointed."

Mackey decided to leave Agee with Lagrange and headed back to the train with Billy.

"I'm beginning to change my opinion of

Lagrange," said Billy. "He's not the dandy I thought he was."

"He'd better not be," Mackey said as they reached their car. "Because something tells me we're going to need all the guns we can find."

Chapter 15

Back in their cabin aboard the train, Mackey looked out the window at the moon that cast an uneasy glow on the Montana landscape. Fall was about to give way to winter, and the warm greens would soon be covered by a blanket of white until spring.

He had taken off his hat, his coat, and his gun belt. He had left them all in the other room just for a while to enjoy the scenery for once. There was something to be said for the helplessness of train travel. He did not have to be mindful of Adair or the trail or of where the best watering holes might be or where to camp for the night. He didn't have to worry about any predators stalking him in his sleep. Neither the two-legged or the four-legged variety.

Instead, all he had to do was sit there and look out the window. For the first time in as long as he could remember, he wasn't playing the role of sheriff or captain or husband or leader. He was just a man watching creation roll by on a pretty moonlit night.

Mackey had never been a prayerful man, not before the army and certainly not since, but the scene caused him to recall a verse in the Bible. *To every thing a season.*

For the land. For men, too, he supposed. *And a purpose to every thing under heaven?* Well, he wasn't so sure about that part. He could think of quite a few people who served no purpose at all except to make life's journey even more arduous than it already was.

It made him naturally wonder if he, himself, had a grander purpose than just hunting criminals and shooting people.

The moonlit night as they sped through the prairie had made Sheriff Mackey more than a bit philosophical, but fortunately, Billy Sunday was there to keep him from delving too deep into his own thoughts. "Stop."

Mackey looked over at his deputy, who was in the process of cleaning his Sharps rifle. "Stop what?"

"Brooding. I can hear you brooding from all the way over here."

Mackey went back to looking out the window. "Just enjoying the scenery, is all."

"You would be enjoying it if you weren't brooding so much. That stuff Agee said to you back there at the end. When he got that final thrust of courage in him before Lagrange slapped him down. What he said is bothering you. That stuff about you not being brave."

Normally, Mackey had no cause to disagree with his deputy. The man knew him so well, he usually had him pegged right. But this time, he was wrong.

"Fifty dollars."

"The amount of money Agee got paid?"

"Exactly. It's a hell of a lot of money for a telegrapher to get paid just to tell them which train to rob."

"I'd say it's worth it," Billy said. "After all, without Agee's tip, they could rob a train that didn't hold anything. Might make it difficult to come up with Agee's fifty dollars."

"That's just the thing," Mackey said. "Fifty dollars is a hell of a sum for the robbers to guarantee each month, especially when they often hit trains that carried jewelry or art or other things they couldn't sell quickly."

Billy seemed to catch on to what he was saying. "And they always paid him in gold coins. Not all of the passengers would've had gold coins. Some of them might have greenbacks or letters of credit."

"There were always at least five men hitting the train," Mackey continued. "According to the papers, the thieves got little more than a thousand dollars after each event. Split five ways, then carving out a little for Agee might not seem like much, but fifty dollars is hard for men who don't work regularly to come by. Guaranteeing that sum in advance could prove to be a problem, especially if they hit a train that's lighter than expected."

"What are you saying?"

178

"I'm saying that fifty dollars is a pretty specific amount that could be hard for robbers to come by if their sole income is robbery. It might mean something. It might not mean anything, but it's a fact that sticks out in my mind is all."

"That the only thing sticking out in your mind?" Billy asked. "You sure none of that other nonsense Agee said is bothering you?"

"It wasn't anything Agee said as much as what I've already been turning over in my mind. About things changing. About things being different than I think they should be."

"You'd better be talking about the changes back home and not about yourself," Billy said. "Because if you believe anything that twitchy little bastard said about you, you're wrong."

"Nope. Just wondering what fighting a man like Grant gets me. So what if I don't like him? So what if I don't like everything he's doing in town? Hell, so what if he even wants to become mayor? Why should I stand in his way?"

"You heard about that?" Billy winced. "I was trying to keep that from you. Who told you? Pappy?"

"Doc Ridley." He turned from his view of the mountainside. "If you heard it, too, why wouldn't you tell me?"

"Because I don't go to you with every rumor I hear." Billy pulled the cleaning rod from the barrel of his rifle. "I heard a few of the old-timers

179

talking about it. They talk about a lot of things. Figured it would make its way to you on its own steam. I didn't want you getting worked up about something that might just be a lie."

"Grant sure as hell sounds like a candidate for something."

"Yes, he does, and there's not a damned thing you can do about it," Billy said. "Not from here. Not from the front porch of the jailhouse, either. The election's in a month. If he runs, he'll probably win. We've just got to deal with the consequences if he does."

"There's talk about him installing a real police force. Abolishing the sheriff's department."

"That would be part of dealing with the consequences that I just mentioned." Billy set aside his Sharps for a moment. "You've got to keep things in perspective, Aaron. Six months ago, you and me were ready to walk away from Dover Station. Head to California and see what we could make of ourselves there. But Katherine was too sick to go, so we agreed to stay around for a while. Nothing wrong with that, and I don't have a single complaint. If Grant runs and the people choose him, we make the best of it. Mr. Rice likes you. Maybe we get a job with him." He looked around the ornate railcar. "I'd be lying if I said this didn't beat the hell out of sleeping in the back room of the jailhouse."

Mackey smiled in spite of himself. "Wish I could tell if I was against Grant in particular or against change in general. Wonder if my opinion of the man is clouding my judgment of him."

Billy wiped down the barrel of his rifle with a cleaning rag. "Him coming out of that man's tent just before I was attacked isn't a matter of opinion, Aaron. That's a flat-out fact. And him meeting an anarchist at all is damned suspicious, much less meeting him in Tent City. Trust your instincts, Aaron. They're usually pretty good. I ought to know. They've helped keep me alive for the past ten years."

Mackey looked away from the window. Billy had a knack for saying the damnedest things at the right time. "Thank you for that."

"Shut up." Billy tossed his rag aside and began feeding cartridges into the Sharps. "You can thank me by quit doubting yourself. Dover Station and Grant will take care of themselves. Right now, we've got a passel of murderers stalking this train."

A heavy knock came at the door and Mackey told them to come in. It was Kennard the conductor.

"The train engineer reports seeing that bonfire right where you said it would be, sheriff. On the far side of the Talon River. We're already starting to slow down, just like you ordered."

"What did I tell you, Aaron?" Billy loaded

the last cartridge into the Sharps. "Focus on the business at hand."

Mackey stood up and began putting on his gun belt. To Kennard, he said, "Anyone complains, just say we're letting the engine cool down."

"Most of the passengers are either asleep or too drunk to notice," the conductor said, "but I'll tell them that if they ask."

Mackey and Billy pulled on their coats and hats. Mackey holstered his Peacemaker in the belly holster and grabbed the Winchester. Billy had kept his gun belt on the entire time and grabbed the Sharps.

"Lead the way," Mackey told the conductor. "The sooner the better."

The conductor led Mackey and Billy through the sleeping cars and the dining car, and through the passenger cars where people were attempting to sit upright in various states of unconsciousness.

The train had come to a gradual, but complete stop by the time they reached the head of the last passenger car before the tender car that stored the water and coal for the engine.

Kennard opened the door and they were immediately greeted by a cold nastiness in the night air. Mackey was glad that the wind was little more than a breeze or he and Billy would freeze while they waited.

The conductor lit a lantern but stayed close by the doorway. He looked nervous, and it was not just due to the cold. "Are you sure that fire is a good sign, sheriff? I mean, we usually don't stop for such things, being out here on our own and all, especially at night."

"I told our scout to ride ahead and signal us if he found anyone waiting for us farther down the line. That bonfire means he must have found something." He saw the worried look on Kennard's face hadn't changed and added, "It's good news. I promise."

"I've already lost two good friends on this run, sheriff, so forgive me for being cautious. But what if the bandits caught one of your friends and are using that fire as a trap for us?"

Since Mackey was beginning to get annoyed, he let Billy answer that question. "We've got two good friends out scouting for us. They've been hunting and trapping in this territory their whole lives. There's no way anyone could get close enough to them to hurt them, much less make them betray us."

Mackey could see Billy's words still had no effect on the conductor. He didn't want that kind of concern around him. Fear could be as infectious as the plague, and the sooner the man was out of his sight, the better.

Mackey took the lantern from the fat man. "We'll take it from here. Why don't you head back to the boxcar and make sure the stableman has our horses saddled? But he's to leave Adair where she is. She's liable to take a bite out of him if he tries to take her outside. She doesn't like people much."

"Kind of like her owner," Billy added.

If Kennard heard that, he did not show it as he hurried inside to the general warmth and safety of the train.

Mackey stepped to the edge of the stairs and held the lantern high, swinging it back and forth three times before stepping down the stairs and doing the same thing from the ground. "One of the Boudreauxs should've seen that."

Mackey set the lantern on the bottom step and leaned against the train, waiting. It was better down on the ground. He could see better, too, though it was still too dark to see much, even with the moon.

The dust from the coal and the smoke from the boiler engine were beginning to hurt his eyes. And even though he had fully recovered from his bout of pneumonia several months before, his lungs were still a bit raw. "Could go for a cup of coffee right about now," he admitted. "Take some of the chill out of the air."

Above him, Billy leaned against the railing, keeping an eye out. "Coffee would just make us jumpy. Or make us have to make water. Either way, best if we don't have it."

Mackey glanced up at his deputy. He had a way of putting things into perspective. "There's that, I guess."

Billy pulled out some paper from his shirt pocket, then a pouch of tobacco from his coat, and began rolling a smoke. The lack of wind made this possible. "Think we should tell Lagrange about this?"

"If he wakes up, we'll include him," Mackey said. "If he doesn't, no loss. I don't want to have to worry about him pushing to come with us."

Billy tapped tobacco into the rolling paper. "He handled himself pretty good up until now."

"That's because everything until now has been indoors. Lagrange is a smart man and probably a capable one. But I don't know how he handles himself outside, and going up against a group of train robbers is a damned awkward time to find out."

A skitter of rocks hitting the railbed snapped Mackey and Billy alert. Each man brought up his rifle, but did not aim it as no target had yet presented itself in the darkness.

"I did that on purpose," Jack Boudreaux called out from the darkness. "Didn't want you shooting me on my way down here. But you two should be quieter. I could hear you all the way at the top of the hill."

Mackey knew Billy could never pass up an

opportunity to tease the Boudreauxs. "Wanted to help you find your way in the darkness. Was afraid you'd get lost."

"Never got lost in the dark yet, goddamn it."

Jack, like his twin brother, Henry, was land-work lean and of medium height. Both sported thick dark hair and strong features that women seemed to find irresistible, not that the boys put up much of a fight when a lady tried to charm them. Mackey had pegged the Boudreauxs to be around twenty-five years of age, but given their affection for single and married women alike, the sheriff was amazed they had lived even that long.

Mackey waited until Jack had made it all the way down the incline before asking questions. "You lit the fire, so I take it you found something."

"I most certainly did," Jack said. "Me and Henry found a camp about three miles away. Five men, all of them armed. Two pack mules with them. They didn't do too much to hide themselves, because I don't think they care much about anyone finding them."

"Recognize any of them?" Billy asked.

"We didn't risk getting that close," Jack said, "even at night. But they're armed to the teeth. We watched them strip down while they made camp. Each man's got two rifles and two pistols, though they only sport one. Second

186

pistol's either tucked in their shirt or in the back of their belt. They're not big talkers, didn't call each other by name, either. They just ran through what they'd just done to the track and how they planned on robbing it first thing in the morning."

"You see what they did to the track?" Mackey asked.

"They pulled up a couple of sections and cast them off to the side," Boudreaux told them. "Figure they'll either derail the train if it can't stop in time or they'll get it to stop and rob it when it does. They've got the men and the guns to do it, Aaron. Those boys move like they know what they're doing."

Mackey was not as concerned as young Boudreaux. "So do we. Where's your horse?"

"Up the hill about a hundred yards back tethered to a dead tree. Why?"

"Head back up there and wait while Billy gets his horse," Mackey said. "He'll ride with you to meet your brother. Billy will place you boys where he needs you."

"Needs us?" Jack repeated. "Hell, we figured we'd surround the bastards from behind and disarm them that way."

Mackey wished that would have been possible. "You said these boys knew how to handle themselves. You behind them and me in front of them. One of us is liable to be dead including all of them. Was kind of hoping to keep one of them alive. The way Billy will show you is better."

Jack was not a dumb man, but he had never been the assertive type. He held out his hand to gauge the weather. "Better hope the wind stays this calm or the long guns won't offer much from a distance."

"We'd better hope for a lot of things."

Mackey stepped off the other side of the train and walked back toward the boxcar where their horses were stored. Billy followed.

"Feels good to be off that damned train for a bit," Billy said as they walked. "Miss not having the ground under my feet. Miss not having all the room I want to spread out."

"The more room you have, the less money they make," Mackey said, mindful of where he stepped in the darkness. The muted light from the shaded windows of the train cars did not offer much in the way of guidance. "You clear on what I need you to do?"

Billy began to repeat it verbatim. "Spread the Boudreauxs and myself on either side of the tracks in a raised position. I draw a bead on the leader. The Boudreauxs aim at the two on either side of him. You drop your left hand, we kill them."

"Good memory."

"Hell, Aaron. We've only gone over it twenty times since dinner. When you weren't brooding, that is. Only problem is the math. Since there's five of them and we shoot three of them, that'll leave two remaining. How do you want to handle them?"

"They're my problem," Mackey said. "Just make sure you don't shoot anyone else unless I'm hit or dead. I'd like to grab one of these bastards and get them to talk if I can."

"You think they'll give you the chance?"

"One of the last two just might," Mackey allowed, "especially when they see their leader dead. But I suppose we'll find out soon enough, won't we?"

The sky began to darken as the majesty of the false dawn faded before the true dawn began. Mackey glanced back at Billy as they approached the boxcar. "I can hear your mind working from here, so might as well spit it out."

Billy came clean. "Don't like you going up against five men alone. Not strangers, anyway."

"I won't be alone. I'll have you and the brothers backing me up with the rifles. That makes all the difference."

"Four against five is better odds," Billy said. "Might make them think twice about doing something stupid."

"Robbing the train in the first place was stupid," Mackey said. "Whatever happens today

189

is their doing. Besides, the leader is looking at three murders. He's less likely to go peacefully."

The boxcar came into view in the weak morning light. "You know I'm with you either way."

"Yeah. I know."

Chapter 16

When they reached the horse car, the stableman was already outside holding Mackey's and Billy's mounts. Billy's horse was a chestnut roan mare he'd never gotten around to naming.

Mackey's horse was a black Arabian named Adair, a gift from the men of his last post before he was asked to resign from the cavalry. The men had found her in a herd they had taken from a Mexican horse thief, though no one knew how the man had come upon such a majestic animal.

Adair strained against the rein when she caught Mackey's scent on the wind. The stableman seemed just as anxious to let her go as she was to be free. She trotted over and nuzzled against Mackey's shoulder.

"I know you hate it in there," he said as he patted her neck. "Time to get to work."

The stableman handed Billy the reins of his horse. "You've got yourself a damned nasty animal with that one, mister. I've heard Arabians are spirited, but that demon tried to bite me three times."

Mackey slid his Winchester into the scabbard, then checked his gear to make sure it was all still there. "Conductor tell you to leave her alone until I got here?"

"He did," the stableman admitted, "but I've been handling horses my whole damned life and never backed down to an animal yet. Don't intend on starting now, either. That mare is spoiled. Needs a good beating if you ask me."

Mackey slid his foot into the stirrup and hauled himself up into the saddle. He never felt quite as comfortable on the ground as he did on horseback.

He brought Adair around and looked down at the stableman. "What the hell did you just say to me?"

The stableman looked like the sort who was accustomed to speaking his mind whenever it suited him, but at that particular moment in time, looking up at Mackey peering down at him from atop his horse, speaking his mind did not appear to suit him very well. Instead, he quietly pushed the ramp back in the cattle car.

"Yep," Billy said. "Like owner, like horse."

Mackey and Billy brought their animals about and began moving south along the tracks at a decent trot. The horses had been standing still for a day or so. He wanted to warm them up first before they met the robbers.

"You'd best run ahead and join Jack. I'll give you three plenty of time to get into position. Figure on me being there just after sunup."

"We'll be waiting." Billy brought the roan around and took off at a gallop to meet Jack Boudreaux at the head of the train.

Mackey reached down and patted Adair's neck again. "Come on, baby. Let's go to work."

He clicked his teeth, and the horse began walking toward the roadblock. Mackey didn't even have to use his heels. She knew where she was going and seemed eager to get there.

The edge of the sun had just begun to appear over the eastern horizon when Mackey saw the five mounted men standing in a line across the ruined track bed. The rails had been pulled up and the ties cast aside.

Mackey had never been a railroad man, but he knew enough about them to know how much work it took to pull rail. It was hard work, harder than men who stole for a living should have been willing to do.

He remembered what Agee had said back in Chidester. How he had always been paid fifty dollars in gold after tipping off the gang about which trains to rob. Not greenbacks, not jewelry, but gold. The whole system—the intimidation, the listening in on the telegraph signals, and even the payoff—seemed too organized for common bandits. Yet three people had died since the robberies began, and Mackey couldn't understand why. A train engineer, a brakeman, and a passenger protecting his wife. The robbers had been so disciplined about some parts of their scheme and so careless about others.

Mackey nudged Adair to walk up on the railbed as they approached, her shoes clapping loudly against the wooden ties still intact. The mounts of the robbers in front of him stirred as Mackey approached, but the line held.

He didn't look around to see if the Boudreauxs and Billy were in position. He knew he would not be able to see them anyway.

Adair stopped twenty yards in front of the men without any prompting from Mackey. She had been through similar situations with her rider many times before. She knew what to do.

Now that he was closer, Mackey saw all five men had bandanas covering their faces. The man in the middle sat taller than the other four and was much broader than his compatriots. He had a rifle resting by its stock on his left hip. The others were all leaner and smaller. The one on the far left looked to be the youngest, but the bandana made it difficult to tell.

The man in the middle leaned across his saddle toward Mackey but did not break the line. "Morning. You lost, mister?"

Even in the dim light, Mackey could see the man examining his rig, the Winchester tied to his saddle and the Colt holstered on his belly.

Mackey looked the men over as he spoke. "You the leader here?"

"Yes, sir, I suppose you could say I am." The

194

voice was unfamiliar. "And just who the hell might you be?"

"Name's Aaron Mackey, and I'm placing all of you under arrest."

The name hit each of the men like a gust of wind. Every one of them reared back a bit and looked at each other.

The only one who did not react was the leader. "That so? Last I heard, Aaron Mackey was the sheriff up in Dover Station."

"Still is," Mackey said. "Mr. Rice asked me to put a stop to these robberies personally and that's exactly what I'm doing. Right here and right now." He looked at each of the four other men in turn. "You boys throw down your guns nice and easy and come along with me. You have my word that no one will get hurt."

"*Mister* Rice?" The leader spoke to his men without taking his eyes off Mackey. "You hear that, boys? Sheriff Mackey's mighty respectful for a lawman with such a dangerous reputation, don't you think?"

The man to the left of the leader said, "Sure is, boss. The way I heard it, he beat Bear Harper to death with his bare hands."

The man to the right of the leader added, "I heard he handed over Darabont to be skinned alive by savages."

"Heard that one myself," the leader said, "after he savaged the good sheriff's woman, of course."

He leaned forward in the saddle. "I get all them details right, sheriff?"

Mackey stopped looking at the men and focused on the leader. "Some, not all. Doesn't matter much anyhow. Only thing that matters is my breakfast."

Three of the men in the center of the line laughed. The two on the outside just sat as still as they could manage and looked scared.

"Your breakfast?" the leader said. "I suppose that's a pleasant thought, seeing as how it's your last one. Why's your breakfast so important."

"On account of my not having it yet," Mackey explained, "least of all my coffee. And as Bear Harper could tell you, I'm not a pleasant man before my coffee. Makes me impatient as hell, and seeing as how I'm a man who likes to keep things at an even keel, I intend on enjoying both on time at eight o'clock sharp."

The leader said, "Sorry to disappoint you, sheriff, but I can't see that happening. We're going to shoot you dead, show your body off to those people on the train back there, and take every cent they've got."

"You boys have had a good run, but it's over." Mackey raised his left hand. "You're all coming back to the train with me. Upright or over your saddle, makes no difference. Make your choice, because time's wasting and my breakfast is getting cold."

The other men looked at the leader, who did not move. "You don't have the slightest idea what's going on here, do you, sheriff? But, seeing as how I respect what you've done for your town, I'm going to make a proposition to you. You ride on back to that train and have your breakfast and we go on our way. No harm, no foul. Call this one a draw. How's that sound?"

"Sounds good to me." Mackey kept looking at the man. His left hand remained in the air. "Not sure what the three men you killed might think of it, though."

The leader smiled. "Fine, sheriff. Have it . . ."

The man's rifle flinched.

Mackey dropped his left hand.

Thunder boomed from the hillside as a single round from Billy's Sharps punched a hole through the center of the leader's chest, knocking the man from his horse.

Two of the men behind him jerked and fell from their saddles as bullets slammed into their chests as well.

The last two robbers struggled to keep control of their mounts as the horses of the dead men scrambled to run away.

Mackey had already drawn his Colt and aimed it at the older of the two men, who had dropped his rifle when his horse bucked. He was tugging on the reins with one hand while groping for his sidearm with the other.

"It's over!" Mackey yelled. "Don't do it!"

But the man grabbed his pistol and began to pull it as Mackey fired. The shot caught him in the left shoulder. He rocked back from the impact but managed to hold on. Mackey fired again and, this time, shot him through the chest. The man dropped from the saddle as the frightened animal sprinted away and joined the other three bounding through the field to the left of the train tracks.

Mackey shifted his aim to the last bandit, who was in a ball on the ground, hands held away from him. His horse was racing off to join the others. "Don't shoot! I give up!"

"Unbuckle your gun belt and stand up slow."

Mackey had the Peacemaker track the young man as he slowly unbuckled his gun belt and got to his feet. He kept his hands in the air and his head bowed.

The sheriff looked over the bandit as he heard Billy and the Boudreaux brothers riding toward them. Mackey saw the boy's jacket and pants bore specks of blood.

"You shot?"

The young man hesitated. "I don't think so. And I don't want to get shot finding out."

"Any other guns or knives on you?"

"Got a knife in my boot," the young man said, "but no guns."

"Pat yourself down for holes," Mackey ordered him. "Just do it slow."

The Boudreauxs arrived as the young man finished searching himself for wounds. "I'm not hit, so the blood's not mine."

Mackey was glad for that much at least. A wounded man would've been a nuisance this far away from the train. To Henry, he said, "Where's Billy?"

"Off to grab one of the runaways so this one can ride."

Despite the rising sun, Mackey could feel the air turning colder.

Jack shivered and said, "I don't want to be out here any longer than I have to. I say this last bastard here can double up with Henry if Billy's gone too long."

But Henry Boudreaux was not having any of it. "He ain't riding with me. I could smell the son of a bitch all the way back in the hills. I've got no intention of getting fleas."

"Well he sure as hell ain't riding with me," Jack argued. "Your horse is fresher. I'm the one whose been riding around all night by myself."

As the argument continued, Mackey closed his eyes. The Boudreauxs were among the best trackers and hunters he had ever seen, but they were a handful to deal with at any other time. "Knock it off. Billy will find his goddamned horse."

The sheriff turned his attention to the boy, "Got a name?"

"Wilson. Joe Wilson." He was looking down at the corpses that had once been his partners. "God, you really did kill them, didn't you?"

"And you would've been right down there next to them if you'd gone for your gun," Jack told him.

But Wilson was too shocked to be scared. "They're gone. Even Tom. Christ."

Now that the Boudreauxs were there, Mackey opened the Colt's cylinder, removed the spent brass and replaced them from cartridges on his belt. "Is Tom the name of the leader?"

"Tom Macum. Rode with him up here from Omaha. The others were already with him by then." He pointed down at the three other corpses. "Johnny Boy, Sam Dennis, and Tom Custer. We just called him Cus on account of Tom already being Tom, I guess." He slowly lowered his hands and muttered to himself. "Gone now. All of them."

Henry caught Mackey's eye. "This boy's a bit touched."

Mackey ignored him. The name meant something to him. "Tom Macum? From Stansfield?"

Wilson looked like he had just woken up from a bad dream. "I think so. Maybe. I don't know. We didn't talk much about things like that."

"Pull the mask off his face." Mackey trained the Peacemaker on him. "And if you make a play for any of his guns, you're a dead man."

Wilson did as Mackey told him. When the sheriff saw the face of the dead man, he recognized him as Tom Macum of Stansfield, Montana. He owned a ranch about an hour's ride north of town. Had a wife, too, as Mackey could remember. He did not know if Macum had any children, but that hardly mattered now.

The only question Mackey had was why a man like Macum would be robbing trains in the first place. He had never known the man to break the law before.

Mackey asked Wilson, "How many trains have you robbed with these men?"

"Three times. All of them went peaceful. Not the times when they killed folks."

"Of course, you weren't," Mackey said. "Charge will be murder all the same." He decided there'd be plenty of time to question him about the particulars on the train to Olivette once they fixed the rails, but he had to be certain of something first. "This all of you? Your whole gang?"

"As far as I know," Wilson said. "It was always just the five of us. Now, it's just me, I guess." He lost himself looking at the hole in Tom Macum's chest. "Just me."

The young man lurched forward and lost his supper on the side of the tracks. Mackey looked south and saw Billy Sunday riding back his way trailing another horse behind him.

To the Boudreauxs, he said, "Looks like you boys will be riding solo. Billy's found this boy a horse."

Mackey took in a deep breath of cold air and let it fill his lungs before he slowly let it out. Mr. Rice's robbers were dead, a prisoner left alive to capture, and Billy had tracked down a horse for the prisoner. All before he had enjoyed his first sip of coffee.

It was shaping up to be a fine day after all, and the sun wasn't completely up yet.

The Boudreaux brothers hung back and flanked the queasy Wilson as Mackey and Billy rode a little bit ahead.

"Nice shooting back there," Mackey said.

"I took the mouthy one to be the leader," Billy explained, "so I plugged him first. Jack and Henry took the other two."

Mackey had figured that had been the way it had played out. "The leader was Tom Macum."

Billy never reacted to anything, but he reacted now. "You sure? Tom Macum from Stansfield?"

"He's back there on the tracks with the other four," Mackey said. "I saw his face after it was over, and Wilson confirmed it. I didn't know the others, but Tom is a shock."

Billy kept riding. "Tom must've been in town a dozen or so times I can remember. Used to bring his cattle to market twice a year. Can't think of a time when he stepped out of line or gave anyone any trouble."

"Well he made up for it by starting to rob trains," Mackey said. "I wouldn't have believed it, either, but he's lying back there on the tracks as dead as the rest of them."

The two men rode back to the train in silence for a time until Billy said, "You thought something was off about this whole thing from the beginning. Agee, the money, now Tom Macum? What the hell does it all mean?"

"I don't know," Mackey admitted, "and I don't think that kid we caught will be able to tell us much. Even when he does snap out of whatever fog he's in, he was a follower, not a leader. Macum was always a smart businessman. If he was smart enough to be able to rob trains without us getting wind of it before now, then he wasn't stupid enough to trust a green kid like Joe Wilson with any details."

"So who do you think has the answers?" Billy asked. "Agee doesn't know anything, and the rest of the gang is dead."

"We'll give their bodies a thorough going-over when we get them on the train. See if there's any kind of notes or anything on them like we found on Ernst back in Tent City. It's a long shot, but it's worth a try."

"I can track those horses if you want," Billy said. "They were headed off in the same direction, which was south. Could be that they're heading back home."

Mackey couldn't dismiss the idea as quickly as he would have liked. Billy Sunday was a hell of a tracker, but there was no telling where those horses were headed. He had already lost one dear friend on a solo tracking mission against Darabont. The death of Sim Halstead had damned near killed both him and Billy. Mackey could not afford to lose his best friend, too.

"I wouldn't want you riding out alone," the sheriff said. "I'd prefer one of the Boudreauxs go with you."

"It's a one-man job, Aaron. Don't need two. And I won't do anything stupid, either. Just riding after a bunch of scared horses is all. They might've just been running scared for all I know."

"You know horses as well as I do," Mackey said. "You know they were headed home. I'm just worried about what'll happen when you find them. Remember what happened to Sim. I don't want the same thing happening to you, too."

"Sim was trailing people who knew they were being followed," Billy argued. "These horses are just following their instinct. I'll read the trail, maybe track them for a day or two, and meet you back in Olivette. Sound fair to you?"

It sounded more than fair. It sounded like the best thing Mackey had heard all day, but it did not make him like the idea any better. "That kid we caught said he rode with Macum on only three of the robberies. Given that there were seven robberies and Macum had five men each time, it stands to reason he's got others with him. Others who might be where those horses are headed. I'll approve it if you promise me you'll be careful."

"Don't know any other way to be. I'll ride ahead to the train and pick up provisions before I head out."

Chapter 17

Billy rode ahead to secure provisions from the train's cook while Lagrange rode toward Mackey on a brown Appaloosa. Despite his city clothes, he seemed to handle the big horse with ease. "Two rode out and five came back. I take it two of them are your outriders and the man in the middle is your prisoner."

"Says his name is Joe Wilson," Mackey said. "The rest of his crew is dead. We'll pick them up when the train gets closer to the damaged rail and the crew repairs the damage."

"How much damage is there?"

"A section of track and all the ties," Mackey said. "Doesn't look like they burned anything, so the engineer and some volunteers should be able to get us back on track in a few hours. We'll be late into Olivette, but I can't remember the last time anyone was in a hurry to get there."

"I'll leave it to you to break the bad news to the conductor," Lagrange said. "I don't think the man likes me very much, and the feeling is mutual. I'll be glad to take the prisoner off your hands while you and your friends get cleaned up."

Mackey was a bit surprised. "And here I was thinking you'd be upset that we didn't ask you to ride out with us."

"I know my skills and you don't," Lagrange said. "It only makes sense you'd want to face the robbers with men you knew and trusted. I would have felt exactly the same way."

His opinion of Lagrange improved all the time. He called back to the Boudreauxs. "This man's name is Robert Lagrange. He's from the Pinkertons. He'll take the prisoner back to the train while you boys clean up. There's a cabin for you boys all to yourselves. You should be pretty comfortable."

"What about you, Aaron?" Hank called out. "You sleeping with the horses?"

He tipped his hat to Lagrange as the Pinkerton man took the reins of Wilson's horse and led prisoner and mount ahead of them. He crossed the tracks in front of the engine and rode past the passenger cars with Wilson in tow.

It was hard for him to believe that everything had ended that quickly, but it had. "Me? I'll clean up later. For now, I'm going for my coffee."

But the screams from the train that cut through the morning air told him the coffee would have to wait.

He brought Adair into a full gallop with the Boudreaux twins right behind him.

Mackey brought her up short in front of the first car behind the tender car. He slid off the saddle and threw up the reins to Billy, who had ridden back to meet them. His Sharps was already in his hand. "Want me to go in with you?"

"No. I need the three of you to stay out here until I see what happened."

Mackey climbed up to the first car and went inside. He kept his hand close to the Peacemaker without actually drawing it. No sense in scaring people until he knew exactly what he was up against.

As soon as he entered the train car, he saw the reason for the screaming right away. A dandy in a fine blue suit and waxed moustaches was standing in the middle of the aisle, holding a knife to a young lady's throat.

At first, Mackey thought it might be Lagrange, but this man was taller and older than Lagrange by about ten years.

Mackey drew the Peacemaker and cocked it as he aimed it at the man. "Put the knife down before someone gets hurt."

But the dandy only pulled the lady closer and held the blade at her throat. Now, Mackey could see that it was a straight razor, not a knife.

"Not on your life, sheriff. I'm going to tell you how this plays out. You're going to get us three horses from the boxcar back there. Then you're going to let me, that boy you just arrested, and this pretty young thing I've just met ride out of here. You'll agree to stay on the train and won't follow us. You do that and maybe, in a few miles, I cut this young lady loose."

She screamed as the man yanked her hair. "You

know how to ride, don't you darling?" The dandy grinned. "If not, I'd wager you'll learn soon enough."

Mackey kept the Peacemaker aimed at the attacker's head as he walked slowly forward. "I've got three men posted outside, boy, and another coming at you from behind. The only way you're going anywhere is in a box unless you let her go."

The man pulled the woman with him as he backed up the aisle, away from Mackey. "Stay right where you are."

But Mackey kept coming. And the Peacemaker did not waver.

The passengers screamed as the man stumbled and almost fell. But he kept his balance and the blade at her throat without cutting her.

Mackey used the distraction to close the distance between them by a step or two.

From the back of the car, Mackey heard Lagrange call out, "Back away from the girl or you're dead."

The dandy turned around just long enough for Mackey to make his move. He rushed forward to grab the blade, but was too late.

The man slashed out at Mackey, but missed wildly. The sheriff burst forward and kept the attacker's arm extended. Passengers screamed and ducked out of the way as the woman broke free from his grip.

The man landed a left hook on Mackey's jaw, but the sheriff's grip on the knife hand didn't falter.

Lagrange rushed from the back of the train and slid his forearm under the man's neck and tried to wrestle the knife from him. Mackey uncocked his pistol and brought the barrel across the right side of the attacker's face.

His grip on the knife held, so Mackey did it a second time, then a third until he finally went down and the knife skittered under the seats.

Mackey holstered his gun as Lagrange dragged the unconscious man out of the car backward. When they reached the dining car, Mackey flipped the unconscious man on his stomach and patted him down for weapons while Lagrange twisted a tablecloth and used it to bind the man's hands behind him.

"You're going to need a towel for his head," Mackey said. "He's bleeding pretty bad."

"Of course, he is," Lagrange said as he swiped some cloth napkins from an unoccupied table and wrapped them around the man's head like a bandana. "You caved his head in. That tends to cause some bleeding."

Mackey held the napkins in place while Lagrange worked. It may not have been perfect, but it was better than allowing him to bleed to death.

"Any idea who he is?" Mackey asked.

"I saw him when I first boarded the train," Lagrange said, "but that was it. I never took him for working with the robbers."

"I didn't take their leader for being a robber, either," Mackey admitted, "but it looks like today's my day for being surprised."

Lagrange tied a third napkin tight over the man's ruined face. "Let's hope we get to the doctor in Olivette in time for this one to tell us anything."

Chapter 18

Knowing the train would be delayed for a couple of hours before it resumed its trip to Olivette, Billy wanted to track the horses as quickly as possible. After the chaos with the madman on the train, Mackey ordered him to go on with his original plan, claiming tracking the horses was now more important than ever.

He got a day's worth of provisions from the train's cook and headed out immediately. The mystery of where the horses were headed and if they were headed back home had only doubled after the events on the train. How big was Tom Macum's gang? How many people had he brought in to help him? It seemed like it had to be more than the five other men who they had found with him.

With the surviving members of the gang either dead or unable to talk, Billy knew tracking the horses gave him the best possibility of getting some answers.

Based on the small amount of provisions he had found at the gang's campsite, he knew they had to live close by. They hadn't brought enough with them for more than one night in the field, certainly not enough for a long ride back. They had to live close by. He hoped the dead men's horses would be able to show him the way.

Horses were smart animals, much smarter than the dime novels from back east or most people gave them credit for. After fleeing the gunfire, the four horses that had escaped reverted back to nature and formed a small herd. He could tell by their hoofprints in the dirt that one had assumed the leadership role and had led them in a relatively straight line through a small stand of trees, then a deeper forest. Most of the land was flat and, given that it was so close to winter, there was little grazing available. The animals were not wandering in search of food. They were heading for the one place they knew the food would be plentiful. Home.

Billy Sunday had no trouble following their tracks and droppings on the packed dirt of the forest floor. He could tell by the length of their respective gaits that they moved with purpose and speed. They knew where they were going.

Billy knew it, too, when he broke through the trees and found himself at the edge of a snow-covered clearing at the foot of a mountain range. A ranch house with a decent-sized barn to the right sat in the distance. A thin wisp of smoke trailing up from the chimney told him someone was home. And, judging by the way the horse tracks fell, they had headed straight for the warmth of the barn.

Billy decided he could still learn something from the horses, so he moved his mount back into the tree line and rode the long way around toward the barn. When he drew next to it, he broke cover of the trees and tied his horse to a fallen log at the edge of the tree line. Given that the house was occupied, he knew a man on foot was less threatening than a man on horseback. And if it came down to shooting, he'd still be able to get to his horse and ride into the cover of the forest before they got close.

The corral was empty, and all of the hitching posts in front of the house were unoccupied. That meant the horses were in the barn, probably unsaddled. He'd be a mile or so away before anyone came after him.

Billy pulled his Sharps from his saddle and began walking toward the barn. He stepped as lightly as he could through the snow, but it was impossible to be totally quiet. He rounded the front of the barn and found one of the doors was open. He looked inside and saw the horses he had been tracking were in their stalls, unsaddled and munching away at hay.

Someone had removed their saddles and fed them before Billy had gotten there. The horses had made better time than he'd thought. Someone was home. Time to ease out of here, ride back to the train, and get Aaron and the others to come with him.

As he turned around, he heard the sound that could only be hammers of a shotgun being thumbed back. A woman's voice said, "Don't move, you black son of a bitch."

Billy slowly set his Sharps against the barn and raised his hands. He could tell from the thickness in the woman's voice that she had been crying and recently.

"My rifle's against the barn and my hands are nowhere near the pistol on my leg," he said. "I'm going to turn around real slow so you can see I'm not trying to steal anything."

Billy began turning slowly to his left, so the woman would see the star pinned to that side of his coat. "You'll see I'm no threat to you or anyone else."

He saw the woman lower the shotgun the more he turned. She was a plump woman, in her late forties, with grayish hair and puffy red eyes. "You're a sheriff?" Her voice finally cracking.

"Deputy Sheriff Billy Sunday, ma'am. From up in Dover Station."

"I've heard of you. But you're from Dover Station?" She lowered the shotgun completely. "That's more than a day's ride away. What the hell are you doing all the way down here?"

Billy had no intention of telling her anything until she was away from that shotgun. "I'd be a mite more comfortable if you'd put that shotgun down and let me lower my hands, ma'am. It's a damned cold day for standing still, if you'll pardon my language."

She lowered the shotgun and Billy picked up his Sharps. "I think it's best if I close the barn door so the horses stay warm. Don't want them catching pneumonia, now do we?"

"No, we don't," she said. "I probably should've done that myself, but I was too surprised by seeing them all come back like that without Tom or the others."

Billy shouldered the barn door closed and threw the latch that would keep them shut. "I hate to be a bother, ma'am, but could we go inside for a spell? I'd like to warm up before I head back."

She began heading back inside and left the shotgun next to the door. "Got stew on, so you can help yourself. Was expecting Tom and the others to come back for lunch, not just their horses."

Billy left the shotgun outside and shut the door behind him. The farther away she was from the weapon, the better.

She stopped short just inside the doorway. It was a large kitchen with the kind of open fireplaces that served to heat the rest of the house and heated food, too. She looked up at him with swollen, reddened eyes. "You know, they say strange things happen in threes and today's no exception."

She seemed to be in an awkward state of mind, which suited Billy just fine. If she was Tom Macum's wife, she knew all about the hardship of living out in this part of the world. She knew death was always just out of reach and ready to move in at the slightest opportunity.

She knew her husband must be dead, but had not gotten around to believing it just yet. Billy was happy to let her ease into the idea rather than allow it to land on her all at once.

He decided to keep her talking. "What would those three things be, ma'am?"

"The first is that those horses came back on their own." She handed him a plate from the wooden table and sat down in a rocking chair next to the roaring fire. "The second is that you're down here all the way from Dover Station. The third, I suppose, is that you're a, well, a Negro I guess is the proper term. Never had one of your kind in my house before."

"Honored to be the first one, ma'am, and I appreciate your hospitality."

But the woman did not seem to hear him as the tears began to flow. "Why did those horses come back by themselves, deputy? You had something to do with that, didn't you?"

He set his plate back on the table. "You've lived out here a long time, ma'am?"

"Over thirty years," she said. "Ma and Pa brought us out here when I was a little girl."

"So you know how things are out here," he told her. "How unkind it can be."

She looked down at her apron and used it to wipe away her tears. "Why did them horses come back from the west? Tom and the others were supposed to be tending to our herd to the north. We ain't got nothing in the west. Why would he and the others be over there?"

"What others, ma'am?"

"Tom, Joe, Johnny, Sam, and Cus," she told him. "Been with us ever since we managed a stagecoach stop and telegraph office before Tom got into ranching a few years back."

Billy had not known much about Tom Macum's life before ranching. And he had no idea the man had managed a stagecoach stop or a telegraph office. "So Tom's your husband?"

"He was." The woman began to weep heavily. "Because he's dead now, ain't he?"

Experience kept Billy from trying to console her. He had learned that, in times like these, the harder and sooner the reality hit, the better everyone was. Death was as final as it got and there was no way to sugarcoat it. No sense in trying, either.

"I'm sorry for your loss, ma'am." He checked around for other pistols or rifles nearby. He did not see any, not even hanging on the wall above the door or the fireplace. "I truly am."

"Were you there when it happened?" She

looked up at him without anger in her eyes, only questions. "Can you tell me why it happened?"

Like grief, Billy believed truth was better when it was learned, not told. "Tom and the others weren't tending to the herd in the north. Where do you think they were?"

She ran her finger along a seam of her apron. "Why do men lie to their wives, deputy? They depend on us for so damned much. They ask us to be so strong for them, but they think we're too weak to stand the truth, so they lie to us, thinking we're too stupid to know the difference."

"What lies, Mrs. Macum?"

"About where all the money was coming from," she said. "About that new barn out there going up three months ago. And another one just like it at our place in Stansfield. Didn't he think I'd know he didn't get all of that money just from selling horses and cattle? Tom had never been poor, thank God, but he'd never had enough money to throw around like that. Not until that snake crawled back into our lives."

Billy felt sweat begin to break out all over his back, the way it always did when he was close to something that was about to happen. And he was very close now. "What snake, Mrs. Macum?"

She looked up at him with a mixture of sadness and rage in her eyes. "The same one who's changing your town for you. That bastard James Grant, that's who."

Billy leaned against the wall. There it was. The link Aaron had been looking for. The link Mr. Rice would want to hear. A direct link between the train robberies and James Grant. "He the one who started giving your husband all of this extra money?"

"Five hundred dollars a month, near as I can figure," she told him. "Not that I ever saw it, but I knew how much it was on account of him taking less from the till than he used to. Never added to it, though, not even after he built them new barns. I imagine he was spending the money on something else, though I don't know what."

But Billy knew what. Paying for a cadre of men to rob the train wouldn't be cheap. It would take money to keep them ready for him whenever they got the call. A call Tom Macum could hear since he had once run a telegraph office.

Billy felt like he needed to sit down but wanted to keep her talking. He had to get her to come back to the train with him so she could tell Aaron all of this herself. Otherwise, it was just supposition on his part. "What do you think he was doing, Mrs. Macum?"

"Robbing trains, most likely," she said. "Not that he had any damned business doing that. I read the papers, deputy. I knew when those attacks happened and where. I knew Tom and his men weren't here when those robberies

220

happened, so I had my suspicions. And when his telegraph equipment disappeared one day, I knew something was going on. Tom changed, too. He had never been a jolly man, but he'd been affable enough. He changed once news of the robberies started appearing in the papers a few months ago."

She looked away, toward the window and the snow-covered meadow Billy had just ridden through. "I even asked him about it once. He stopped talking to me for a week after that. Can you believe that? His own wife. Way out here, just the two of us. Not a word for a week." Her eyes narrowed. "That's when I knew something had happened and I knew James Grant was a part of it. We'd known him years ago, back when we both ran stations for the stagecoach. Train lines only made business better for us, and James Grant was attracted to money the way bees are to honey. Nobody likes being poor, but Grant made a business of being wealthy. Even though there wasn't much money to be had in that business, it didn't matter. He just needed to have more than the rest of us. The biggest stop. The most amount of liquor. Even women, believe it or not. Got to be so that people stayed on at his place so long, they had to make up time. Drivers often skipped our station altogether, or only stayed long enough to water their horses and use the privy. People suffering poorly from a night of drinking usually don't have appetites for apple pie and home-cooked meals, deputy."

She kept talking and Billy kept listening. "So Grant bought out our share in the coach stop, which we used to set up our ranch. We hadn't heard from him until about six months ago while we were in Stansfield. He came by and told us how prosperous he was. Said he'd been hired by Silas Van Dorn to be his personal manager, though neither Tom nor I knew how that could've happened. Grant had always been an ambitious man, but working for a man like Van Dorn didn't make much sense. Then I was asked to leave the room while Tom and James huddled around the fire, whispering to each other like a couple of old washwomen across a fence. Things changed after that."

Her eyes got that faraway look again. "I guess you could say that was the day Tom and the others began to die. It wasn't today. It was six months ago. They were already dead and didn't even know it yet. Nothing I could've done about it, either. Could I?"

Billy was not sure if she was talking to him or to God or to herself. He answered anyway. "Ma'am, was there anyone else Tom used to work with? Any other men who used to . . . help him other than the men who were with him today?"

"Out here?" She winced, though it looked

like it was meant to be a smile. "There's always someone out here looking to make some money. Problem is finding the men, not getting them to do what you need. Tom used to take different men with him to tend to the herd, he said, but I guess I knew it meant train robbing. I know there was one man in particular he liked to work with. Dave Aderson. Big bastard with scars on his face. I never liked him much and told Tom to never let him in the house. Always got the worst feeling from him, though I can't say why. You ever get a feeling off a person like that, mister?"

Billy followed her gaze out the window. "This Aderson ride a big black paint and wear a brown slouch hat?"

Mrs. Macum became more aware of herself. "I don't remember the kind of hat he wore, but I remember his horse. And yes, I believe it was a black paint. A beautiful animal for such an ugly man. Big, too, which a man his size would require. Why do you ask? Do you know Dave?"

"No, ma'am. But he's riding this way right now. And, things being what they are between you two, it's probably best you get to your bedroom and find a place to hide."

Billy watched Aderson approach from the front window. It was difficult for the rider to see him in the shade of the house, especially on horseback.

Billy intended on allowing the man to get even closer before he stepped out onto the porch. The black paint was breathing heavy, a clear indication that Aderson had pushed the animal hard for quite a distance.

Billy had no way of knowing Aderson's intentions in advance. He may have heard what had happened at the train and was riding to see if Tom had made it. He also may have just been stopping by to see if Macum had any work for him.

Or he had been an outlier at the robbery, the way the man in the train had been a member of Macum's gang, too. He could be here to silence Tom's wife because she was the only other person who knew James Grant was behind the robberies.

Given Mrs. Macum's descriptions of Aderson's disposition, Billy was betting it was the third option.

Rider and horse had been well within the range of his Sharps since they'd broken through the clearing, but Billy decided against opening fire until he knew why Aderson was there. He had his suspicions and instinct, but he did not know for certain. He had promised Mackey he would avoid a confrontation if at all possible. And if at all possible, Billy Sunday would do just that.

He waited until Aderson was within less than fifty yards of the house before he opened the door and stepped out onto the porch. He stepped out slowly and shut the door behind him. He kept the Sharps visible, but the butt of the rifle high on his hip and aimed to the sky. He wanted Aderson to see it, but not think it was pointed at him. No sense in provoking something if he did not have to.

Aderson brought the paint up short, about thirty yards away from the Macum house. He was as big as Mrs. Macum had said he was and just as ugly, too. A thick brown beard did little to hide the scars that crisscrossed the left side of his face. They were of varying depth and length and had probably been received at different times. Billy had no idea how a man could get scars like that, except that he was fairly certain they had not happened during choir practice.

The rider brought his tired horse under control. "The hell are you doing here, buck?"

Billy thumbed the tin star on his jacket. "Name's not Buck. I'm Deputy Billy Sunday from Dover Station."

Aderson's scowl changed, as if the name meant something to him. "Dover Station's a long way from here, boy."

"That's what everyone keeps telling me. And the name's Deputy Billy Sunday, mister. Not boy."

Aderson looked around the area before saying, "What brings you to the Macum spread?"

"I was going to ask you the exact same thing."

"Good thing I asked first, then."

"I'm law, remember? My questions take priority. Tell me why you're here."

"I'm here to see Tom about a job," Aderson said. "Told me to come by after breakfast, so that's what I've done."

Billy looked at the amount of breath smoke coming from the horse's nostrils. "You live a long way from here?"

"Not too far," Aderson said, "not that it's any damned business of yours. Why?"

"Because that horse has done some hard riding, Mr. Aderson, and this is not hard riding land. It's fairly flat, and the snowfall was light and uneven at best. That animal's lathered up, kind of like she was running away from something. That would mean you were running away from something, wouldn't it?"

He slowly lowered the Sharps until it was aimed at Aderson. "What were you running from, Aderson?"

The man's eyes squinted. "You know my name?"

"Yes, I do. And now I want to know why that horse is in a lather. And if you make any sudden moves, I'll fire. I don't think I have to remind you of what a Sharps can do to a man at close range."

The paint began to fuss, probably sensing

the tension in the air. Aderson brought it under control. "No thanks. I've seen enough of what that damned thing can do from a distance already, you murdering son of a bitch."

Aderson's pistol cleared leather just as Billy squeezed the rifle's trigger. The massive slug struck the big man high in the center of the chest and blew him out of the saddle.

As the black paint ran off, Billy brought the rifle up to his shoulder and aimed it down at the fallen man in case there was still any fight left in him. But there wasn't enough left of the man's chest for there to be much of anything left of him at all.

Billy kept the rifle aimed down at him as he took the pistol away from the dead man. He did not like to take chances, not even with corpses.

Billy turned when a solitary gunshot came from within the house. He turned and ran inside, cursing himself for not noticing another rider. Had he missed something? Had Aderson just been a decoy?

But when he burst into the bedroom, Sharps at the ready, he found there had been no other rider and that Billy Sunday had not missed anything, save for the pistol the Macums kept in the bedroom, probably for self-defense.

Only this time, Mrs. Macum had used it to take her own life. She had placed the gun barrel under her chin and squeezed the trigger.

Billy lowered his rifle as he sank against the doorway. His only proof of a link between James Grant and the train robbery had just put a bullet in her brain.

Chapter 19

In the doctor's office in Olivette, Mackey closed his eyes as he waited for the doctor to finish patching up the bandit he had slugged on the train. The man had drifted in and out of consciousness since Mackey had hit him with the pistol, but the bleeding seemed to have stopped. As there was no real doctor on the train, Mackey had to wait until the train reached Olivette before he knew if the man would survive.

He looked at Billy, who stood in the doorway rolling another smoke. "I hope you're not blaming yourself for the Macum woman. You didn't make her put that pistol to her head any more than you made Aderson draw his gun."

"Should've found a way to make her feel safer. Maybe she wouldn't have—"

"We're not lawyers or doctors," Mackey said. "We don't deal in maybes. We deal in what is. Maybe if you'd gone back there with her, you would've gotten trapped by Aderson and he could've killed you both. Maybe she would've shot you on account of what you did to her husband, before shooting herself. What happened was bad enough. No need to make it worse by regretting it. You're alive and they're dead. At least now we know there was a link between

Grant and Macum. We wouldn't have known that unless you'd ridden out there like you did."

"Can't prove it, though."

"Couldn't prove it even if we had her signed and sworn testimony before a judge," Mackey said. "It's just hearsay, but lucky for us, we're not going to a court of law or appearing before a judge. There's only one man we've got to convince, and he's got his doubts already. Mr. Fraser Rice."

Billy licked the cigarette paper and closed it. "Could be this man you brained knows something we can write down and have him sign."

"It's possible," Mackey said, "if the idiot working on him doesn't kill him first."

The doctor at Olivette worked out of an old barn behind the whorehouse off the town's Main Street. Given that treating sporting ladies of various social diseases was likely the doctor's surest source of income, the location of the doctor's office was more out of practicality than anything else. It also dimmed Mackey's hopes that the doctor could treat the man's wounds beyond giving him something for a persistent itch.

In the portion of the barn that served as the doctor's front office, Mackey was seated on a charred pew from the church that had burned down some time ago, though no one could quite remember when or how. The doctor had made a half-hearted attempt to sweep some of the straw out of the place, but a good portion of it still remained in the cracks of the sodden wooden floor.

"I can still smell the animals," Billy said from the doorway. "How the hell can a doctor work in a place like this?"

Mackey smelled it, too. "Makes house calls whenever he can, I'd imagine."

There was considerable talk of the town of Olivette generating the same level of interest from Mr. Rice and his partners as Dover Station currently enjoyed, but Mackey did not see much possibility in that. The town of Olivette had cropped up on a forgettable rocky plateau that had neither scenery nor grazing land nor trees for logging. Some miners had managed to scrape out a living on the sparse amounts of copper in the hills, but not enough to make a proper town out of the wind-scoured place. He hoped no one was holding their breath waiting for investment, lest they die of suffocation.

A glass shattered and a woman's cackle followed by a tinny rendition of "Old Dog Trey" echoed in the alley. Billy glanced behind him. The place of ill repute looked almost quaint against the purple sky of the setting sun and the lamplight in the windows. "At least someone's having a good time."

"Just glad it's not our town," Mackey said.

"Last whorehouse scuffle we broke up caused us a hell of a lot of trouble."

Billy looked thoughtful for a moment. "Wonder what's going on back home. Election's only a couple of weeks away. Wonder if Grant threw his hat in the ring."

"Probably making sure no one else is going to run against him," Mackey said. "His ego couldn't stand opposition, though he'd probably beat anyone who stood against him."

"Heard your old man might run against him," Billy said as he lit his smoke, "though it was just a rumor."

Mackey had not heard that one yet, either from Billy or his other sources. "The only place Pappy is running to is the bank to deposit the small fortune he makes off the Dover Station Company every day. He loves to talk politics, but he's no politician. He'd resign his office within a week out of boredom."

Mackey could have gone on about his father's lack of political acumen, but the doctor trudged out from one of the old stalls he used as a place to treat patients. He dunked his bloody hands into a bucket of water and dried them with a filthy towel.

Mackey pegged Doctor Brenner to be a wiry man of about fifty who was too thin for his frame. Mackey thought he had the look of an opium fiend about him, reddened sunken eyes and pale skin. The sheriff didn't think he was fit enough to work on an alley cat, much less a human being, but given how the man in question had held a woman at knifepoint and swiped at him with a razor, a cat doctor was better than he deserved.

Brenner tossed the towel to the side and took a bottle from the bottom drawer of his desk. He looked at Mackey as he pulled out the cork. "You the one who did that to his face?"

"I am."

After two deep swallows, Brenner came up for air, but didn't put the cork in the bottle. "What the hell did you hit him with? That train out there?"

"Butt of my Peacemaker. Why?"

"Because you caved in half his skull. I had to take his eye."

Mackey had not thought he had hit the man that hard, but hadn't given it much thought either way. "I hit him until he dropped the razor."

The doctor looked like he wanted to say more, but thought better of it. He took another belt instead. "Guess he shouldn't have tried to cut you."

Mackey stood up. "He awake?"

"Drunk as a skunk on account of me having only whiskey and no ether. Never had much call for it since I've been here. I ain't been a surgeon since the army, and even then, it was closer to butchery than medicine."

But Mackey didn't care about the drunk's life story. "Can the man talk or not?"

"I said he was drunk, not unconscious. Bandaged him up as best I could, but he'll never be pretty again." Brenner regarded him with the bottle in his bony hand. "I wouldn't go hitting him anymore if that's what you're asking. I bandaged him up as well as I could, but he'll bleed out if you move him too much."

Mackey looked back at his deputy. "Keep an eye out for anyone we don't know. Holler if you see anyone."

Billy raised his Sharps and laid the stock on his hip. "Take your time."

Mackey went in to see the patient. From behind him, he heard the doctor say to Billy. "Your friend's not a forgiving man, is he?"

Billy didn't answer.

Mackey found the injured man lying on a cot that looked like it had once served as a trough, now with a couple of planks across it to support a thin mattress. The patient was lying flat on his back with the right side of his face completely bandaged. An empty bottle of whiskey was on the floor beside the makeshift bed. Mackey didn't know if he'd finished the bottle or if the doctor had. He figured they had both done their part to kill it.

The doctor may have been a drunk, but Mackey

could tell he clearly knew how to apply a field dressing. The right side of the man's head was neatly bandaged from just above the cheek to the top of his head. His good eye widened at the sight of the sheriff standing before him. Some men might have recoiled at the sight. Others might have felt proud to see what had happened to a man who had tried to harm him.

Mackey did not feel anything at all except curious.

The wounded man's good eye widened when he saw his attacker standing before him. "You come to gloat, you son of a bitch?" His speech was slurred from whiskey.

"No. Came here for some answers. What's your name?"

He raised his bandaged right hand with two planks of wood strapped to either side of it. "Doc says my wrist is fractured in two places and I've lost an eye." He winced from pain and he lay flat again. "I'd say you've gotten enough out of me for one day."

Mackey looked at the man's bandages. "You held an innocent woman at knifepoint and tried to stab me. You're lucky you're still alive."

"You call this lucky? You call this alive? Doc says I'll never be able to deal a hand of cards again."

"But at least you can walk." Mackey looked down at the man's knees, then back at him. "For now."

The wounded man's breath caught. "You wouldn't."

"I'm still waiting for an answer to my question. And if you lie, don't count on the rummy who patched you up being able to save you a second time."

The man's good eye closed in defeat. "Name's Gerald Swain out of Mississippi."

The name actually meant something to Mackey. "The gambler?"

"I was," Swain said, "right up until I came up against you."

Mackey had heard of Gerald Swain many times before over the years. He had made his name and fortune as a cardsharp on the grandest riverboats on the Mississippi. Men came from all over the country—and some said the world—to play Swain for high stakes on the paddle-wheeled vessels that roamed the mighty river. Though Mackey had never met the man, Swain was one of those characters he had heard about once, only to have them remain frozen in his memory forever.

Mackey imagined Swain as a dashing riverboat dandy with money to burn and beautiful women on his arm in every port along the river. That mental picture was a far sight away from the broken, bandaged men before him. "How the hell did you get here? Montana's a long way from New Orleans."

Swain's good eye closed slowly. "I guess that's the point. Found myself pretty far from New Orleans, too, once I'd worn out my welcome on the river. My reputation preceded me, and the captains all wanted a bigger cut of my winnings for allowing me to gamble on their vessels. I had to leave the river entirely and set up permanently in New Orleans. It's a pretty city, but an expensive option for a man of my tastes, so I found myself a wanderer again. I wound up in Kansas, where the gaming hall bullies were even less amicable than riverboat captains, which speaks volumes about the character of both sets of individuals. My prospects were dwindling as fast as my funds when I met a man with an interesting proposition."

Mackey leaned against the stall frame. "What was his name?"

"Tommy Macum," Swain said. "He's one of the men I assume you killed yesterday. You would have led him back in chains otherwise."

Mackey leaned against the entrance to the stall. At least now he had another living witness that Tom Macum was working with Grant. "You ever heard of Macum before then?"

"Sure," Swain admitted. "He'd run stagecoach stations and a telegraph office in a few places. When he approached me about becoming a train robber, my instincts told me to get the hell out of there. Now I wish I'd shot the son of a bitch

237

rather than becoming just another notch on the belt of the great Aaron Mackey, the Hero of Adobe Flats and the Savior of Dover Station."

Mackey winced at the titles. "So you've heard of me?"

"I'm not the only one here with a reputation that precedes him, sheriff."

Mackey had no interest in flattery. "You said you met Macum in Kansas?"

"He met me," Swain told him. "Said he'd been searching me out because he had a proposition to make me. That's when he asked me to join his friends in robbing trains."

A bout of pain coursed through him and he cried out, reaching for the bottle. "Can I get another, please?"

Mackey found another bottle on a shelf on the far side of the stall, but did not take it. "Keep talking. If I like what I hear, maybe you'll get some relief."

Swain groaned through the pain. "If I don't get whiskey now, I don't talk."

Mackey took the empty bottle and smashed it on the ground beside Swain's bed. "Either you keep talking, or I drag you out of bed and through that glass. Understand me?"

"A butcher and a torturer," Swain spat. "My, how your family must be proud."

Mackey grabbed hold of the gambler's leg and began pulling him from his bed.

Swain quickly resumed his story, "I asked him how he had heard of me but he refused to answer. I had seen him around Abilene for a couple of days before he approached me. He saw how desperate I had become. He knew I was out of money and was in no position to turn him down, so I listened. Because he bought me a drink that I couldn't pay for on my own."

"That's all it took?" Mackey asked. "The price of a glass of whiskey?"

"The fall from grace was a little more gradual than that, but by the time Macum found me, yes, that's all it took. Macum managed to make it sound like I was lucky he was letting me in on such a sweet deal. He said he was one man shy of a gang and asked me to join him. He said it was sure money and practically no risk to speak of."

Mackey wasn't convinced. "You've been around long enough to know if something's too good to be true, it usually is."

"Desperation can make a man believe all sorts of damned fool notions," Swain said. "But when Macum told me how sweet the deal actually was, even I was convinced. He said he had a well-heeled backer looking to cash in on robbing trains up in this part of the territory. He said that since I wasn't known up here, no one could recognize me, so I'd make the perfect ace on the train to make sure none of the passengers got too brave. He even boasted that he had a man on the railroad who would tip him off whenever a train was ripe for the taking. He said the amount we took didn't matter because we would get paid either way, no matter what we got from the passengers."

Mackey knew his next question would be his most important. "How much?"

"Fifty bucks a week in gold whether or not we pulled off a robbery. Plus, we got to keep whatever we took from the passengers."

There was that number again, Mackey thought. The same as Agee told him. Fifty dollars in gold coins. "That strike you as strange?"

"Sure it did," Swain admitted. "So did the notion that the backer wouldn't want a piece of the haul. But, as I said before, I was in no position to complain or require an explanation, so I accepted Macum's deal."

So far, everything Swain had said matched what Mackey already knew. "Macum tell you who he was working for?"

"He refused to tell me," Swain said. "I asked him several times, but Tom was a crafty one. He never let anything slip unless he wanted to tell me. He said the less anyone knew about the whole operation, the better. He wanted me to be the group's inside man on the train, to blend in with the passengers and tamp down any troublemakers on board. If nothing happened, I stayed quiet and handed over my stuff during the robbery just like everyone else, except I always got my stuff back later. In the event I had to back up Macum and his men, I'd ride out with them."

Swain looked toward the wall. "That's why I grabbed the woman. I figured it was time for me to get young Joe and ride the hell out of there back to Macum's ranch. Not very gallant of me, I know, but I assure you she was never in any real danger. I had the back of the razor to her throat, not the blade. I didn't want to risk hurting her."

"So you slashed out at me instead." Mackey looked at Swain's injuries. "And look at where it got you. You lost an eye, a hand, and bought yourself one last dance at the end of a rope."

"I've done nothing deserving a hanging." Swain pushed himself upright in the bed. "I had no hand in those killings, Mackey. Young Joe will tell you that. I signed on well after that business."

Mackey shrugged. "For your sake, I hope you're right, though a judge will probably see it differently. Accessory after the fact is the proper legal term. And seeing as how much Mr. Rice hates people stealing from him, I wouldn't put a plug nickel on your chances, Swain."

Swain sounded much more sober now. The threat of death by hanging had a way of chasing the booze from a man's system. "You've got to be able to do something for me, damn you. I've told you everything I know. And it's all the truth. You know that. I can see that you know it. It matches up with what others have told you, doesn't it?"

"Would you be willing to put all of this in a statement in front of witnesses?"

The man moved his bandaged hand. "I'm right-handed, or at least I was. But I'll repeat everything I've told you in front of witnesses and make my mark beneath it. It's a mark I've made in dozens of gambling dens from here to New Orleans."

That would give him more evidence for Mr. Rice and, ultimately, a judge. But he needed more. More, perhaps, than Swain's sodden mind could offer just then. "You've told me a lot of things," Mackey said, "but you didn't tell me what I wanted to know. Who was Macum's backer? Who was giving him all this gold he paid out each week?"

"And I already told you he never said. I pushed and prodded. Hell, I even got him drunk and called on a sporting lady who owed me a favor to show him a good time. I tried like hell to get it out of him, but he never cracked. I know there were other people in on the plan, a big bastard by the name of Dave Aderson, but he sure as hell wasn't giving out gold to anybody. That's the God's honest truth, or as close to it as I could ever get."

Mackey knew Swain was too drunk and hurt to lie convincingly, but there was something he was holding back. Something he might not have even known he was holding back. He pressed the wounded man further. "You're a professional gambler. You made your life watching people. Understanding them. Well, so have I. I know you must've spent a lot of time with Macum and his bunch. You must've heard something about who was paying you."

The gambler closed his good eye. "I was saving this for later."

"There's no later here, Swain. There's just the here and now. Tell me what you know."

"It's just a guess and you don't strike me as the type who takes well to guessing." Swain's eye remained closed for so long, Mackey feared the man had passed out. His breathing became shallow, and his entire body relaxed. Mackey was about to kick the prisoner awake when he said, "Whoever Macum was working for, it was someone who can put his hands on hundreds of dollars in gold pieces at a time. Someone smart enough to pick a competent man like Macum to run the show instead of a criminal who'd go too far and kill a whole trainload of people."

"Macum and his bunch killed three people as it was."

"He said they'd given him no choice in the matter. The engineer tried to hit one of the boys with a wrench, and the conductor he killed pulled a gun. And the passenger he killed knocked young Joe on his ass and set to kicking hell out

243

of him. Tom said he had no choice but to shoot the poor bastard."

Just then, Mackey did not care about the killings. He needed to make that last link between Macum and Grant. "Get back to the money man. Tell me more about him."

"I got the feeling whoever was paying him was close by on account of him never having a problem paying us before and after a job. Macum never took a cut of the take, either. Just let us split it evenly among the four of us, at least on any job I was on."

Swain opened his eye and looked at Mackey. "Someone was paying him good money to hit the railroad, sheriff, and I couldn't tell you the first reason why. The money was so good, I didn't care much, either. That's the truth, too. Now you can drag me out of this here bed and across that glass on the floor like you threatened before, and I won't be able to tell you any more than that. That's all I know because that's all I was told. I didn't even know about the three killings until after I'd signed on. I was in it for the money, not the blood."

"In my experience, the two usually go together." Mackey kicked the shards of glass out of the stall. He didn't want the gambler getting ideas about using a piece to take his own life. "I'll be back later with a lawyer if I can find one and a couple of witnesses if I can't. We'll get all of this down on paper and you can make your mark. You do that, and I'll talk to Mr. Rice on your behalf when I see him. If I catch him on a good day, you might just get ten years from a friendly judge. I know that's a long time, but that part's out of my hands. You have my word on that."

Swain's head bobbed as he swallowed hard. Drunk or sober, healthy or hurting, being told you were about to lose ten years of your life was not an easy thing to hear. "I'd appreciate that, sheriff. I'd also appreciate it if you got the hell out of here and let me get some rest. You'll get your damned statement after I rest a spell."

Mackey watched the wounded gambler's will finally give out as he fell asleep. He waited a few moments to make sure he was still breathing before leaving the stall.

The doctor lowered his bottle as Mackey walked by him on his way out. "Wasn't enough to cave in the man's skull, but you had to threaten to drag him across broken glass, too? The Hero of Adobe Flats. The Savior of Dover Station." He spat at a cuspidor by the desk but did not have enough on it to make it that far. "You must be awfully proud of yourself."

Mackey stopped and pointed out at the whorehouse across the way. "You proud of feeding off desperate women, Doc?"

The doctor sneered as he looked him up and down. "You make me sick."

"The whiskey's making you sick," Mackey said. "Save some of that for your patient. He's going to need it where he's going. I'll be back later to take his statement, and I want him able to talk when I get here. Mr. Rice will see to it that you're compensated for saving his life. Until then, do yourself a favor and keep your mouth shut and your opinions to yourself."

Mackey and Billy walked through the alley between the whorehouse and the stables where their mounts were kept.

Billy asked, "Get anything out of him?"

"Got enough to get him to give us a statement on paper," Mackey admitted. "We'll come back later with Lagrange and get his statement. We'll need a couple of the passengers to serve as witnesses. That'll delay their trip to Butte a little longer than they'd like, but they've got no choice. I'll telegraph Mr. Rice now and let him know the latest."

"Not going to tell him everything," Billy said. "I don't trust the telegraph lines, especially with Grant getting a copy of every telegram sent."

"You're not the only one," Mackey said. "Mr. Rice doesn't seem to trust them, either."

Chapter 20

If he had not been so angry, James Grant would have enjoyed Murphy's fear. He held the yellow sheet in front of him. "When did this telegram come across the wire?"

"Late last night," Murphy said.

"I thought I left instructions to be immediately notified of any telegram leaving the last known location of Mackey's train?"

Murphy scrambled for his pad and dropped it. "You did, sir, but it was late, and I didn't want to disturb you."

"I'm not aware that the word 'immediately' has a time limit on it."

"I know, but I thought you were asleep and I didn't want to wake you. It's just a telegram between Mr. Rice and the sheriff meeting in Butte. There's nothing to tell."

Grant resisted the urge to backhand the son of a bitch. News of Rice being anywhere near the territory, much less in it, was of major importance.

But he knew how much the people of Dover Station liked to talk. He had done a good job of making sure they spoke in his favor up to this point. And with his major announcement at hand, he knew throttling the town's telegrapher could only cause more trouble than it was worth.

Grant balled up the yellow paper and tossed it across the office. "From now on, if you come upon any telegram from Mackey or anyone even mentioning him, you are to bring it to me immediately. No matter the day, no matter the hour. I don't care if it's midnight or lunchtime or anytime in between. Do you understand me?"

Murphy quickly picked up the pad he had dropped. "Yes, sir. I didn't mean to anger you. I'm sorry."

He decided to use the mistake of allowing his temper to get the better of him to his advantage. Murphy flinched as Grant patted him on the back. "No harm done, Joe. I hadn't made myself clear before, but now I have. Thanks for showing it to me when you did."

Murphy smiled, relieved that the storm of his employer's anger had passed and all was well. But Grant saw something else in the little man's eyes. Something that hadn't been there before.

Awareness. Knowledge that there was another side to the affable Mr. Grant he had never seen before. Grant knew the memory of the incident would fade with time and continued praise, but it would always be there like a rock just beneath the sands.

The idea was to use Murphy's newfound awareness to his own advantage when the time was right. It was one of the many skills James Grant had acquired over the years.

He pulled out his gold pocket watch from his brocade vest and compared it to the Regulator clock on the wall. Both timepieces said it was a minute before three in the afternoon. The watch had cost more than his father had made during an entire lifetime of punching cattle and plowing fields. Grant was proud that he had the money to be able to buy it. He intended on having more.

He snapped the watch shut and tucked it back into his pocket before buttoning up his coat. "Keep up the good work, Joe. Talk to you soon."

The telegrapher tipped his cap as he stepped outside. He didn't bother closing the door behind him, keeping the cold wind out of the office. If Murphy wanted it closed, he could do it himself.

Walter Underhill was waiting for him outside, leaning against a post while watching a couple of women purchase train tickets. The fact each woman was standing beside her husband did not deter him from looking. Nor did it deter the women from stealing glances at the large Texan with the flowing blond locks.

Grant cleared his throat. "Hope I'm not keeping you from any important business, Underhill."

"Not at all." Underhill tipped his hat to the blushing ladies as they looked away, their husbands oblivious. "Where we off to now?"

"Katie's Place," Grant said as he began to walk. "I have business to discuss with Mrs. Campbell."

"What kind of business?"

Grant had always been careful of what he allowed Underhill to see. He knew the former lawman had become close to Mackey and Billy Sunday. He had grown tired of hearing the old-timers in saloons gas on about their exploits during the siege. When he had first come to Dover Station at Mr. Van Dorn's request, Grant shouted out "the Savior of Dover Station" as a joke during a spirited debate over how many Darabont men Mackey had personally killed. The name took on a life of its own and Grant used it to his advantage whenever it served him. The town could use all of the heroes it could get. Not only did the name help improve the town's image, it irked Mackey to no end.

"Business that concerns her hotel," was all Grant told him as they walked past the Municipal Building toward the hotel. Construction had resumed full tilt since Eddows's ill-fated plan to execute Ross. He had brought Mohr to town in the hopes his message might strike a chord with some of the workers. He had never expected a simpleton like Eddows to take it literally.

But now that Ernst Mohr was dead, Grant would use the radical's death to his own advantage. The only question was how? Should he seize on underlying resentment towards the sheriff and claim Mohr's death was caused by Mackey's heavy-handed administration of the law? Or should Grant vow to use his office as mayor to stomp out the element that attracted such rabble in the first place?

The only decision he had made was that he was running for mayor. After his meeting with Mrs. Campbell, he would know the nature of his candidacy.

Underhill brought Grant's thoughts from the future and back to the present. "This is the second time you're meeting with Mrs. Campbell in two weeks."

"I wasn't aware I was paying you to be my secretary, Underhill. I thought I was paying for your gun."

"You're paying for my help," Underhill said. "And advice comes with that help. Sniffing around Aaron Mackey's woman is not a prescription for good health."

Grant straightened his topcoat. "My interest in Mrs. Campbell is purely professional. And even if it wasn't, the sheriff is still a married man, so Mrs. Campbell cannot technically be his woman."

"Don't know what it says in a town record, James. But I do know Mackey's mind, and he and the Campbell widow are as close as you could get to being married without the vows or the hardware. I suggest you don't get in the habit of having too many business dealings with her in the future on account of the sheriff not liking it."

"I don't give a damn about the sheriff's likes, Underhill. I do as I please."

He stopped himself before he said any more. He had said quite a bit as it was.

But soon, Aaron Mackey's opinion wouldn't account for much in Dover Plains or anywhere else.

It was time for James Grant to enlist Mrs. Campbell in a coin trick he had seen at a carnival once in Nebraska.

The carnival hack called it: Heads I Win, Tails You Lose.

It was almost half past three by the time Mrs. Campbell came to the front parlor of the hotel. He had been waiting so long, Grant began to wonder if that idiot Sandborne boy had forgotten to tell her he was calling for her.

Grant had always been a patient man. In fact, his patience had often been his salvation, the quality that had separated him from the rest. The frontier had taught him patience and the power of persistence. Of knowing when to act, when to watch, and when to strike. And now, as he sat in the elegant front parlor of Mrs. Katherine Campbell's hotel, he was planning his boldest strike since coming to Dover Station.

He rose when Mrs. Campbell glided into the

room in that sophisticated East Coast manner Grant had always found appealing. He judged her to be around forty, but only because he had prided himself on his powers of observation. The tiny lines that appeared around her eyes when she offered him that indulgent smile whenever he visited her. As if he should count himself fortunate he was receiving that much from her.

He comforted himself in the knowledge that very soon, he would be in a position to grant indulgences and not her. His first step toward that goal began now.

"Mrs. Campbell," he said as he rose to greet her. "You're always a vision."

She wore a plain blue dress, as Grant knew was her custom during daytime hours. The dress had not been fashioned to accentuate her long legs, but Grant was able to admire them just the same. After all, he had always been a most observant man.

"Good afternoon, Mr. Grant." She sat without offering him her hand. He took the lack of formality to be a sign that she may be finally warming to him. "I understand you wish to see me again, though I can't imagine why. I'm still considering your request to rename the hotel 'Campbell House,' but I'm afraid I haven't quite made up my mind just yet."

He could have sat and listened to her speak for hours. That high-class Bostonian accent she had enthralled him. Not out of any sense of love or attraction, but because he wondered how it would sound when her world crumbled before her very eyes.

"I understand it's a woman's prerogative to take her time in making a decision," Grant said, "but I'm here on a related matter. I know you're a busy woman, so I'll get to the heart of it. I wish to purchase this hotel from you. Tonight. In cash."

Since the day he had come to town six months before, he had observed the Campbell widow from near and far. He had always admired her grace and poise, the way she held herself in all occasions. True, it was odd that she never left the hotel, not even to stand in the thoroughfare. It was rumored that this was due to some phobia she had acquired while she was held by Darabont and his men.

It made his enjoyment of watching her fluster at the idea of losing her hotel that much better.

It took her a moment to regain her composure, but she still looked flushed. "Mr. Grant. I was just considering changing the name of the hotel. I hadn't expected you to offer to buy it outright."

He gave her the line that had worked so well on so many other people in town. "I apologize for the sudden nature of my request, but such is to be expected in a town on the rise. As you have undoubtedly seen, Mrs. Campbell, Dover Station is certainly that. Ideas and actions that often take days or weeks at other, more sensible times, take only hours in our present environment."

He leaned forward, respecting the proper distance between them. "That's why I need your answer tonight. By tomorrow at the latest. Events in town are moving faster than even I could have foreseen. On the business front and, might I add, on a more personal front, too." He looked down at his hat with that practiced look that had conveyed sincerity to so many in town before. "I'm afraid I'm not at liberty to discuss the details at the moment, nor the necessity for the urgency, but I assure you it is quite necessary."

He thought he saw a hint of dampness appear on her well-powdered brow. He had to fight himself to keep from smiling. Finally, a crack in that elegant Campbell façade.

She blinked before replying, "It would take me at least several days to give you a fair price."

Yes, the crack in the façade had formed, but the longer he waited, the quicker the fissure would be repaired. He could not allow that to happen, so he kept at it. "Mrs. Campbell, I cannot impress upon you enough how vital it is that you make your decision now. Tonight, I can offer you top dollar for the hotel. I have seen the town's records and know how much you paid for the property three years ago. I know you have made several improvements since then and, given that existing buildings are a commodity in town, I am prepared to pay you handsomely, but I am afraid my offer expires when I leave this room. That's why I must have your answer now."

As Mrs. Campbell sat back in her chair, Grant could see a degree of calmness had come over her. She had weathered the storm of initial shock and indecision and had managed to right herself once more. Grant had already lost the element of surprise, but was very much still in the game.

She said, "Your idea of handsome might be very ugly to me, Mr. Grant."

Grant admired her spark. "Name your price, then, and let us reach an accord."

"But I've already told you that I'm hardly in a position to do so. Any sum I give might be too low or too high without having the time to give the matter its due consideration. I appreciate your need for urgency, but the sale of my home and business is not something I take lightly. If you press me for an answer, I'm afraid that answer will have to be no."

Grant had been hoping she would say that. But he persisted for the sake of his performance. "A fair number today is better than no number tomorrow, Mrs. Campbell."

He watched her think it over. The deflated shut-in acting very much the Bostonian lady of culture. "A lady could be forgiven for hearing a measure of dark intent in your words. Surely, I must be mistaken."

You're not mistaken, Grant thought, but said something quite different. "I apologize for my tone, as threatening you couldn't be further from my mind. All I meant to convey is that tonight I can afford to be generous. Next time, should there be a next time, this may not be the case."

"But if I refuse your offer on your terms, why would I think there would be a next time? After all, men don't like to be rebuked, especially by a woman."

He watched her look out the parlor window at the late afternoon strollers and wagons moving along the boardwalk and thoroughfare just outside the hotel. *My hotel,* she was undoubtedly thinking.

Grant could not let her think too long. "Mrs. Campbell, I need . . ."

She continued as though she had not heard him. "I am curious about the sudden urgency to acquire my hotel, Mr. Grant. I find it rather odd and, for the life of me, I can't understand the reason why. It wouldn't have anything to do with Sheriff Mackey being out of town, would it?"

Grant held his ground. "I'm trying to make you an offer to purchase your hotel at a fair price, Mrs. Campbell. I have no idea what role the sheriff's absence or presence could possibly play in this negotiation."

"Is that what this is, Mr. Grant? This feels less like a negotiation and more like an ambush, like something that would happen to a stumblebum who finds himself dragged into an alley beside one of the saloons you chose to build rather than constructing houses where the newcomers could live."

Heads I win, Grant thought, and tails you lose. If she had accepted his offer, he would own the hotel. But she appeared to be choosing anger instead. He could use that against her when the time was right. "Mrs. Campbell, I meant no offense."

"I believe offense is the sole reason for being here. I believe you came to either push me into selling this place or to frighten me. You may rest assured that neither tactic will work. If and when the time comes that I decide to sell my hotel, I will do so. Until then, I will hold on to it and run it as I see fit, although I'm still considering changing the name to Campbell House per your suggestion."

She stood up and so did Grant, out of politeness. She added, "Now please leave before I have you escorted out."

Grant smiled as he slowly turned his hat by the brim. "By whom, Mrs. Campbell? The Sandborne boy Aaron hired to play deputy while Aaron's out of town? I wouldn't give much for his chances."

"I don't need anyone to help me throw anyone

out of my own hotel." She pointed to the door. "Get out. Now."

He bent slightly at the waist and made his exit, slipping on his hat as he did so.

In his mind, he saw which way the coin had landed. *Tails, Mrs. Campbell. You lose.*

Chapter 21

In the warm luxury of his private railcar in Butte, Mr. Frazer Rice, Chairman of the Rice Van Dorn Company, reread Swain's sworn statement about his part in the train robberies. When Rice was finished, he looked across the desk at the man who had given it to him. "And you're sure this is legal?"

"As legal as it can get," Mackey said. "That's his sworn statement made in front of me. Got an attorney who was a passenger on the train to witness it. That Pinkerton named Lagrange witnessed it, too."

"Sounds like that Pinkerton man I hired came in handy after all," Rice said. "I wasn't sure he would. I'm glad he was of some use."

"I may have use for him still. In fact, I'd like to have him return with me to Dover Station, if you don't mind the added expense."

Rice waved off the idea of money. "I don't care about cost. I care about your reasons for needing him."

"Lagrange has never been to Dover. No one knows who he is. I've got a feeling that could be an advantage for us, things being what they are."

"It's the way things are in that town that concern me." Rice frowned as he tossed the affidavit on his desk. "Place has turned into a goddamned mystery to me since I left."

"I thought you might be feeling that way," Mackey admitted, "when you sent that telegram directly to me. But I didn't want to say too much over the lines, since there was no way of telling who might be reading it later on."

"Prudent as ever, sheriff. I keep forgetting you're not a shitkicker like the rest of them out there. You're a West Pointer, by God, and I'm grateful for it. I think you're the only man in that whole damned town I can trust."

Mackey waited for Rice to say more, but watched him drum his fingers on the desk instead. Mackey figured it was best to just sit quietly and watched him brood. Sometimes, silence was a great teacher.

Mr. Rice was older than the sheriff by more than twenty years, though he bore none of the expansions or frailties that often occurred with advancing age. A bald head and silver muttonchops gave him the sophisticated air befitting one of the wealthiest men in America.

Rice stopped drumming his fingers "Do you know I haven't heard from that bastard Van Dorn in a month? I send him requests via the mail train on a weekly basis and never get a response. And even before then, the responses were so damned terse, they were hardly worth the time it took to send them."

Mackey was surprised. "You mean you've had no contact with the town except through me?"

"Oh, I get plenty of construction reports and information on our holdings," Rice said. "A package shows up on the train each week like clockwork. But whenever I ask Silas a direct question about something or tell him I want something done, he never replies. Just sends another report. The damnable part of it is that he makes any changes I tell him to make, but my questions go unanswered."

Mackey had an idea why things had gone that way, but he needed to be sure. "Was Mr. Van Dorn always like that?"

"Never. That weasel never had the spine to defy me like this before," Rice said. "Hell, he used to go overboard by giving me too much information. Now I can't get a word out of him. Makes no damned sense."

"Unfortunately, it makes plenty of sense if you consider James Grant is Van Dorn's right hand."

Rice took a cigar from the humidor on his desk and bit off the end of it. "I heard he'd hired an assistant of some kind." He spat the cigar end into a cuspidor by his desk. "I even encouraged him to find the right person to help him. Silas is a brilliant man, maybe the smartest man I've ever known, but getting things done is not his strong suit."

Rice held the cigar but did not light it. "What can you tell me about this Grant fellow? Silas was awfully vague when I asked him about Grant's particulars."

Mackey told him what he knew. "He's about forty or so. Nice looking and easy to like. At least that's how he comes across at first. I heard he spent most of his life knocking around the Midwest. Ran a stagecoach line and a telegraph office here or there. Managed ranches, owned a bar. Even was a lawman for a time in Nebraska according to some stories, but I don't believe everything I hear."

Mr. Rice grunted. "Unfortunately, Silas doesn't have your discerning character. Or personality. Hell, I don't think the man even has a personality. He's a bookish, quiet little man who'd never venture outside his house if I didn't make him come to the office every day. But given Silas's awkwardness and gullibility, I think it's damned likely that he has allowed this Grant character to have more influence over our investments than he should. But that shouldn't preclude him from responding to me, especially when I sent him a private letter inquiring about Grant's position in the enterprise."

Mackey had come to this meeting prepared to convince Mr. Rice of Grant's plan to take over Dover Station. He was glad it didn't look like he'd have to work that hard to do it. "I doubt he ever saw the letter, sir. Jim Grant's got him pretty well hobbled."

Rice's eyes narrowed. "You think Grant would have the temerity to hold back a personal, confidential correspondence I sent directly to Silas?"

"Silas didn't reply, so I'd say there's a good chance he's intercepting his mail."

Rice thumbed a match alive and brought the flame to his cigar. "The impetuous bastard."

Mackey kept talking while Rice lit his cigar. "Grant is a smooth operator, sir. He's gotten pretty popular in a short amount of time. Been smart about it, too. He keeps his name out of the papers, probably on account of he knows you'll see them, but the quotes you read from Silas are James Grant's words. He's done a lot to make your company very popular in town, too. The businessmen like him. The workers like him. The townspeople, too, and they can be pretty fickle with their affections. In fact, I can't think of anyone who doesn't like him."

Rice pointed the cigar at him. "Except you."

Mackey didn't deny it. "I'm not in the business of trusting anyone. But no, I don't like him. I think he's too sweet to be wholesome."

Rice puffed away at his cigar, a thin cloud of smoke hanging around him like a dirty halo. "What's he after? He's not stealing from us. I have the books checked independently with our bank in town. Everything seems to be in order on that score. He keeps his petty cash reasonable and he doesn't pay himself an exorbitant salary. The materials are all accounted for, so he's not stealing from us. My people back in New York think I'm crazy for worrying the way I do. They think I should be over the moon about what's going on in Dover Station, but I know there's something wrong, sheriff. I can feel it in my bones, and my feelings are never wrong."

Another puff on his cigar, then, "You tell me Grant is up to something, and I believe you. But what is it?"

Mackey saw no reason to sugarcoat it. "Power."

Rice laughed. "Sounds like he's got all the power he needs right now."

"Not for him," Mackey explained. "A man like Grant always wants more. And with town elections coming up in two weeks, I think he's going to run for mayor. That'll give him all the power he needs, at least for a while."

Rice slowly lowered his cigar toward the crystal ashtray on his desk. "You can't be serious."

"I'm not one for jokes, sir."

"But he's an employee of the Dover Station Company. Silas has him overseeing all of our operations. How the hell can he run the town and do his job at the same time?"

"The office of mayor has always been a part-time position," Mackey explained. "And the way Grant has charmed the people these last six months, he's practically the mayor anyway. No one else wants the job, and the acting mayor, Doc Ridley, just wants to practice medicine. No one will run against Grant, and even if they did, he'd win. I imagine he's going to declare his candidacy while I'm gone."

Rice flicked his ash and almost broke the cigar. "He'll have the town in a stranglehold if that's the case. I won't let it happen."

Mackey knew he had to proceed carefully. If he did not address the matter exactly the right way, it could send Rice on a disastrous course that would only benefit Grant.

"No offense, sir, but he's had plenty of time to solidify his position, and there's not much you can do to stop him."

Rice's temper sparked. "What the hell are you talking about?"

Mackey produced the letter he had taken from the lining of Ernst Mohr's jacket. "He has taken the time to give himself plenty of options, sir. Take this letter I found on a dead radical in Tent City named Ernst Mohr. I can't read it because it's in German, but I can make out enough of the words to show someone wrote to Mohr to come to Dover Station. Probably to raise hell."

Rice held out his hand. "Give it to me and I'll make out all the words for you. Name wasn't always Rice. It was Rickenbach before my grandfather came to this country. The name might've

266

been shortened, but the family's German traditions remained."

Mackey gave him the letter and watched him read it. "Your reading of the letter's not far off. He was told to go to Dover Station by a Mr. Macum who told him he'd find fertile ground there. It says a train ticket and some money were enclosed in the letter for his trouble." Rice handed the letter back to Mackey. "Seems damned vague to me. Too vague to get me on a train to someplace in Montana. My guess is that this Macum and Ernst Mohr either already knew each other or Mohr knew he should be expecting a letter. Either way, I don't like it."

Mackey tucked the letter back into his pocket. "Neither do I, sir. But I hate to tell you that your options are limited."

Rice's eyes narrowed. "A man does not attain my position in life without having plenty of options available to him, sheriff."

Mackey remembered what Katherine had told him. A man like Rice couldn't be told what to do. He had to make it seem like it was his idea. "Let's say you send a letter to Van Dorn to fire Grant. Who will he get to replace Grant? You've got half a dozen large buildings being built right now, not to mention managing the ranching, mining, and logging operations your company controls. You say Silas is brilliant, but he hasn't paid attention to the daily operation of things since you left town. And if I have Grant pegged right, I'll bet he's kept just enough from him to make himself indispensable."

Rice gritted his teeth. "Cemeteries are filled with indispensable men, sheriff."

"Yes, sir, and there are plenty of good companies buried right next to them."

The wealthy man thought about it, then said, "I'll give you a letter to hand deliver to Silas personally, spelling out all the reasons why I want that son of a bitch Grant fired. He might have the rest of the town charmed, but not you."

"I'll happily deliver it," Mackey said, "but I don't think it'll make a damned bit of difference." As Rice's face reddened, he quickly added, "Because Silas is in no position to replace him overnight. What's more, Grant's been slowly bringing in his own people for the past couple of months to back his play."

"People? What kind of people?"

"Gunmen in the guise of supervisors," Mackey said. "They've kept a low profile and haven't bullied anyone without cause, but I know the type. They're on the payroll and they do their job, but one word from Grant and they'll be at his side in a heartbeat. Armed, too."

"How many are we talking about?"

"At least twenty," Mackey said. "By the time I get back, maybe thirty."

Rice pounded his desk. "Damn it! How did things get out of hand so fast?"

"He did it smart," Mackey told him, "and he did it slow, bringing them in one or two at a time and giving them jobs. They're going easy now, but if Grant gives the word, they'll take the town by force if necessary. I can try to stop them, but he's so popular, it'll be tough even without gunplay."

Mackey raised one finger at a time as he counted off everything he believed Grant had done. He spoke quicker than he normally did, because, as he began to speak, more of the story began to make sense to him. "First, he organized men to rob your trains to dampen enthusiasm about the town. He had access to gold, so he was able to pay them to keep them interested. If the robberies continued, he'd only get more power as he could bring his own people in to open businesses in town. But now that I've stopped it, he can take credit for it.

"Second, he brought in an anarchist to stir up some of the workers, but I put a stop to it. He took credit for it, but he can easily blame me for allowing the man to operate in the first place.

"Third, he's popular with everyone, and so is the company. You fire him, he looks like a martyr and he turns public sentiment against the company. They'll burn straw versions of Silas Van Dorn on Front Street. Hell, my own father's making so much money off the company, he'll probably light the match."

Rice left his cigar in the ashtray and rubbed a hand over his bald head. "Good God."

But Mackey wasn't done. "Fourth, as mayor, he's in a position to pass laws and regulations that could slow your development of the town to a crawl, forcing you to pay him off. He knows you've invested too much in the town to back off now, and you can't make a case for incompetence. In short, he's dug in deep at Dover Station and there's not much we can do about it."

Mackey lowered his fingers into a fist. "I'm just sorry I didn't see everything he was planning until now. I never bought his act, but I didn't think he was capable of this."

Rice lifted his head from his hand. "You think he's capable? Well, by God, you're about to get a lesson in what true capability is. I have friends in lots of places, son. I'll have the territorial governor send in men to seize the town."

"You'll just make Grant a martyr," Mackey reminded him, "and you have your investments to think about. All removing Grant would do is hurt a lot of people."

"Then I'll head to Washington, talk to the president. God knows I've given that ungrateful son of a bitch enough money over the years. I'll have him send in the army and maintain order!"

Mackey had been afraid that was the direction

Rice would go. When all else failed, the wealthy called in the army to do their fighting for them. "Do you have the current layout of the town in your records, sir?"

"I have it right here." Rice took a set of plans from the credenza behind his desk and unrolled them. "Every building that's scheduled to be built is right here."

Mackey had to stand to get a better look at the map. It was not every day that a man saw his hometown reduced to the edges of a paper.

He did not like what he saw. "I've only seen a partial rendering of this. And I'm afraid Grant has taken it upon himself to change this some."

Rice's eyes narrowed. "How?"

"The angle of the buildings on the edge of town is different. He's built them in the shape of a wedge, with narrower streets than what's shown here. The buildings don't have any windows and no alleyways to speak of, either."

Rice took a closer look at the plans. "That's not what we agreed upon. Why, he's changed everything."

"And practically built himself a fortress," Mackey told him. "The buildings create narrow pinch points into the town that could easily repel the army with just a few rifles at key locations. Front Street is wide open, but Grant's people could turn that into a shooting gallery. The army could take the town eventually, but not without destroying a lot of property and killing a lot of innocents. I can't think of a general who'd order it, even in the territories."

Deflated, Rice sank back into his chair and pushed himself away from his desk and the offending plan of Dover Station.

"Well I can't allow him to stay unchecked, and I can't get rid of him. I can't fire him, and I can't arrest him. What the hell am I supposed to do? Just let this son of a bitch get away with bilking me? With attacking my railroad and killing three people? Do you have any idea what will happen to me if word of this gets out?"

Mackey lowered himself into his seat. He made it a point to look away while the man calmed down. He could not sell him on what he knew had to be done. Rice had to come to the conclusion himself.

After a few puffs on his cigar, Rice looked at him through the smoke. "You have a plan, don't you?"

"Not a plan, but it's the only way I can think of that comes close to addressing this."

Rice said, "I'm a man of many skills, Aaron, but divining the intentions of others is not one of them. Tell me what you're thinking."

"I need you to contact Washington," Mackey said, "but for a different reason."

Chapter 22

Mackey and Billy began to gather up their things when the conductor announced they were approaching Dover Station.

Billy had been worried about Aaron since he'd returned from his meeting with Rice days ago. He had barely said a word morning, noon, or night. He stared out the window mostly, whether it was light enough to see anything or not.

Now that they were close to home, Billy decided to chance a discussion. "You've been quiet."

Mackey pulled on his coat. "Never been known as a conversationalist, Billy. You know that better than anyone."

"Also know you get quieter when you get nervous. And since I've never known you to be this quiet, you're probably nervous as hell about something. Can't say as I blame you. I'm nervous right along with you. We're headed into a dangerous situation, Aaron. Just wish you were a little more talkative so I'd know what exactly to be nervous about, given that we're spoiled for choice in the concerns department."

It was the first hint of a smile Billy had been able to get out of the man in a week. "Talking about it won't make it better."

"But talking will help us be better organized. Grant's sure as hell organized, so we'll need to be, too. Hell, Aaron. We're not wading into a saloon to break up a fight or gunning down men robbing a bank. We need to talk about what we're going to do, and we might as well do it in here where the walls don't have ears."

Aaron finally looked away from that damned window. "Guess I've been brooding. Everything we do hinges on how well Mr. Rice's correspondence with Washington goes. Everything hinges on that. Even then, it might not be enough, but it's more than what we have now."

After returning from his meeting with Rice, Mackey had told him what the man had in store. He did not believe it would have much of an effect, but it could not hurt, either. "I see Lagrange is still on board the train. You going to use him in town?"

"I've asked him to move through town and find out how many gunmen Grant's got on his side. He could come in handy if we need an ace up our sleeve."

Billy understood that way of thinking. "The way Macum had Swain on the train in case anything went wrong."

"Something like that, I guess."

Both men braced themselves as the train began to slow down as it approached Dover Station.

Billy watched Mackey look out the window

again as the train passed the remains of the land that had once been the JT Ranch in the distance. Black dots moved across the land the way ants moved toward the scraps on a picnic blanket. Only they weren't ants or black dots. They were cattle and horses and riders and farmers tending to chores on another cold Montana morning. They were part of the future of Dover Station, whatever that future might be.

Aaron surprised Billy by saying, "I don't know if we're right anymore, Billy. I don't know if Grant is the problem, and I'm beginning to wonder if we are."

Billy had known his friend to get melancholy before, and the only cure for it was to get him talking until he found his way through it. "What do you mean?"

"That's what I mean." Mackey pointed out the window. "So much change. There was a time when we knew everyone, good and bad. Now, every time I go to sleep, I wake up and the whole damned town seems to have gotten a little bit bigger every single day. Every train, wagon, and stagecoach brings in more people who change it all just a little more.

"Buildings going up and coming down. Workmen, tramps, whores, and all the rest. It's not ours anymore, Billy. It's not home. It's different now, and that's neither good nor bad. It's just the way it is. They like what Van Dorn and Grant are doing, and I can't say as I blame them. I'm just trying to make sure I dislike the men for the right reasons."

The train jerked again as the engine began to slow down even more as they got closer to the station. Billy wished his friend had spoken up yesterday so he would have had the time to talk him out of this nonsense. He was in a dangerous mindset, given how close they were to home.

Billy spoke fast. "People like to follow, Aaron. Makes life easier that way. Men like Silas Van Dorn and James Grant like to lead and make money off it in the process. Never yet met a man who was good all the way through. Never yet met a man who was bad all the way through, neither. Grant might've done a lot of good in this town, but he's still responsible for the deaths of three innocent people."

"I can't prove that," Mackey said, "and Swain's affidavit isn't going to convince anyone."

"Maybe not," Billy allowed, "but you have it, and that could be enough. Men like Van Dorn and Grant have money, and money gives them sway. That's the way it is, and that's the way it's always going to be. If it's not money, it'll be something else, but it'll always be about a small group of men telling a larger group of men what to do because most people think following is easier."

The train hitched as the brakes began to kick

in. The new stockyards at the south end of the station rolled by, and Billy knew he was out of time.

But he got a little help by way of a canvas banner stretched across Front Street. It read:

VOTE FOR THE FUTURE
JIM GRANT *for* **Mayor**
WALTER UNDERHILL *for* **Chief of Police**

Mackey looked away from the window and sank back in his seat. "Looks like the rumors before we left were right. Grant's made his intentions official. A new era for Dover Station has begun."

Billy knew they only had a few minutes before the train pulled into the station, so he talked even faster. "This isn't about change or the past, Aaron. This is about something a lot more permanent than that. It's about the law. The law remains no matter what, just like the land lasts through snow and drought and fire. Seasons change, but the land remains. Same thing with the law. Grant could get himself elected governor, and it wouldn't change the fact that he broke the law when his men killed three people. And one way or the other, the law's going to hold him accountable."

He pointed out at the grand new station building that had just slid into view. "If it doesn't, then

277

none of all the new buildings or fancy streetlights in the world mean a goddamned thing."

Mackey stood up after the train came to a halt. "You always know exactly what to say, don't you, Billy?"

"No, sir. I just have a knack for knowing what you need to hear and when you need to hear it."

He picked up his bag from the couch on the other side of the car. "How many times you practice that speech, anyway?"

"The truth doesn't need to be practiced, just said." Billy was glad that whatever cloud had covered his friend had passed. He saw another banner for the Grant/Underhill election draped across the front of the station building, glad to be able to change the subject. "Sorry to see Walter's name up there. I've actually grown to like the man. Can't believe he's fallen for any of Grant's nonsense."

"What was that you just said about money influencing everything?" Mackey asked. "Being a lawman again is what brought Walter to town in the first place. Stands to reason he'd want to be the new chief of police under Grant."

Billy slung his bag onto his shoulder. "Wonder what that'll mean for us and the sheriff's office."

Mackey opened the train car door and stepped out on to the station platform. "Guess we're about to find out."

● ● ●

After getting their horses from the stable car, Billy rode to the jailhouse while Mackey rode Adair to Katie's Place. He had only been gone two weeks, but the amount of construction between the station and the hotel amazed him. Every street had a canvas banner bearing Grant's and Underhill's names across it. The wooden skeletons of no fewer than eight buildings had been erected since he left. Several buildings that had been half-built before he left had been completely finished.

He imagined Grant's campaign for mayor had spurred the crews to work around the clock. More completed buildings would make him look even better. It would show the good people of Dover Station what he could do when he put his mind to it. Each of the buildings was three stories tall, probably built to get rid of Tent City once and for all. No sense in risking ill will with the voters by having them pass an eyesore like Tent City on their way to the voting place.

Amid the din of the hammering and the sawing that echoed throughout the town, Mackey caught a glimpse of Van Dorn House.

Mackey pulled Adair to a halt when he saw a new sign above Katie's Place that read "The Campbell House" in large letters carved into the wood.

It wasn't the sign that bothered him. It was

the three men, all sporting pistols on their hips, lounging in chairs on the porch.

Mackey drew his Winchester from the saddle boot and aimed it at them. "You on the porch. Throw up your hands and do it slow."

None of the men threw up their hands. None of them moved, either. The one on the far left only smiled. "Welcome back, sheriff. We've been waiting for you."

Mackey shifted his aim to him. "You deaf, boy?"

"We've got permission from Mr. Underhill to wear these guns. He sent us to fetch you over to see Mr. Van Dorn and Mr. Grant. They're anxious to see you."

The one in the middle added, "After you've had a chance to clean up, of course. We understand you've been busy during your trip. Mr. Van Dorn likes his guests to be clean when they come to visit."

Mackey fired, putting a round into the porch board between the man's feet. "Guess you men are hard of hearing. I gave you an order. Either you follow it or you get shot."

The man on the left said, "And I told you we got permission to carry these guns from Mr. Underhill."

"And it's not his permission to give," Mackey said. "Either you leave your gun belts on the porch, or I leave you on the porch. What's it going to be?"

The man on the far right had not spoken yet. He looked older than his partners, and Mackey took him to be the leader. "Do what he wants, boys. Might as well humor the son of a bitch for the time being. Won't make much difference in a week anyway."

Mackey ignored the comment as he watched the men unbuckle their gun belts before they stood up. Each of them held the belts by the buckle and slowly laid them back on the chairs.

Mackey kept the rifle trained on them as they moved away from their guns. The older of the three said, "Mr. Van Dorn still wants to see you as soon as possible, sheriff. I suggest you don't keep him waiting. He's not a patient man."

"You can tell him I got the message and I'll be along. You boys can pick up your guns at the jailhouse later on tonight."

Two of the men stepped off the boardwalk and headed toward Van Dorn House. The leader stayed behind a second longer. "That's the last time you'll disarm me, Mackey. Understand? Next time you try to take my gun, it'll end different."

"Ending will be the same." Mackey urged Adair forward. "Me standing over you with a rifle, just like I am now."

The leader held up his hands as he slowly backed away. "Enjoy yourself, Mackey. While you can, anyways."

Mackey kept the men covered until they were well up the hill to Van Dorn House. Buggies and wagons had to move around Adair as horse and rider refused to move for anyone.

Mackey lowered his rifle and climbed down from the saddle. He kept the Winchester with him as he tied Adair to the hitching post in front of the hotel and gathered up the three gun belts with his free hand.

He walked inside the hotel and was surprised when Katherine almost tackled him. She threw her arms around his waist with such strength, he had to fight to keep his balance.

"Thank God," she whispered. "Thank God you're back alive."

As he ushered her into the parlor, she had to walk sideways as she refused to let him go.

He set the rifle and gun belts on one of the tables in the parlor. None of the customers who lounged as they read papers and drank coffee seemed to be bothered by the display of affection. "What the hell happened?"

"Everything." Her voice quavered, but she did not cry. She told him about Grant's proposition to buy the hotel and her refusal. "Now I know why he was in such a hurry," she added at the end. "The next day, those banners started appearing all over town about him running for mayor and Underhill running for chief of police. I don't know why buying this place was so damned important to him, but it seemed to be."

Mackey had no idea, either. And he didn't care. "Did he hurt you?"

"No," she admitted. "He didn't threaten me in any way. He left me alone until today, when I woke up to hammering and sawing just after sunup. When I came downstairs, three men had Josh Sandborne at gunpoint while they took down the old sign and put up that new sign. 'Courtesy of Mr. Grant,' they told me, the bastards."

"Where's Sandborne now?"

"Resting in his room," she said. "The girls are tending to him now. He tried to fight them off and they beat him something awful. Doc Ridley says he'll live, but he'll be a long time healing."

Mackey felt the blood begin to rush to his head, the way it always did when anger settled over him. "Was Underhill part of this?"

"No, he wasn't," Katherine said, "and neither was Grant, but the men definitely worked for him. Said they did anyway."

Katherine must have felt a change in his touch, because she pulled away from him and took his face in her hands. "I need you to stop right now, Aaron. I need you to stop being angry and listen to me. I know how you get when you lose your temper, but you can't do that because that's what Grant wants. He's hoping you'll lose your temper and do something foolish. Something he'll be justified to kill you for, and he'll get away with it, too. The people are elated he's running for mayor. Even your father has been giving speeches for him. And he has more than just moral support, Aaron. He has gunmen, too."

Mackey had figured as much. "How many?"

"I've seen him with no fewer than ten at any one time, but I think it might be as many as thirty." She held his face tighter and shook it. "I only told you what happened because those men refused to leave the porch. I don't want you barging into Van Dorn's office and causing trouble. They'll shoot you dead, Aaron. You and Billy if either of you give them the slightest reason."

"They tell you that?"

"They didn't need to tell me," she said. "I've seen it. I know how men like that operate. You can't beat them by fighting them, Aaron. You can only beat them by outthinking them. That means you can't let them goad you into a fight you can't win."

She pulled his face closer to her and looked deeply into his eyes. "I've waited so long for you, Aaron Mackey, I won't lose you to them. Not over this. If they want the town, let them have it. You are more important than their greed and selfishness. Your life is more important than anything, and we can overcome anything as long as you and I are together."

He reached up and gently took her hands from his face, kissing her hands as he did so. "I'm not angry, and I won't do anything stupid, I promise. I've just got to get ready for my meeting with Mr. Van Dorn. Got some news of my own I need to give him."

"But you'll come back to me right after, won't you? I need to see you're still alive, Aaron. Please. I've been through so much already, I can't take the idea of losing you, too."

Seeing such a strong woman be so weak made him pull her close to him. "I'll come back, and I'll be fine. I promise. You won't lose me, and I'll never leave you again. Not now. Not ever. Understand?"

She held him tightly, and he felt her breathing slow as he held her close. She pulled her head away from her chest and said, "Maybe you really should take a bath before you go over there. You do smell kind of harsh."

Chapter 23

After bathing and shaving, Sheriff Aaron Mackey checked in on young Sandborne. One of the women they had rescued from Darabont's clutches, Jessica, he thought was her name, was tending to his wounds. Sandborne had two black eyes, the result of a broken nose and busted lip. He seemed to be hovering in and out of consciousness, so Mackey beckoned Jessica into the hallway.

She closed the door behind her as she stepped outside.

"I didn't want to wake him up," Mackey said. "How is he?"

"He's very bad," she told him. He caught the hint of a Mexican accent as she spoke. "His nose has been broken and his ribs may be broken. We will have to tend to his wounds for a very long time. He sleeps a lot."

"Just keep on taking care of him and let me know when he wakes up. If I'm not here, tell him I was grateful for the way he protected Mrs. Campbell."

"He spoke of you many times." She looked at the floor. "He said he is sorry that he could not do a better job."

"He did the best job he could against over-

286

whelming odds." The words he had just spoken struck him immediately. In some ways, he was like Joshua Sandborne had been right before Grant's men started replacing the sign. Mackey could either fight smart, or fight stupid, as this man had done. Though instead of lying in bed for his mistakes, Mackey had no doubt that Grant or one of his people would put him in his grave.

"Just keep an eye on him for me," Mackey told her, "and thank you for what you're doing for him."

As he walked away, she surprised him by saying, "Will you kill the men who did this?"

The question stopped Mackey dead in his tracks. He turned and answered as honestly as he could. "I hope to. I don't think it'll be today or tomorrow, but soon. I'll do it as soon as I can. You can tell him that. I think he'll understand."

She offered a half-hearted smile as she opened the door to Sandborne's room and quietly shut the door behind her.

Mackey wished he could've had a better answer for her, but it was the only one he had at the moment.

When Mackey stepped downstairs, he found Katherine and Pappy talking in the hotel's front parlor. Pappy was sporting a fashionable new blue suit with thin pinstripes. It was an outfit that was supposed to make him look sophisticated, but the stripes only accentuated his bulk. Not an ounce of it was fat, and all of it was as much muscle as a man his size could carry.

He had become quite a prosperous man since the Dover Station Company had come to town. Since he had hired Brian Mason as an assistant, Pappy's store was the only dry goods merchant in town.

The elder Mackey broke off his conversation with Katherine when he saw his son. "Well, if it isn't the hero of Dover Station himself, all dressed up and ready to make an impression."

"Grant send you over here as a scout?" Mackey asked. "Maybe gauge my mood before I head over there?"

"Haven't scouted for anyone since Sherman, by God," Pappy said. "And that was war. I'd never scout my son for anyone's benefit except his own."

"Or yours, depending on how you look at it." He looked at Katherine and smiled. "I'll be back right after my meeting, I promise."

She began to say something, but Pappy cut her off. "No need to hurry off so soon, boy. I'd like to talk to you for a moment before you go up there to talk with Mr. Van Dorn and Mr. Grant. They're aware of the delay and understand its importance."

Mackey pulled on his hat and kept walking toward the door. "Then you'd better speak your mind while I'm moving, because I've got a couple of things to say to them while I'm at it."

He stepped out onto the boardwalk and replaced his rifle in his saddle scabbard before climbing on top of Adair. That's when he realized there was no other horse at the hitching post. His father had walked all the way from his store to the hotel.

When Mackey eased Adair into the thoroughfare, his father said, "Aren't you going to wait for me?"

"You want to talk, you'll have to do it on foot, Pop. And shame on you for walking where you could've ridden. Never thought my old man would've turned into a city boy in such a short amount of time."

"Insolent bastard," Pappy said as he stepped into the frozen mud of the street. "Making your poor father walk while he's trying to talk some sense into you."

"You've always had plenty of wind for any situation at hand. I can hear you just as well from up here as I can down there or in Katherine's parlor. You've got something to say, might as well say it from there while I make my way up to Van Dorn House."

"You were practically born on horseback," Pappy said, "so I suppose it's only fitting I try to change your life while you're on a horse, too."

Mackey smiled. "That's what Grant tell you to say?"

"It's what I've decided. Grant's got nothing to do with it. I take it you've seen the signs about Grant and Underhill running for mayor and police chief respectively."

"They've been kind of hard to miss."

"I warned you about that when we talked before you left town," Pappy reminded him. "I told you change was coming, and it looks like it's here. That's what I want to talk to you about. I want to talk to you about the future."

"And I'll bet you see men like Grant and Underhill as the future in town, is that it?"

"I see them building on the foundation me and other men who built this place out of the wilderness laid down for them," Pappy said. "I see no good reason to fight them merely out of a contempt for change. And I see no reason why you should fight them, either."

Mackey wanted to tell him about the three men who had died during the train robberies Grant had sponsored, but decided against it. As the biggest gossip in the territory, Pappy read all the papers and already knew about the deaths. Since none of the stories had implicated Grant, he'd never believe the man had anything to do with it. And Mackey was in no mood to take the time to convince his father of anything.

"If you can't beat them, join them," Mackey said. "You're turning over a new leaf, Pop. You never used to be so obliging."

His father walked closer to Adair and whispered up at his son. "Remember that big building going up across the street from the jailhouse? They're calling it the Municipal Building. They're saying it'll be a proper town hall with a records department, a court, and a headquarters for the new police force they're looking to start. No sense in fighting a battle that's already over, boy. A battle from which we can profit."

"You mean you can profit," Mackey said. "Not me."

"That's what I've come to talk to you about. There's no reason why you can't have a piece of this, too. A larger police force means less work for you and Billy. Means there probably won't be a need for a sheriff after next week. Why, I hear Grant and Underhill already have thirty men ready to sign on once the election is over."

"Billy and I were elected, Pop. Same as Grant probably will be if he runs next week. He can't throw us out of office just because he's of a mind to."

"He can and he will," Pappy argued, "and I say good riddance. You two have spent enough of your lives trying to make this place peaceful. You defended us from Darabont. You're a hero. Time to cash in on it and let other people take the risks for a change. That's why I'm asking you and Billy to resign your posts and come work for me. Fifty-fifty, right down the line."

Mackey closed his eyes and let the cold air wash over him to calm him down. He had been offered many a bribe before, but never by his own father. "How can it be fifty-fifty if there's three of us?"

"Well, fifty percent for me, and you and Billy come to your own arrangement. Why, the people will line up to shake the hand of the man who saved Dover Station from the heathen hands of Darabont and his men. I'm already making more money than I can spend as it is. With the two of you there at my side, we could be three times bigger than we already are this time next year."

"You're already bigger due to Mason selling out to you when he joined up with Grant," Mackey said. "Where do you expect this extra growth to come from?"

"From the town, of course. People need things we have. Always will. We're the only store in town, and Mr. Grant gave me his personal assurance that it'll stay that way, too."

"If you can get me to sign on with you, of course," Mackey added.

"He never mentioned that."

"But I'll bet he implied it clear enough," Mackey said. He wanted to give Adair her head, to let her run and take them away from the town. From the shouting and the banging and the sawing that never stopped from sunrise to sunset every single day, including Sunday. Away from the intrigue that had settled over the town. Away from the greed and the dishonesty. Dover Station had never been an Eden, but it had never been like this until the company came to town. Until Van Dorn's incompetence handed the town to Grant.

But Mackey knew he could not ride off or run away. He had no intention of doing it, either. He had too much to stay for right here in town. Too much to fight for.

And three dead men to avenge. Men he had never known, but who deserved justice anyway.

"Mason might've sold out to you, Pop, but I won't. I hate to turn you down, but I've got no choice."

Adair bucked when his father reached up and grabbed her bit, pulling her to a halt. "Damn you, boy, I'm not talking about selling out. I'm talking about cashing in. Life's about choices, and you've got a choice to make now. Your Mr. Rice left Van Dorn in charge of this place when he went back to New York. Van Dorn has Grant running things for him. There's nothing any of us can do about that, and quite frankly, I have no complaints. You're over thirty, son. It's time to play the cards you've got instead of waiting for the hand you want. And you happen to be holding a damned fine hand, if you ask me. Let Underhill and his boys deal with the drunks and the drovers and the bar fights. Let him get shot at and run down bandits. You've done your time and served honorably. Hell, with the reputation you've got after Darabont, you could run for mayor yourself one day soon if you had a mind. After that, maybe even governor."

Pappy surprised Mackey by leaning forward and grabbing his son's hand. Hard. "It's time to do what's right, not what you want. Be smart enough to know when to cash in your winnings, boy. You're an educated man, Aaron. Use it, don't waste it. I'm asking you to enjoy life instead. Mary wouldn't let you do it, but Katherine would."

The mere thought of the wife who had abandoned him made him sit taller in the saddle and glare down at his father. Had Billy been there, he probably would have said Mackey had "lit the West Point candle."

"Let go of my horse, Pop. Let go of her, or I'll put the heel to her sides and drag you through the mud."

Even Brendan Mackey took pause when his son got that look. He let go of the animal. "Aaron, listen to me."

"I have been listening to you all the way since the hotel and all I've gotten for my trouble is annoyance. Mary left because she wanted me to be something I wasn't, just like you want me to be now. I'm still the sheriff of this town, and I've got a duty to uphold. That's exactly what I'm going to do, too, until the law says otherwise. Until then, I've got a meeting to attend. You wouldn't want me to keep your masters waiting, now would you?"

Mackey didn't drive his heels into Adair's sides. He just let up on the bit, and the horse took off on her own steam. She was a natural runner and a sensitive animal, too. She always seemed to know when her rider wanted to go fast, and she ran fast now, up the hill, where he pulled her toward the cold shadow of the Van Dorn House.

Mackey didn't dismount right away. Instead, he took in the view of Dover Station and saw how much it had changed in the past five months since he had been on this spot. It had been just the bare bones of a house then. Now it was a cold monstrosity of gingerbread ornamentation and steep eaves.

But there was no finer view of the town from any other perspective. And as he looked out over the changing landscape, he saw a sight that made him gasp. He looked at Katie's Place, the new Campbell House, and saw Mrs. Katherine Campbell standing in the middle of the thoroughfare in front of her hotel.

It was the first time she had stepped off her own property since Mackey had brought her back.

And despite the great distance between them, he could see her standing alone, shielding her eyes against the sun to see him.

Mackey stood high in the saddle and waved.

His heart warmed when she waved back.

He climbed down from the saddle and tied Adair to the hitching post. Katherine's strength had restored him. And nothing Van Dorn or Grant could do or say could stop him.

Chapter 24

The inside of the Van Dorn House was even colder than Mackey remembered. With every shade pulled down and every drape drawn, the entire house was devoid of any natural light from the outside world. Oil lamps cast flickering shadows along the oak-paneled walls and bookcases of the study. The air was heavy and stale.

If Mackey hadn't known differently, he would have thought the house had been ancient before the town of Dover Station ever existed. In truth, the house was less than six months old. Mackey couldn't understand how such a new building could become so dingy so quickly.

He imagined the solitary nature of the builder and occupant may have had something to do with it.

Since neither Mr. Van Dorn nor Mr. Grant had looked up from their ledger since the butler had shown him into the study, much less offered him a seat, Mackey noticed the bookshelves lining the walls of the study were already filled with tomes whose titles he could not make out due to the lack of light. He was tempted to take a closer look, but refused to give either Van Dorn or Grant the satisfaction of his curiosity.

Instead, he chose to stand quietly beside an uncomfortable chair while the two men huddled over one of the many ledgers piled atop the cluttered desk.

Mackey imagined this scene had been staged for his benefit; the two men who controlled the fate of his town making the sheriff wait as they tried to fit him in to their busy schedule. But Mackey had stood at attention waiting for colonels and generals while lead and arrows flew and men died. Standing in a dank study was nothing in comparison.

The time did give Mackey a chance to finally get his first good look at Silas Van Dorn in months. Mr. Rice's investment partner was thin to the point of being scrawny, with sharp features, and thick spectacles perched on the bridge of his narrow nose. His pale skin seemed to glow in the candlelight.

Upon his first trip to Dover Station six months before, Mr. Rice had mentioned Van Dorn was forty, though he looked even older than Pappy. His stringy gray hair and woolly muttonchops may have been in fashion in New York, but they made him look out of place in Montana.

The ornate wooden desk was a wilderness of books and papers. Mackey couldn't understand how either of them could make sense of such a mess. But he bet James Grant knew where every paper was and the purpose it served, even if

Silas Van Dorn did not. The man from New York did not strike Mackey as the type who troubled himself with such details. If he did, he would not have allowed Grant to assume so much control of his company.

Mackey watched Grant standing behind his employer, pointing down at a column in the ledger. Grant had changed his appearance in the two weeks Mackey was away on Mr. Rice's errand. His dark brown hair was cut closer and his moustache neatly trimmed and waxed to a subtle curl at the ends. His dark suit had been tailored to accentuate his broad shoulders, and his brocade vest gave him a leaner look. He looked more like an executive than the laborer he had been. He looked more like a candidate than a cowhand.

But Mackey noticed the hand he used to point at the numbers was thick and calloused. Grant's hands that had seen years of hard work other than counting money.

Mackey smiled to himself. Grant could spend as much as he wanted on fancy clothes and hair wax, but he would never change what he was. And he knew men like Van Dorn would only let him go for so long before they reminded him of that. He wasn't one of them. He would always be a hired hand, whether it was here as his assistant or in the new Municipal Building as mayor.

He watched Van Dorn and Grant whisper

as they appeared to reach some accord on the figures they were reviewing. Van Dorn closed the thick book and set it aside with the reverence an altar server might have for the Bible. Mr. Grant scooped it up and placed it in the bookshelf to the left of the desk.

Mr. Van Dorn looked at the sheriff over the rim of the spectacles. "Ah, Sheriff McKay. Forgive us for keeping you waiting. My assistant and I were so taken by our business that we have forgotten our manners."

"Last name's Mackey, not McKay."

Van Dorn took the correction well. "Again, I apologize. My East Coast inflections make me pronounce words in a unique way. Well, at least unique in this part of the world. No offense intended." He gestured toward a chair on the other side of the desk. "Do please sit down and make yourself comfortable."

Mackey reluctantly took a seat. The seat was intentionally deep, forcing him to sit tall. He did not like the idea of looking up at Van Dorn. He liked the idea of Grant looking down at him even less.

Grant slid the ledger into the bookshelf and faced Mackey. "Good to see you, Aaron. I understand you had a productive trip. Mr. Van Dorn and I are most anxious to hear about it."

But Mackey wasn't anxious to tell them. "Then I'm sorry to disappoint you. Mr. Rice asked Billy and me to handle a personal matter for him, which we did. I imagine he'll tell you about it personally if he's of a mind to."

Van Dorn cleared his throat, making a weak sound as he did so. "Your loyalty to my partner is unquestionable, sheriff, even admirable. But as it could take some weeks, perhaps as long as a month, for word to reach us from Mr. Rice's offices in New York, and given the fact that your success or failure directly affects his company's investments here in Dover Station, don't you agree that it would be more efficient if you simply told us what transpired?"

"We've read the news accounts of what happened," Grant added, "so we know you killed those murdering bastards who were robbing our trains. Good for you. But we would like to know how it happened directly from you. As you know, I was also a lawman once, so I appreciate how delicate these matters can sometimes be. I assure you nothing you tell us will leave this room. We're particularly curious as to why you were gone for so long."

"Because I met with Mr. Rice personally down in Butte." Mackey reached into his pocket and handed an envelope across the desk to Mr. Van Dorn. "He wanted me to give this to you personally, Mr. Van Dorn."

James Grant took hold of it, but Mackey did not let it go. "He said I was to hand this directly to Mr. Van Dorn and only to Mr. Van Dorn. Not you."

Grant withdrew and Van Dorn took the envelope with great effort. "What does it say?"

"I'm not accustomed to reading other people's mail. He told me to give it to you personally, and that's what I've done."

"Consider your mission a success," Van Dorn said. He then handed the envelope to Grant, who slipped it into the pocket of his jacket. "We'll read it later after you've given us an account of your exploits."

Mackey already knew what the answer would be, but he had to ask anyway. "I'd appreciate it if we could speak privately."

"We are speaking privately," Van Dorn said. "Mr. Grant here is my right hand in all things regarding Dover Station and this company. Anything you say to me, you can say to him."

"He's also running for mayor," Mackey said. "And what I have to say is best kept off the campaign trail."

But Van Dorn laughed it off. "He's running unopposed, sheriff. There won't be much electioneering to be done before the ballots are cast. And after he is elected, the office of mayor is a part-time position, so he will continue to work for me. Why, in his capacity as mayor, he will also be your superior, won't he?"

"For a time," Grant said, then quickly

added, "We're still trying to determine the law enforcement jurisdictions in town."

"Sounds to me like you've already got that worked out," Mackey said. "Got Walter Underhill running as chief of police."

"So you've seen the signs?" Grant said. "I didn't know if you've noticed them since your return."

"Can't spit in town without hitting one," Mackey said. "You made a good choice. Walt's a good man."

"I'm so happy you approve." Van Dorn folded his thin fingers on his desk. "Now, as much as we have enjoyed discussing the state of local politics with you, sheriff, I'll politely ask one more time for an accounting of your activities while you were gone. After all, Mr. Underhill had to serve as the sheriff in your absence, taking him away from duties he might otherwise have been performing for the company. I think that entitles us to an answer to our reasonable question."

Mackey had tried to do this the right way. He had tried to get Van Dorn to speak to him in private. He had lived up to the spirit and the letter of Mr. Rice's request, so all that was left was the truth. Mackey saw no reason to be polite any longer.

He was glad the handle of the Peacemaker was within easy reach across his belly. Grant might not like what he had to say.

"Before I left," Mackey began. "I found out that your stationmaster in Chidester had intentionally misspelled words in telegrams he sent for each train that had been robbed. Each train had something worth stealing, so I knew it wasn't just a coincidence."

"Mr. Agee?" Van Dorn said. "Are you sure? I understand he's been with the railroad for quite some time."

Mackey looked at Grant as he replied. "He was paid fifty dollars a month in gold by a big ugly man with a scar to tip off which trains had loot. Sometimes the trains got robbed, sometimes they didn't. Agee went along with it because the gold was delivered on the first of every month, and the big guy threatened to kill his family if he didn't do it. I had him send out a similar message tipping off the robbers that our train was ripe for a robbery, and the robbers took the bait."

"What happened to them?" Grant said a little too quickly. "I mean, the news accounts said some of the men were killed, but they were rather vague."

"That's because I was vague with the reporters," Mackey said. "I killed four of the six robbers, but kept two alive. That's how I was able to track down the ringleader and the man who was paying them."

"The big man," Van Dorn said. "The one with the scar?"

"His name is Aderson, or at least it was until

Billy Sunday shot him dead. But no, he wasn't the ringleader. A guy by the name of Tommy Macum was. The real question is who was paying him to rob your trains."

Grant lifted his chin and almost kept the tremor out of his voice. "Well, sheriff? Did you find out who it was? The man atop the pyramid?"

"Whoever it was," Mackey began, "knew Tommy Macum, had enough access to gold to make sure everyone was paid their fifty dollars in gold on a regular basis, and had a vested interest in seeing the town's prospects weakened for their own benefit. A gambit that cost three good people their lives."

Grant returned Mackey's glare. "You have a problem answering direct questions, Aaron. Do you know who is behind all of this or don't you?"

"I've gotten sworn statements from the two surviving robbers and from Agee, and I have enough common sense to see where everything points. And it points to you, Grant."

Grant smirked. "Why am I not surprised?"

"Come now, sheriff," Van Dorn gasped. "I enjoy a joke as much as the next man, but this is hardly the time for humor. All of your evidence is purely circumstantial."

"Maybe for a judge," Mackey said, "but not for Mr. Rice. That letter you handed to Grant? That's his termination letter signed and sealed by the man himself."

"Preposterous," Van Dorn said. "James, let me see that letter."

Grant's hand trembled as he reached inside his jacket. Mackey watched the hand, hoping he would come out with something more than just the envelope. Something that would give Mackey all the reason he needed to kill this man, but all he held was the envelope, which he handed to Van Dorn.

The banker opened the letter and quickly read it, before refolding it and placing it back inside the envelope. "This is absurd. He's obviously been influenced by the sheriff's clear bias against you. Don't give it a second thought, James. All of this is built on the rumor and innuendo of train robbers and a hayseed lawman. I'll handle the matter directly with Mr. Rice. You're to continue with your duties as if nothing happened."

"Yes, sir." Grant glared at Mackey. "It will be an honor."

"Excellent." Van Dorn struggled to get to his feet and Grant rushed to help him. For a man of forty, Van Dorn moved like he was eighty. "Now, I am afraid you must excuse me, sheriff, as it is time for me to take a rest. Your weather here in this wilderness seems to be too pure for my diseased city lungs. I'll leave it to James here to show you out."

Mackey remained seated as Van Dorn began coughing. Grant guided him toward the doorway, where the butler took Van Dorn by the arm and guided him upstairs.

Grant quietly closed the door and looked at Mackey. "I apologize for Mr. Van Dorn's early departure. He is a city man, born and raised, and of a different disposition than you and me."

"Meaning he's not a killer?"

A smirk from Grant. "Meaning he prefers remaining indoors with his books and his poems and his ledgers rather than associate with men of our sort, much less our harsh climate."

"I'm not so sure about that," Mackey said. "He seems to enjoy your company just fine."

"I'm an employee, not an associate, Aaron. He pays me to handle the things he either can't do on his own or doesn't want to do. I follow his orders, at least for now. That's part of the reason why I wanted to talk to you today."

That surprised Mackey. "Even after I just handed your boss instructions to fire you?"

Grant winced. "That was certainly an awkward moment. For you, I mean. I'm sure that didn't go quite as you had imagined it would, did it, Aaron?"

"I didn't expect it to go one way or the other, to tell the truth. Though I'll admit I'm sorry that the only thing you pulled out of that pocket just then was an envelope."

"No fear about that." Grant opened his jacket wide. "I'm unarmed. The truly powerful in this world have more effective weapons at their disposal than guns."

"Says the man who's never been shot at."

"Oh, I've been shot at before," Grant said as he took a seat behind Van Dorn's desk. He looked right at home. "In fact, I've been stabbed, kicked, thrown, and just about anything else you could think of. Even got set on fire once by a whore down in Laramie. But that's a story for another day. Those things are in the past. You and I are more interested in discussing the future, aren't we? Or at least we should be."

"Depends on your idea of the future. You've got dreams of running this town from that brand-new Municipal Building you've been working on for yourself and from this . . ." He looked around the shadowy office. "This rabbit warren or whatever the hell it is. Your vision of the future involves you having this town coming and going. My vision of the future is the sight of you in prison for the three people you got killed when you ordered Macum and his men to rob those trains."

"That's a rather bleak vision of the future from my point of view," Grant admitted. "I see things differently, a time where all of us enjoy our lives in peace and comfort."

"Whatever crystal ball you're looking through has a hell of a big crack running through it."

"No crystal balls or tea leaves or Chinese fortunetellers for me, thank you. Why, a blind man could see what's happening here. Why can't you? It astounds me that you don't appreciate all I've done for you lately. Or at least tried to do for you, anyway."

"Then how about you spell it out for me? After all, 'hayseed lawmen' like me are a bit dense about such matters."

"For starters, I've been damned good to your family," Grant said. "I've made your father a wealthy man and intend on making him wealthier still if he'll let me. And I think he will. I've further added to your legend by calling you the Savior of Dover Station. A happy accident, I'll admit, but one that has worked especially well for you." He wagged a finger at the sheriff. "People will be writing books and songs about you one day, and I won't get to see a penny of it."

"Seeing as how you'll be long dead by then, you sure as hell won't."

Grant frowned as if in contemplation. "I also tried to help that widow you're sweet on. Mrs. Campbell. Katherine Campbell has such a nice ring to it, doesn't it? All things lacy and fine. I stopped by to see her several times, as a matter of fact." He raised his face to the ceiling and closed his eyes in memory. "My, she's a handsome woman, Aaron. Refined. Cultured. Nothing at all like the rough-hewn variety we grow out here. Not common like you and me."

"You'll get no argument from me," Mackey

said. "Still can't figure out how she knows which piece of silver to use with each course at dinner. Pretty good judge of character, too. Guess that's why she turned you down flat when you tried to swindle her place out from under her."

"Swindle?" Grant said. "Why, I offered to buy her out at a fair price of her own naming, but she refused to even entertain the notion. She said she had to talk to you first, but you were out of town again on your crusade for Mr. Rice."

"You didn't like that, did you? Guess you're not used to women saying no to you."

"No, I'm simply not used to people being so blind to their own interests." He leaned forward and folded his hands on top of the desk. "You see, I was trying to buy her out to help you."

"And just how would that have helped me?"

"By freeing you up to leave. To take the money I was going to give her and move away from here. Start up a new life somewhere else far away from here."

Mackey was beginning to grow interested. "And just what makes you think I'd ever want to leave my hometown?"

"Because I know you hate me, and if you don't hate me, you certainly think I was involved in those robberies, even though you'll never be able to prove it. Not with Tommy Macum and his wife dead and gone. A man of your high principles would never support me, and I know you'd never work with me. That's why I'm making the decision for you by not giving you any choice in the matter. You see, Aaron, your time here is over. As soon as I'm elected mayor—and, despite your feeble attempt with Van Dorn just now, I *will* be mayor—I won't have any use for you or your colored deputy."

Mackey furrowed his brow. "Billy's black? Shit, Jimmy. He never mentioned it to me. Damn, you know a man for ten years, you think he'd mention something like that. Just when you think you know all there is to know about someone."

Grant laughed. "Your attempt at humor is lost on me, Aaron. You're done in Dover Station. You're just too stupid to know it."

"Flattery is the last resort of the desperate," Mackey observed.

"While stating the truth is a virtue of the wise," Grant said. "After my election, I'll dissolve the sheriff's office, and we'll have a brand-new police force to keep law and order around here."

"Staffed by the gunmen you've been slowly bringing into town for the past month or so," Mackey added. "Too bad Van Dorn never leaves this house. He could see it for himself."

"He sees what he wants to see," Grant said. "And what neither of us want to see is you around here anymore. You've outlived your usefulness. You're part of Dover Station's rich and colorful past. I'm part of its future, and there's no room for you in it."

"That so?"

"It certainly is," Grant went on. "I hear statehood's right around the corner, and this town's in a prime position to be one of the most important cities in the state. Hell, I even plan on changing the name to Dover City once I get people used to the idea."

"Why not Grant City?"

James Grant slowly shook his head. "The more you speak, the more I'm convinced it's time you go off and do something else. I tried my damnedest to give you every reason in the world to leave, but that woman of yours sure is stubborn. Kind of like that horse of yours. What breed is it again? I can't hardly remember."

"Thought an old cowboy like you would be able to retain such knowledge, Jimmy. She's an Arabian."

Grant snapped his fingers. "As dark as she is spirited. Just like that deputy of yours. And your woman."

"Anything you've got to say about Deputy Sunday you can say directly to Deputy Sunday. I wish you would. Don't think you'd like the way it turned out."

"I mean him no ill will. He's a brave man, despite his condition, and I'm sure he'll find his place in this world when he leaves town with you."

"Maybe he'll stay. Run for mayor."

"No, he'll leave when you leave," Grant observed. "I'm sure of it. You have a way of inspiring loyalty in people, Aaron, something I've never been able to do. Not in the way you do it, anyway. I have to charm and cajole people into liking me and, when that fails—as it ultimately does—I have to force their hand. Blackmail usually works best, but it won't work with you. Your life is an open book, so there's nothing I can use to persuade you to leave."

He opened the desk drawer.

Mackey pulled the Peacemaker and aimed it at Grant. "Don't do anything stupid, Jimmy."

The company man raised his left hand and slowly lifted an envelope with his right. "I merely wanted to demonstrate that you weren't the only one who had correspondence today, Aaron." He elbowed the drawer shut. "I'd like to lower my hands now."

Mackey tucked the pistol back into the holster and took the envelope Grant offered him. He opened it up and had to read the paper twice before the words made sense to him.

"That's right, sheriff," Grant said. "I was able to get a territorial judge to grant you a decree of divorce on the grounds of abandonment. As you're the only claiming party and there's no

313

official contest to the contrary, all you need to do is sign that and you'll be free of your ex-wife, Mary. No need to thank me, though. Think of it as thanks to a hero on behalf of a grateful township."

Mackey held the decree in his hand, not quite sure he understood it. Not the document itself, but the reason why Grant had gone through all of the trouble to get it signed. "You really want me gone, don't you?"

Grant spoke without the slightest hesitation. "As soon as possible. And now, all you have to do is sign that document and show it to any judge who'll marry you. I'll even be glad to do the honors myself once I'm elected if it'll get you out of town any faster. Of course, it all hinges on you being able to get Mrs. Campbell over her anxiety, but I'm sure you can manage."

Mackey felt an unsettling stillness come over him. "How'd you find out about that?"

"Come now, Aaron," Grant laughed. "I know Dover's a booming town, but it's still a small town. People talk. They see things. They know she's been addlebrained since Darabont savaged her, and who could blame her? More the credit to you, I say, for being willing to take on a woman with such a mark against her name. Why, bad enough to allow herself to be taken alive by a man like Darabont, but to have been taken by him while working in a house of ill repute? Not too many men would put up with a woman who has so many difficulties, such as they are."

Mackey threw a straight right hand that caught Grant flush on the left cheek, knocking him out of the chair and on to the floor.

By the time the sheriff came around the desk, Grant was still lying on his side without having much luck.

"Katherine was helping a woman give birth when Darabont took her. A woman knocked up by one of the good citizens of this fine town who refused to claim the baby as his own. But you don't need to worry about that, Grant. Katherine's my business. So is Billy, and so is this town. And I'll be goddamned before I let a carpetbagger like you come in and take over."

"No one will stand with you," Grant said. "They'll all turn on you the moment I tell them to. Even your own father will back me."

"I don't care what anyone else does, including Pappy." Mackey put a boot on Grant's back and pinned him to the carpet. "But I do care about the three people you got killed during those train robberies. And all the glad-handing and backslapping in the world isn't going to change that. I plan on putting you in jail the second Mr. Rice gets a judge who'll swear out an order for your arrest. Then I'm going to be there the morning you hang. Until then, I've still got two years left on my term as sheriff. You stay away from me and my family or next time, we won't end our conversation on such good terms. Do you understand?"

Mackey let up just enough weight off Grant's back so he could answer. Grant spat, "You're a dead man, Aaron. You think you'll last two years? You won't last two weeks!"

The sheriff pulled the Peacemaker and pressed the barrel hard against Grant's temple. He knew killing him right here would solve all of his problems. He also knew Grant's death would cause more problems than he could imagine. He had made a deal with Mr. Rice to spare Grant's life. He had to live up to his side of the bargain. He had to give Mr. Rice time to work.

But Grant didn't need to know that. He pressed the barrel harder against Grant's temple. "Tell me you understand what I said."

"I understand, you son of a bitch."

Mackey pressed the barrel harder into his temple.

Grant yelled again, "I said I understand, damn you! What more do you want from me? Blood?"

"Not right now." Mackey stood up and tucked his pistol away. "I'll get that soon enough. Until then, you can run your company and you can run for office and stay the hell away from me. You don't, there'll be trouble."

Mackey stopped when he reached the study door. "Crossing me would be the dumbest thing you'd ever do, Jim, and you're not stupid. You're a smart man. So smart, you knew Mrs. Macum was dead. That's funny, because Billy and I didn't mention that to anyone and we're the only people who knew. How'd you find out?"

By then, Grant had made it up to his hands and knees as he tried to shake the cobwebs from his mind. He acted like he hadn't heard the question, but Mackey knew better.

He decided not to force the issue. But he made a point of slamming the door behind him.

Chapter 25

As he sat in the Rose of Tralee Saloon, one of the newer places in town, Charles Everett Harrington of *The Dover Station Record* sipped his whiskey as he listened to Pappy's third telling of the Siege of Dover Station of the evening.

Harrington had heard his old friend tell the tale no fewer than a hundred times in the six months since the incident, mostly for the benefit of the newcomers to town. He noticed Pappy was drunker than normal on that particular evening, though the newspaperman could not imagine why. The dry-goods business was booming like everything else in town and likely to only improve as the town grew.

Harrington wondered if Pappy had experienced some difficulty with Aaron. His son was usually prickly, even more so after such a long time away from home. One of the few failings the younger Mackey possessed was his ignorance of how easily his mood affected his father. One of the many failings of the elder Mackey was his indestructible visage. It was only when one spent a significant amount of time with him, particularly late at night while sharing a bottle of whiskey in a loud saloon, did one learn how truly sensitive Brendan Mackey could be. He may have won the Congressional Medal of Honor in the War Between the States, but had a soft spot in his warrior heart, particularly where his son was concerned.

Harrington could only guess at the reason for Pappy's excess that evening, but he enjoyed how the liquor had put him in good voice as he brought his triumphant tale of siege and salvation to a rousing close.

"And that's exactly the way it happened, my friends. Eight men rode out and eight men returned with a complete accompaniment of the women stolen by the heathen horde in tow. Darabont suffered savage justice at the hands of the mighty Blackfeet Indians on the very same night as those poor women enjoyed hearth and home, thanks to the bravery of none other than the Savior of Dover Station himself, my son Sheriff Aaron Mackey, and his loyal deputy Billy Sunday. All of this happened one thousand, eight hundred and eighty-eight years after the good Lord above sent His only son to die for our sins."

Pappy raised his glass of whiskey. "So let us make a toast to the tale of the humble home we call Dover Station. Those who believe me can buy me a drink for having the pleasure of saying you met the man who sired such a heroic figure. And those who do not may kiss my royal Irish ass."

Harrington watched everyone in the saloon cheer and thump tables at the conclusion of Pappy's performance. Even the stoic Walter Underhill and his men raised their glasses. Neither Underhill nor his new men were known for their good humor, but it was Harrington's experience that Pappy's stories often brought a grin to even the grimmest countenance.

Most of the men called over the saloon's Young Roses, as the waitresses were called, and flicked coins and tossed greenbacks at them to buy Pappy a drink.

Yet through the shouts for more drinks and more stories, Harrington heard one voice ring out as clear as it was shrill.

"I've got a third option, you donkey bastard. How 'bout you kiss my ass and keep your goddamned mouth shut?"

Most of the men whooped and hollered at the suggestion, including Pappy himself.

Harrington noticed Underhill looking around. The Texan's booming voice cut through the noise. "That better not've been one of mine who said that."

A scrawny, bedraggled man whose prairie hat had seen more than its share of harsh weather got to his feet. Harrington didn't know this man's name for certain, but believed he had heard him called Trammel at some point.

"I ain't one of yours, you rebel bastard. I'm one

of Jim Grant's own men, by God, and I don't take orders from you or any other man walking."

Harrington looked through the crowd and saw Trammel was one of a table of three newcomers he had seen running errands for Grant and Van Dorn over the past month, Trammel and his friends usually bringing people to and from the Van Dorn House at all hours of the night and day.

Underhill reached out for the man without standing up. "Quit your yapping and have a drink. You're sobering everyone up by barking like that."

But Trammel easily avoided Underhill's grasp. "I told you I don't work for you, and you don't get to boss me, neither. I'm not drunk, and I've got a mind to have words with that mouthy foreigner over there whether you like it or not."

Harrington watched Pappy stop in mid-drink, before slowly lowering his glass to the table. The newsman had long known there were few things in this world that could rouse his old friend to anger than referring to him as a foreigner. Although he had spent his tender years in Ireland, like most Irish, he considered himself as American as any native son.

Pappy turned and faced the man. "Well, if it's words you want, I've certainly no shortage of those, as any man here will say." The crowd laughed. Pappy did not. His large fists hung at his sides like an ape. "And if it's a lesson you need, you'll find me a fair teacher."

It was at this point that Harrington noted that young Trammel made the great error of pushing a chair out of his way as he stormed toward Pappy. "I've had just about enough of you and your damned family, grandpa! Pushing people around like they ran this town!"

When he drew close enough, Trammel threw a haymaker at Pappy's chin. It was a blow he easily evaded, despite being forty years older than his assailant. Pappy buried a massive left hand deep in Trammel's stomach before throwing the gasping man back against the bar.

"Knock it off," Pappy warned, "before you get hurt."

Whether it was merely bravado or the fog of war, Harrington could not be certain, but something caused young Trammel to launch himself at Pappy. The storekeeper connected with a powerful right hand to the jaw that rendered Trammel unconscious before he hit the sawdust on the saloon floor.

All but Underhill and Harrington cheered as Pappy stepped over Trammel's body to face the two men at the table. A strand of thick gray hair fell over his eye. "You ladies wish to express an opinion, too, or are you too delicate to fight?"

Harrington ran from the saloon amid the scrape of chairs on wood and shouts of men joining battle. Someone needed to get the sheriff before this spiraled out of control. And Harrington was just the man to do it.

Down at the jailhouse, Mackey drank coffee while Billy asked questions. The sheriff had always admired how his deputy could criticize him without actually doing it.

"You sure hitting Grant was a good idea?"

Mackey flexed his right hand. "Didn't do any harm except to my hand. He was pretty clear he wants us out and his new police force in."

Billy winced at the notion. "Sorry to see Underhill's name on the same sign as Grant's. Just when I was beginning to like him. Can't see him as a police chief, though. That boy couldn't lead a mouse to cheese, much less a police force."

"Walt's always wanted to be a lawman again. I don't blame him for grabbing his chance. He's being used just like Grant is using everyone else."

"Grant's a smart son of a bitch, isn't he?" Billy observed. "Smarter than I thought."

Mackey could not argue with that statement. "The damnable thing is I don't really blame him for what he's doing. He saw a chance to better himself, and he's taking it. I don't like it, but I understand it. Van Dorn's the one I hold responsible. If he'd kept tighter hold of the company's reins like he's supposed to, Grant wouldn't be able to get away with the shit he has."

Billy sipped his coffee. "I checked with Murphy over at the telegraph office." Billy sipped his coffee. "No word from Mr. Rice yet."

"Won't either. It'll be tomorrow at the earliest. Until then, see if you can't find Lagrange. See if he's been able to get a better idea of how many extra guns Grant has hired on since we were gone."

"I did some looking around on my own," Billy said. "I put the number at about fifteen, but that's just those I saw. The real number could be higher than that."

Mackey figured it probably was. "I caught three of his newer boys waiting for me at the hotel when I rode back from the train. Must be new because I never saw them before."

"You punch them in the face, too?"

"Worse," Mackey said. "I made them hand over their guns." He kicked the bottom drawer. "Got them right here. Told them to come ask for them. Haven't seen them yet."

"Probably at the Tin Horn or some other hellhole drinking up the courage to do just that. And they'll be trouble when they do."

"They're trouble drunk or sober," Mackey said. "But if they come here drunk, they can sleep it off back in the cells."

Billy smiled. "Grant won't like that much."

"Then he's going to have to learn how to live with disappointment."

Both men looked up when someone began frantically banging at the jailhouse door. They normally kept it open, but after his fight with Grant earlier that day, he thought it best to keep it locked for the time being.

Mackey pulled his Peacemaker as he called out, "Who is it?"

"It's me, Charlie," Harrington answered through the door. "You've got to come quick. Your father's about to kill someone who was running down you and your pa!"

"Fists or guns?" Mackey asked as he stood up and pulled on his coat. Goddamned Pappy was always getting into something. "This one of Grant's new men?"

"Yes, sir," Harrington said through the door. "Man by the name of Trammel."

Billy stood also, but Mackey held him back. "You'd best sit this one out. Might be a trap to draw both of us out. I'd feel better if you hung back and kept an ear out in case I need you."

"Hell, that saloon is two blocks from here. I can't hear anything from there, especially with the door closed."

Mackey knew that, but couldn't think of another excuse to keep his friend from joining him. "You'll hear it, believe me. If I'm not back in fifteen minutes, come looking for me."

Billy stopped Mackey from opening the door. "I can help you a hell of a lot better from across the street with the Sharps."

Mackey looked at his deputy's hand until he removed it from the door. "Like I said, fifteen minutes."

Billy removed his hand as the sheriff stepped into the cold Montana night.

On the boardwalk, Harrington had to jog to keep up with Mackey's long strides. "How many is he up against?"

"Three," Harrington reported. "He took down one, but the other two were ready to start swinging when I figured it was time to get you."

"You figured right, Charlie. They armed? Drunk?"

"Trammel didn't have a gun when your pa knocked him out. I didn't see if his two friends had guns, but I don't think they did. They seemed to be with Underhill, though they didn't seem to like him very much."

Mackey kept walking. "Can't see Walter having much of a role in this."

"He didn't." The cold air was beginning to hurt Harrington's lungs. "Walt tried to stop Trammel from attacking your old man, but couldn't. Pappy laid him out cold in two punches."

"Pappy's getting old," Mackey said as he turned

the corner toward the saloon. "Not too long ago, he would've knocked out a man with one shot."

"I think he was trying to be nice."

"Good thing I don't have to be."

The wooden planks of the boardwalk in front of the Rose of Tralee Saloon smelled like new lumber. They had not been stained yet and did not sag as much as boardwalks in the older parts of town.

Mackey was greeted by familiar sounds as soon as he opened the smoked-glass door of the saloon. A tinny piano banged out a sing-along he didn't know but others obviously did. Men were gambling and grumbling at all of the tables, the clatter of chips and the thud of glass on wood.

The sheriff began to wonder if Harrington was back on the bottle again. It didn't look like a fight had just taken place or that anyone had been hurt. He knew saloons recovered quickly from brawls, even shootings, but there was something wrong here.

It did not take long for the patrons to recognize him. An uneasy quiet settled over the saloon. The singing and the piano music died away. Sheriff Aaron Mackey was there, and he had not come for a drink.

"I hear someone's been offering to throw me a beating." He looked at all of the faces for his father, but could not see him. "I'm right here if they'd like to try."

The barman held up both hands and got the sheriff's attention. Mackey recognized him as Tom Holden, one of the old bartenders at the Tin Horn. He was a wiry man with quick eyes but short arms when it came to pouring whiskey. "Now, just hold on right there, Aaron. This here place is brand spanking new. Just opened up not a week ago." He pointed at the ornate cabinet and mirror behind the bar. "Got shipped here all the way from San Francisco yesterday. Cost me damned near everything I had. I don't want no trouble in here."

"All the more reason why you should point out the big talkers so I can be on my way."

Mackey turned when he heard a chair scrape across wood and a man twice his size stood up.

Walter Underhill said, "Evening, Aaron. Sorry about the ruckus."

Mackey was in no mood for pleasantries, not even from Underhill. "No reason to apologize. Just point out the coward."

"It was one of my men who got out of line," Underhill said. "I apologized to your father, bought him a drink, and everything's fine now. Pappy went home, and I'll make my boys pay for it. I apologize on behalf of the company and my man. I promise it won't happen again."

"You and my old man had a drink together." He

remembered their first meeting on Front Street six months before, when Pappy told Underhill that Texans were the lowest form of white men alive. "I'd have paid to see that."

"Things change, Aaron. People, too. Your father has. I know I sure as hell have. Maybe you should give it a try."

"I appreciate the sentiment. Now where's the windbag who called me out?"

Underhill shifted a bit so his full bulk blocked Mackey's view. Mackey could feel every eye in the place on him. "Now there's no call for that. I've apologized for my men's behavior and I take full responsibility for everything that happened and what was said. I'd be obliged to you if you could let it go at that."

Another time, Underhill's word would have been enough. But with Grant planning to become mayor and take away his office, Mackey could not appear weak. Not now.

He had no desire to go against Underhill, a man he considered an ally if not a friend. But Underhill was a Grant man now, and he would have to pay the consequences, if it came down to consequences being paid.

"Didn't come here for an apology, Walter. I came here for the coward who threatened my life. I'm not going to ask again."

A young man sprang up from his chair at the same table where Underhill had been sitting. "I ain't no coward, damn you, and I meant every word I done said."

Mackey faced the scrawny man. The right side of his jaw was beginning to swell, no doubt the result of his run-in with Pappy. Given the stubble and mangy hair, he gauged him to be about twenty, but small for his age. "You Trammel?"

"Damned right I am. You took our guns, boy, and I aim to—"

Mackey punched Trammel in the throat. Not hard enough to knock him down, but hard enough to shut him up. He staggered, gasping for breath while Mackey grabbed his collar. "You've done enough talking for one night, boy. You're coming with me."

Underhill moved to block his way. "Just hold on, Aaron. I told you I handled it, and I was sorry. I shouldn't have let the boy run his mouth as long as he did, so if there's anyone to blame here, it's me, not him."

Mackey grabbed Trammel's collar tighter. "He's under arrest for disturbing the peace and being drunk and disorderly. You can bail him out in the morning."

Underhill didn't budge, but lowered his voice as he said, "Aaron, I'm asking as a friend."

Mackey leveled a shot into Trammel's kidney. This time, it was hard enough to make the man crumple, but the sheriff had a good grip on his collar. "Get out of my way, Walt. I won't ask again."

Someone in the saloon said, "You're lucky we ain't armed, sheriff."

Mackey hit Trammel again. This time, his bladder went.

The sheriff looked in the direction from where the voice had come. "Anyone else have something to say? I'm sure Trammel would love to hear it." He made a point of looking each man in the eye. None of them met his glare.

Underhill turned, but did not step out of Mackey's path. "Mr. Grant ain't going to like this, Aaron. He won't like it one damned bit."

"I don't give a shit what Grant likes. He's not mayor yet. And when he is, I doubt I'll give a shit then, either."

Mackey shoved Trammel out the door and onto the boardwalk. He collapsed into the mud of Davis Avenue.

As Mackey followed his prisoner outside, he heard Underhill say, "It didn't have to be like this, Aaron. It could've gone a different way."

Mackey knew Underhill might've been right. But he saw no reason to respond. He grabbed Trammel by the collar and pulled him along back to the jailhouse.

Chapter 26

Mackey threw Trammel in the cell and locked the door. He came back out to the office and dumped the keys on his desk, before closing the heavy wooden shutters across the building's only window.

Billy had just finished giving his Sharps a good cleaning. "You know this is only going to make things worse with Grant, don't you?"

"That son of a bitch in there spoke out against me." Mackey took down the Winchester so he could commence cleaning it. "I can't let that stand. Not now. Not ever. And I don't think it made things with Grant worse because they can't get much worse."

"You punched him in the face and kicked the shit out of one of his men in public, Aaron. Believe me, it can get worse."

Mackey emptied the cartridges from the Winchester, made sure it was unloaded, and began to clean it. He would do the Peacekeeper next. He had a feeling he would need both before long.

"I'm going to need you to go out tonight," Mackey told him. "Find Lagrange. See if he's been able to find out how many gunmen Grant's got."

"Hate to disobey you." Billy reloaded the Sharps. "But there's no way in hell I'm leaving you here alone. I counted fifteen guns in town, and that's only what I saw. Could be twice that many for all I know. What if they decide they don't like the idea of you arresting their friend? After the liquor hits them, they're apt to show up here armed to the teeth. From what you said, Underhill might even be leading them. You had to protect your reputation, and he's got to protect his own." Billy slid the last shell into the Sharps. "Whole thing is just one big mess."

"This has been brewing for six months now." Mackey ran the cleaning rod through the Winchester's barrel. "It was bound to come to a head sometime. With the election coming up, something's got to give."

"And it sure as hell ain't going to be you," Billy mumbled.

A quiet knock came at the door.

Mackey set his rifle aside and pulled the Peacemaker. "Who is it?"

A woman's voice said, "It's Jessica from the hotel. I have some messages for you."

Mackey's breath caught. In all of the commotion, he had never thought of Katherine. He had never thought about how all of this would affect her.

And she was all alone, with no one to protect her from Grant and his men.

Billy brought the Sharps to his shoulder and aimed it at the door, just in case Jessica hadn't come alone. "Come in."

She opened the door and rushed to Mackey, oblivious to the fifty-caliber rifle aimed at her head. Billy shut the door behind her and threw the bolt.

"Sheriff," she said, "I've got notes from Mrs. Campbell and Mr. Lagrange. They both told me it was important for me to get these to you as soon as possible."

She handed him two sealed envelopes. He had no idea which message was from Katherine and which was from Lagrange, so he just took one and opened it.

Fortunately, it was from Katherine, as he would know her handwriting anywhere:

I have seen Grant's men gathering behind the hotel. I counted no fewer than thirty riders on horseback. All of them armed. They liveried their mounts in the Northend Stable before going their separate ways. I have no idea where they went, but they broke up into different groups. Please be careful, my love.

"Katherine counts thirty men," Mackey told Billy. "They've got their horses at the Northend Livery, and they've spread all over town."

"Too quick to be related to that business at the saloon just now."

"Grant probably sent for them after my run-in with him earlier. Guess trying to get the bastard fired didn't sit too well with him."

He opened the second note, this one from Lagrange. His handwriting was difficult to make out, but Mackey made it out clear enough.

Sheriff—

I've discovered that Grant has hired approximately forty gunmen, with the last twenty to have arrived in town over the past week. I make this assumption based on what I have overheard in the various saloons I have visited throughout the day. Many are expected to join the new police department Grant plans to begin when he is elected mayor. I have no idea what he has planned for them in the meantime, but at least thirty have stabled their horses just behind the hotel.

I will remain here and await further instruction.

Robert Lagrange

Billy said, "Judging by the look on your face, I'm assuming that's not good news."

"Lagrange said we're up against about forty

guns altogether." To Jessica, he said, "Do you think Sandborne is ready to ride yet?"

The young woman's mood brightened. "He's gotten a lot better since you've been gone, sheriff. His ribs weren't broken, just bruised. Except for his nose being tender, he's almost to his old self. Yes, I think he can ride."

"Good." He spoke the words as he wrote them down. "I want Sandborne to introduce himself to Mr. Lagrange and ask him to help guard the hotel while he's gone."

"Joshua's not planning on going anywhere."

"Yes, he is." Mackey kept writing. "I need him to ride out to the Boudreaux place and tell the boys I need them urgently. They're to bring all the guns and ammunition they can carry, then come straight here to the jailhouse."

He put the note back in the envelope and handed it to Jessica. "Be careful getting back to the hotel."

But the young woman didn't move. "You didn't write back to Mrs. Campbell. Women get angry when their men don't write back. She's awfully worried about you, sheriff."

Mackey smiled for the first time since he had seen Katherine standing alone on the thoroughfare earlier that day. "Tell her to help Mr. Lagrange. And tell her I love her."

Jessica giggled as she made the envelope disappear in one of the many folds of her dress.

"Women like hearing that. They like it even more when it's sincere. I'll give them both the message."

Billy opened the door for her, then locked it after she left. If he was worried about their prospects, he did a good job of hiding it. "Forty-to-one odds, Aaron."

"We've faced worse."

"We were mounted cavalry then, on the open range. Not defending a fixed position with just two men and a cantankerous prisoner."

"It's not that bad." Mackey went back to cleaning the Winchester. "The odds are twenty-to-one if you count the both of us. Ten-to-one once the Boudreaux brothers get here. Hell, even better if you throw Sandborne and Lagrange in the mix."

"You'll post Sandborne and Lagrange at the hotel to protect Katherine. You'll die before you let anything happen to her."

Mackey withdrew the cleaning rod and looked down the barrel of the Winchester. "We're all going to die, Billy. Just a matter of how and why."

Billy looked back to where the cells were. "That son of a bitch worth it?"

"No, but this town sure as hell is. Besides, if we go down, we're going to take a good number of them with us."

"Alamo's down in Texas," Billy observed.

"I'd like it to stay there, if you know what I mean."

Mackey set to reloading his rifle. "I was thinking more about the Battle of San Jacinto."

Chapter 27

"Aaron," Billy whispered. "Wake up."

Mackey almost jumped out of his chair. He hadn't realized he had fallen asleep. He had drunk so much coffee after the Boudreauxs had arrived in town that he thought he would be awake for a week. He must have been more tired than he thought.

"What's going on?"

"Underhill's out there with about twenty riders. Haven't made a sound since they showed up a couple of minutes ago. They're just standing there facing the jail."

Mackey got up from his chair. "They armed?"

"Rifle butts on their legs," Billy reported. "All of them repeaters, too."

"Underhill, too?"

"Rifle's still holstered and so is his pistol, but there's no question he's in charge."

Mackey didn't doubt it, either. Underhill had been through too much to play second fiddle to any man, unless that man was Grant.

"Where are the brothers?"

"The Boudreauxs slept on the construction site across the street right where you wanted them," Billy said. "I'd be surprised if they didn't have those men under their guns right now."

Mackey would've been surprised, too. "Let's hope it doesn't come to that."

He got up from the chair and pulled on his coat, then took his Winchester from the rack. He tugged his hat on his head.

"Want me out there with you?" Billy asked.

"I'll go out and face them alone. Lock the door behind me and cover me from the window. If I go down, shoot Underhill if he's still standing. The brothers'll do some damage from up top."

"I don't think it'll come to that." Billy unlatched the door. "If they'd come for blood, they would've started shooting by now."

Mackey wasn't so sure, but he was about to find out. "Just lock the door behind me."

Which was exactly what Billy did.

Mackey saw the twenty blank faces on horseback as he stepped out onto the boardwalk. Every one of them had as dead a pair of eyes as the next. He had no idea where Grant had found this bunch, or maybe it had been Underhill's doing, but none of them were amateurs like Trammel. Each man had clean weapons and hard miles behind them. They looked neither scared nor cocky. They looked like men who had been paid to do a job and knew how to do it.

No, these weren't friends of Trammel's. These men were professionals.

Underhill spoke from the lead horse. "Morning, Aaron."

"Walt."

Underhill glanced at the jailhouse window. "Morning, Billy."

"Same to you."

"Got that Sharps aimed in my direction, I suppose?"

"Ready to turn you into dust if you even glance at your pistol, Walter."

Underhill looked at Mackey. "Best thing about Deputy Sunday is his honesty."

"Only thing better than his honesty is his aim."

Underhill looked around. "Guess the Boudreaux boys are around here, too."

"That'd be a good guess," Mackey said. "What brings you and your friends out so early on a beautiful morning?"

"I'm here to pick up Trammel. Here to pay the fine or whatever else I have to do to get him out of there."

Mackey looked at the ten riders on either side of him. "Didn't need to bring so many to bail him out."

"No, and I didn't have to order them to stow their horses at the livery behind Katie's hotel when they rode in yesterday, either. Pretty stupid way to keep a secret from you, isn't it?"

Mackey had wondered about why they'd done that. Now he knew. He wasn't happy about this, either.

Underhill went on. "Mr. Grant wanted a show

of force so you'd see he's got men to back him. Since he pays me, that's what I've done. And show's all it is unless you make it more than that."

Mackey looked over the men again. "This all of them?"

"Nope," Underhill said. "This ain't even half, and don't ask me more because I ain't gonna tell you. All I'll tell you is that it's more. A lot more. Mr. Grant wanted you to get a notion of what you're up against. He says he wants to reason with you before things go further than they already have."

"He said a lot," Mackey noted. "He made you memorize all that before he sent this parade over?"

"Something's easy to remember when you agree with it. Mr. Grant doesn't want trouble, Aaron. Neither do I. And neither do you. Not this kind of trouble. You've made your point and stood your ground. No shame in letting us bail out Trammel legally so I can give that troublesome son of a bitch the proper beating he deserves."

Mackey looked over the riders. "I don't see Trammel's two friends with you."

"Harrah and Clarke are too hotheaded for a difficult parlay like this, especially where their trail buddy is involved. The men I brought with me today are professionals. Trammel, Harrah, and Clarke are a different sort."

Mackey had only known Underhill for about six months, but what he knew of the man, he knew well. He could tell the Texan was sincere, which bothered Mackey. He decided now was the time to ask him a pointed question, in front of all the hired guns he'd brought into town. "Grant tell you about his role in the train robberies?"

Underhill's brow furrowed. "No. Why would he? They were company trains, but happened south of here. They've got nothing to do with Dover Station."

"That's what you think." He let the thought linger long enough, hoping the seed would take root in Underhill's mind. The big man was brave, but a touch slow for a lawman, at least in Mackey's opinion. "If you want Trammel, the fine's fifty dollars. Pay it, and I'll let you inside to collect him. But you and only you, Walt. Anyone else so much as flinches and the ball goes up."

Underhill told his men to stay where they were as he stepped down from the saddle and tied his horse to the hitching post in front of the jailhouse. He remained in the thoroughfare so he and Mackey were at an equal height when he handed him fifty dollars in banknotes. It was a subtle courtesy that Mackey noticed. "Fifty dollars is a mighty steep price for a few minor infractions."

"Caught him loitering in front of the hotel and brandishing a weapon in public before my meeting with Grant yesterday. Fines pile up for a boy like Trammel."

Underhill kept his voice low when he said, "It'd probably be cheaper just to shoot him now and be done with it."

Mackey stepped back and knocked on the jailhouse door. "Open up, Billy. Walt's paid Trammel's fine."

The bolt slid back and the door swung inward as Mackey backed into the jailhouse and beckoned Walter inside.

To his men, Underhill said, "Stay here and don't cause any trouble. We're here to get Trammel and be on our way. Won't be but a minute."

Underhill ducked his head and turned sideways like he always did whenever he entered the jail, though Mackey noted he didn't need to do either. He was a big man, but not nearly big enough where he had trouble fitting through the doorway. He closed the door behind him. Billy bolted it shut.

Mackey sat at his desk as Billy went back to let out Trammel. "Hope your boys out there don't get nervous about your well-being."

Underhill took off his hat. "I doubt it. Each of them thinks they should have the top spot in this organization. Trouble is, none of them are wrong. They're all top hands, Aaron. Smart, levelheaded, and fair. Mr. Grant didn't go hiring any roughnecks when he put together this bunch."

"Except for Trammel, Harrah, and Clarke."

"Something's always bound to crawl beneath the door when you spill sugar on the floor." He looked over at the oven. "Mind if I grab a sip of coffee? Billy always made a fine pot."

"Help yourself."

Underhill tossed his hat on the desk, got himself a mug, and poured some coffee. He drank the brew and closed his eyes. "Damn, I've missed that."

Mackey took the fifty dollars Underhill had paid him and put it in a deposit envelope for the bank. "You were always welcome here, Walter. No need to have been a stranger."

"But there is now," Underhill said. "On account of me working for Mr. Grant."

"I never tell a man how he can make a living as long as it's legal."

Underhill set his coffee down on Mackey's desk. "Why do you have to make everything so damned hard, Aaron? Jim's not the best, but he's not the worst, either. He's got vision for this town and he's put a lot of people to work. Sure, he's a little too slick for my taste, and maybe I don't trust him as much as I should, but none of that makes him a bad man. Why can't you just let him be?"

"Meaning why can't I just let him push me and Billy out of a job?"

"A job you didn't want when you brought them ladies back, as I recall."

Underhill stopped talking when Billy led Trammel out from the cells at the end of his Sharps.

Trammel smiled. "Mr. Underhill. I—"

"One word out of you, and I'll beat you to death right here. Understand?"

Trammel looked like he wanted to say something but thought better of it. He kept his mouth shut but pointed down at Mackey's desk.

The sheriff knew what he was pointing at. He opened up the bottom drawer and pulled out the three gun belts he had taken from Trammel, Harrah, and Clarke on the porch of the hotel.

He slid the pile of leather and steel across the desk to Underhill. "Don't give them to him until you've got him bedded down wherever he lives."

Underhill grabbed the three gun belts. "Those three will have to earn these back." To Trammel, he said, "Get outside. Lippy has your horse. We'll talk later."

Billy unlocked the door to let Trammel out. He left the door open, but stood back, his rifle trained on the doorway.

When Trammel was out of earshot, Mackey said, "Best tell your boss to quit letting his men walk around armed while I'm still sheriff. He can change that next week when he gets elected mayor, but for now, it's the law."

Underhill pulled his hat onto his head. "You never know when to quit pushing, do you, Aaron?

You've always got to give a man that extra shove to remind them you're in charge when no one really doubted it in the first place."

"Never been a fan of ambiguity, Walter." He could see Underhill had no idea what he meant, so he quickly added, "People act better when they know where they stand. And I'd appreciate it if you made a point of letting your boss know Trammel's fine was fifty dollars."

"Why?"

"Just humor me. If I'm wrong, then no harm done. But if I'm right, well, who knows?"

Underhill turned to leave, but stopped before he went outside. "Hope the next time we see each other, it's under better circumstances, Aaron."

"Keep Trammel and his friends in line and there's no reason why that can't be the case."

Underhill shut the door behind him and led his twenty men out of town in the direction of the old JT Ranch.

With the prisoner gone, Billy opened the door to let in some of the brisk Montana air. Mackey was glad he did. The jailhouse got awfully musty whenever they had a prisoner. It was twice as bad when that prisoner hadn't bathed in weeks before his arrest. Trammel had smelled like he hadn't bathed in a year, so the jail was in more dire need of an airing out than usual.

He watched Billy doff his hat and wave the Boudreauxs down from the scaffolding of the

Municipal Building across the street. "Where do you want me to send them next?"

"Send them home," Mackey said as he went to the stove. "If we need them again, we'll send for them. No sense in having them sitting around here doing nothing. They're just as likely to get into a dustup with Trammel and his friends. We've already got enough to worry about without that."

Billy put his hat back on and leaned against the doorway, watching the last of the riders disappear out of view. "You see the way they were mounted? The way they rode?"

"Former cavalrymen most likely," Mackey said as he refilled his mug. "Just like us."

"Men like that don't come cheap," Billy continued. "They didn't look like rank and file, either. Every one of them looked like an officer, maybe sergeant at the lowest."

Mackey put the coffeepot back on the stove. "That was my impression, too."

"They're not stragglers or hotheads like Trammel and his friends. They're like us."

"No, they're not," Mackey said as he sat behind his desk. "They're not the law. We are."

Chapter 28

Although a good portion of the Great Northern Hotel was still under construction, at least the office had been finished. It was here where James Grant liked to hold meetings that were not entirely suitable to be held in the gloomy, rarified confines of Van Dorn House. He used the Great Northern as the place where he met with tradesmen and businessmen looking to buy property or rent space in one of the Dover Station Company's many buildings, both existing and planned.

It was also where he met with the men he thought of as his Roughnecks. He never publicly referred to them as that, of course, not even in his private papers. For Grant believed that to name a thing was to own it, and he had no desire to assert any ownership of such men. They were unlike the former cavalry officers he had hired to work under Walter Underhill's police force. Those men were professionals and came at a heavy price.

On the contrary, his Roughnecks were disposable. He used them to run minor errands for him, along with the occasional intimidation tactics on various people who needed a good scare put into them. Men like Trammel, Harrah, and Clarke served this purpose nicely.

He had sent them to collect Aaron Mackey in the hopes one of them would provoke the sheriff to shoot one of them, perhaps killing all three. The higher the body count, the better it would have been for him. He could claim the sheriff had overreacted and the time had come for him to resign from office immediately.

Heads I win. Tails, you lose.

If they had succeeded in bringing him to Van Dorn House, then Grant would have known Mackey was a defeated man who was willing to be bought out. He did not think this would be the case, and he had been proven to be correct.

Again, heads and tails.

But it was in forcing the three men to disarm without killing them that Aaron Mackey had made his first great tactical error as sheriff, at least since James Grant had come to town. For the way he saw it, men like Trammel and the others could only be pushed so far before their pride complicated matters. A slight of pride could only be reckoned by the spillage of blood.

Forcing Trammel, Harrah, and Clarke to disarm in public had deeply scarred the pride of the three Roughnecks sitting before him now.

Grant sat back in his chair and looked at each of the men in turn. Trammel still had not taken a bath, despite his specific orders for the man to do so. But, Grant knew some time with hot water and soap would make the smallish man look less grimy and, therefore, less dangerous. His eyes held the sunken, defeated look of a man who had spent too many nights drowning too many disappointments in a bottle of whiskey. But drink had not yet diminished his skill with a gun or his capacity to terrify people, which was why Grant had hired him in the first place.

Harrah was the middle of the trio in every way. He was taller than Trammel, but shorter and not as broad as Clarke. He was a saddle tramp who had grown tired of life on the trail and was looking for a place to settle permanently, or at least until he got the urge to move on again. Grant knew the type. They dreamed of a home and family, but bristled when the prospects of such grew too real. He was good with a gun and a horse and would serve Grant's purposes well.

Clarke was the giant of the group. Larger than his two companions in every way, Clarke was also the quietest member of the group. Some could be forgiven for thinking the big man was stupid, but James Grant was not some people. He knew Clarke may not say much, but when he did, his words deserved attention. He was as quiet as Trammel was mouthy. He was also a much more dangerous man than Trammel could ever hope to be. He preferred a clean-shaven look and took a bath twice a week. He was far from a dandy, but he appeared more professional than the other two.

How the three of them had come to ride together was beyond Grant's comprehension or interest. He knew they were loyal to each other and decided to use that loyalty to his own advantage now that Aaron Mackey had become a dire threat to his plans.

Grant looked at Trammel as he spoke. "I hear you had a run-in with the sheriff and his father. In fact, three separate incidents in one day. I think that's some kind of record."

Trammel launched into an impassioned defense. "I understand you might be cross with me about that, Mr. Grant, but there weren't no drinking involved in any of them cases. You can ask the boys here. Nary a drop was present at either time. I promised you I wouldn't drink while working for you, and I haven't touched a drop in three weeks."

Grant suspected that was true. He'd hung around the various saloons with Harrah and Clarke, but none of the barkeeps or ladies could remember seeing him drink. "I'm more concerned about the run-ins than your sobriety, Trammel. The sheriff seems to get the best of you every time you see him. Even his father, for God's sake. An old man."

It was Harrah's turn to speak up. "He might have gray hair, Mr. Grant, but Pappy ain't no old man. That bastard hits harder than some bulls I've come across. And after the way his son shamed us in public, Trammel here had a right to mouth off at the father like he did. Charging the old boy might've been wrong, but Trammel paid the price for it, so the scales are balanced on that score."

Grant raised an eyebrow. "But you still think Mackey is in your debt?"

"Don't know about no debt," Trammel said, "but he's got an ass-whooping coming. You don't take a man's firearms from him out here and you sure as hell don't do it in public without expecting some kind of reaction. And I tend to give it to him. The three of us together."

Grant looked at Clarke, who up until this point had remained silent. "He speak for you, too?"

"I don't like going against any sheriff, especially Mackey. But there's a way of disarming a man that doesn't show him up in front of the town. If we let him get away with that, then we're no good to you. We like working for you, Mr. Grant, but we've got names of our own to protect. They might not be much, but they're ours and they're the only names we've got. So, yeah, Trammel speaks for all of us, but we don't want to cause any trouble for you and your election."

Trammel spat a long stream of tobacco juice into the cuspidor beside Grant's desk. "Can't imagine you want the sheriff to be showing you up like that, neither. Especially since you've got

Mr. Underhill lined up to be top law dog in this here kennel."

Had this expression of loyalty come from other men, Grant might have been touched by the sentiment. But given the source, he knew their desire for vengeance was born more from their pride than out of any allegiance to him.

It was just as well. He doubted any of the three would still be alive by this time tomorrow anyway.

He removed a small sack from the top drawer of his desk. It hit with the muted rattle that could only be one thing. Gold. One thousand dollars in gold coins.

All three of the men looked at the bag as if it was the angel of the Lord.

Grant smiled. Gold had that effect on people. People like these men he was about to hire to kill Sheriff Aaron Mackey and Deputy Billy Sunday.

"Now that I've got your attention," Grant said, "here's what I want you to do. But you're going to have to do it quickly before we lose the element of surprise."

Katherine was already dressed by the time Mackey woke up the following morning. He watched her as she sat in front of the mirror, pinning her hair into a high bun, the way she always wore it when she worked downstairs.

He loved watching her at moments like this and

appreciated how she could make even the most normal tasks like fixing one's hair look graceful.

"Good morning," she said without stopping. "You're awake."

Mackey smiled. "Guess you saw me looking at you in the mirror."

"No. Just knew you were awake." She looked back at him as she continued to pin her hair. "You slept very peacefully last night. I can't remember the last time that happened. What changed?"

Mackey had no reason for it, except pure exhaustion. He had the benefit of an empty jailhouse and confirmation of Grant's intentions against him. All of the same troubles that faced him yesterday had only compounded in the hours since, yet he felt relieved. Maybe he was finally beginning to lose his mind after all. "Must be the company I keep. Speaking of which, I need Sandborne to stay close for the time being. At least until after Grant is elected."

She finished with her hair and turned to face him completely. "Why?"

"Things between me and Grant have gotten even worse." He decided to leave it at that. The more he told her, the more it would upset her, and he didn't want that to happen. "I'd just feel better if Sandborne was around. I'll have a talk to him before I leave if you have no objections."

"Do you really think things are that bad?"

"I think they could get that way," Mackey said.

"Grant knows I'm on to him, and he's not happy about it. I've only got one weakness, and I'm looking at her. I wouldn't put it past him to use you against me."

"Between Sandborne and Mr. Lagrange, I'd say I'm in the best of care." She smiled. "Bet you didn't think I knew about Mr. Robert Lagrange of New York, but I did. He took me into his confidence after he saw I had given Jessica that note to deliver to you. He's a brave man. Capable, too."

"Expensive," Mackey said. "I'm glad Mr. Rice is footing the bill, otherwise we couldn't afford him."

She came to him, sitting on the edge of the bed as she embraced him.

The warmth of her spread throughout his body. He heard himself say, "I saw what you did yesterday. Stepping off the porch like that. Can't tell you how much that meant to me, especially before meeting Grant like that."

"That's why I did it," she said, holding him tighter. "I thought if you saw I was strong enough to face my fears, you'd be strong enough to hold onto your temper."

He closed his eyes as he allowed himself to enjoy the feeling of her being so close. He didn't have the heart to tell her that he'd been driven to punching the son of a bitch in the face. "I just need you to be careful. And I need you to be on the lookout for something that could be delivered to me here on the post."

She gently pulled away from him. "What kind of something? A package?"

"A box, as I understand it." He ran his hand across her cheek. God, how she glowed in the morning light. "If it comes, I need you to send someone for me right away. If I'm not there, then get Billy and give it to him."

"Is it something important?" she asked. "Something that will make the difference in this fight between you and Grant?"

He did not want to lie to her. He could not lie to her, even if he wanted to. "I hope so. I really do."

She surprised him by kissing him long and tenderly, driving all thoughts of Grant and deliveries from his mind.

Joshua Sandborne told him Lagrange was having breakfast alone in the hotel dining room. He found the Pinkerton reading the morning edition of *The Dover Station Record* with a pot of coffee at his elbow.

Mackey groaned when he saw the headline.

HOW MUCH LAW DOES
DOVER STATION NEED?

Lagrange looked up from the paper. "Makes for some pretty interesting reading, sheriff." He closed the paper and offered it to him. "Want to read it for yourself?"

By then, Jessica had placed an extra mug of coffee on Lagrange's table and brought out a fresh pot.

Mackey took a seat. "How about you save me some time by giving me the short version?"

"You already knew Underhill was running for police chief," Lagrange said, "which, in my experience, is usually an appointed position, but what do I know? The article talks about how Grant is strongly considering getting rid of your office immediately after his election as mayor. Said it would be fiscally irresponsible for the town to have two law enforcement entities when one would do."

Mackey drank his coffee. "Article mention anyone else supporting the idea?"

"Former mayor Brian Mason thinks it's an idea whose time has come. Mr. Van Dorn is also quoted as saying the idea of a sheriff is a quaint notion the town has outgrown thanks to his company's investment."

Neither of those were surprises. Mason had always hated him, and Van Dorn's quote had probably come straight from Grant. "Anyone oppose it?"

"Mayor Ridley thinks the idea of a municipal building and a police department are gross wastes of money that could be spent better elsewhere and sees no reason for a change at this time. Looks like you've got at least one friend in town, Aaron."

Mackey had grown tired of thinking about his future, much less discussing it. "What about you, Robert? You still my friend?"

"Until I get a telegram from New York telling me to board the next train home, I am." He set his mug down. "You got my message about the riders last night?"

"The same ones who paid me a visit yesterday. They came to collect that loudmouth Trammel."

"From what I heard by nosing around yesterday," Lagrange said, "that boy is a handful. He's a big talker and can mostly back it up. The other two who ride with him are called Harrah and Clarke. They're even more capable than Trammel, but not by much."

"You look worried," Mackey said. "Don't think I can handle them?"

"I'm not worried," Lagrange said. "I get paid whether you live or die, though I've grown fond enough of you to hope you live."

Mackey held up a hand. "Don't start getting all weepy on me. I left my handkerchief in my other coat."

Lagrange grinned. "I think you can take them if it comes down to that, but if they come for you, it won't be head-on. It'll be at an angle, and it'll be fast and mean. You need to be ready for that when it happens because, after you disarmed them yesterday, it's going to happen."

"Agreed." Mackey finished his coffee and stood up. "I'd appreciate it if you could stay around here. Mind the place and Mrs. Campbell for me. Help Sandborne if he needs it."

"That boy will need it," Lagrange said. "He'll be good someday, but that day is not today. But now that I have an idea of how many people Grant has, I'll hang around until you tell me otherwise."

"I'd appreciate it."

Mackey had begun to walk away when Lagrange said, "Sheriff, do you think Grant will go against you? With guns, I mean. He's got nothing to gain by it at this point, does he?"

"He knows I've got evidence that ties him to the robberies. And, by now, he probably already knows you're working with me. All the more reason for you to stay close."

"Take care of yourself, sheriff." He tapped the *Record*. "I'd hate to have to read about you in tomorrow's edition."

Chapter 29

Mackey walked out the back door toward the livery where he'd boarded Adair for the night. The groomsman knew enough to keep out of Adair's way. Just feed her and give her water and leave her alone. It was a lesson he had learned through bitter experience. His hand bore the scar as a reminder that she was particular about who touched her.

Mackey gave her black coat a good brushing before he secured the saddle on her. He could not explain the connection he had with this animal. In the cavalry, he had lost count of the number of mounts he had used, but the Arabian had always been different. More spirited, faster, braver than any other mount he had ever known. He placed his Winchester in the scabbard and led her out into the daylight. It was late morning by then and his brief sleep with Katherine had made him feel as though he had slept for a week.

He stepped in the stirrup and swung himself up into the saddle. He never minded walking, but there was no other feeling in the world quite like being on horseback. The world looked different and everything felt different.

You heard things, too.

Like the unmistakable cocking of a rifle.

Adair must have heard it, too, because Mackey's heels had only glanced the horse's flanks before she took off at a dead run.

A rifle shot echoed, but the bullet had gone wide of its mark as Mackey and Adair raced west out of town. Another blast echoed and another miss.

The sheriff had no idea who was shooting at him and did not bother trying to find out. Trying to hit anything from a galloping horse was pointless, and a stray bullet from either side could kill someone in town. Best to get clear of town and find out who was trying to kill him later on.

Mackey looked back when he cleared the last building and saw three men chasing him on horseback. He couldn't see who they were, but could tell they had their faces covered, looking just like Tom Macum and his men had when they robbed those trains.

Mackey guided Adair to the right and up the trail that led into the rocky outcropping that surrounded the town. He brought her around a large boulder just off the trail and quickly dismounted. He pulled the Winchester from the scabbard and slapped Adair in the rump to send her on her way.

But Adair skittered only a few steps away before calmly walking off at her own pace. She had never been one to shy away from gunfire.

Mackey crouched behind the boulder and

waited for the riders to come barreling past in pursuit.

But after several seconds, the sheriff had not heard any riders or shooting. Most horses weren't like Adair. They bucked around gunfire or at least made a fuss. Mackey should have heard something by now, even if the men had been smart enough to dismount and approach on foot.

All he heard was the cold Montana wind blowing in his ears.

He set his rifle leaning against the boulder and drew his Peacemaker as he slowly crept around to get a better look at the trail. He stole a quick glance before pulling back, expecting a bullet to ricochet off the rocks.

But no shot came.

He looked again and saw no sign of the gunmen. He chanced a look out into the trail and saw only one set of prints in the soft dirt.

Adair's.

He heard the booms of rifle fire coming from the town and knew what had happened. The men had not been trying to kill him after all. They had simply tried to run him off while they attacked elsewhere in town.

He scrambled back to pick up his rifle and climbed back on Adair.

The fight was not on the hillside surrounding the town but within the town itself.

• • •

Lagrange hit the floor as soon as the bullet struck the coffeepot, causing it to explode.

He rolled as he fell, knowing the shot had come from somewhere behind him, through the same door Mackey had just used a few moments before.

He drew his revolver as he rolled and came up on one knee, aiming in the direction of where the shots came from. He saw a man by the door with a rifle, sweeping the room, looking for something to shoot at. Why he hadn't seen Lagrange yet, the Pinkerton man did not know nor did he wait to find out. He fired once, ricocheting off the rifle instead of hitting the man holding it. But the impact raised the man's arms, exposing his chest. Lagrange fired twice more, hitting him in the chest both times.

He heard more gunfire, screams, and a shattering of glass coming from the front of the hotel and ran in that direction. He ran through the lobby and into the gaming room next to the hotel's front parlor. Another man with a kerchief pulled up over his face was leveling round after round into the gambling hall. Gamblers had overturned tables, others crouched beneath them, as bullets bit into the wood.

Lagrange drew down on the gunman, only to see the man jerk to the left from the impact of a bullet to the side. The man turned and began to raise the rifle in the direction from where he had been shot when Lagrange fired twice more, striking the man in the shoulder and back.

The man dropped his rifle as he fell to his knees.

Then Lagrange saw young Sandborne run toward the fallen man, place the barrel of his revolver against the man's temple and squeeze the trigger, killing the man for good.

Lagrange raised his hands and yelled, "It's me, Joshua. Don't shoot."

Fortunately, the young man recognized him and lowered his weapons. "You get any?"

"One out back where I was having coffee. Any more out there than him?"

"Nope. Saw three more riding down Front Street when this bastard burst in here and started shooting. He winged Jessica, but I think she'll be okay."

Then he remembered. "Mrs. Campbell! Have you seen her?"

"No, I haven't."

But Lagrange was already on his way to find her.

Despite having been in love with two military men in her life, Mrs. Katherine had never taken enough of an interest in weapons to consider herself proficient. She knew how to handle a gun, of course, but she was by no means a sharpshooter.

But as she tracked the three riders shooting their way up Front Street from the open window of a vacant guest room, she hoped the Winchester was as good a weapon as Aaron claimed it was.

She had grabbed the weapon as soon as she heard the gunfire when Aaron left. She ran upstairs, rifle in hand, and watched the three riders chase her beloved from town, only to turn back when they lost him among the rocky outcroppings surrounding the town.

Now, she looked down the length of the rifle at the men who had shot at her hotel and tried to kill the man she loved. She drew a bead on the central rider and squeezed the trigger.

The rifle bucked more than she had anticipated. Her weight had been off and the recoil knocked her back, making a second shot impossible.

Her arm was too weak to hold the rifle any longer, but she saw the results of her shot. Unfortunately, she missed the rider, but hit the horse. The man had been thrown headlong into the thoroughfare as three more riders fell in with the remaining two. None of them looked back at their fallen friend, who by then had gotten to his feet and ran behind his friends on foot.

The workers on the scaffolding of the new Municipal Building across from the jailhouse scrambled inside as they saw the five gunmen heading their way.

"Mrs. Campbell!"

She turned and saw the Pinkerton man, Robert Lagrange, standing in the doorway. "Are you okay?"

"I'm fine, but I only hit the bastard's horse, not the bastard himself."

Lagrange rushed to her side and helped her to her feet, mindful that she was favoring her right shoulder. "You did fine, ma'am." He looked out the window. The five riders continued up Front Street toward the jailhouse. The man whose horse had been shot menaced people on the boardwalk as they dodged away from him. "The rest is out of our hands."

Katherine knew Aaron had been safe, but he would not be safe for long.

He would rush toward the gunfire. He always did.

Chapter 30

Billy Sunday had grabbed his rifle when he had heard the first gunshot on Front Street.

He was about to open the door when the first rounds began slamming into the thick wood of the jailhouse door. He was not worried about any bullets getting through. The ironwood door was over six inches thick. Nothing short of a cannon would make a dent in the damned thing. The walls were a foot thick and made of stone and plaster. Nothing was coming through the walls, either.

Billy was not worried about anything getting in. He was worried about who was on the other side of the door and about how long they would stay there shooting at him. He wondered where Aaron might be and if he had already been hurt.

He did not know much and would not know much more unless he got out there to see for himself. And with them shooting at him, there was not much he could do. Or could he?

An idea came to him as round after round kept slamming into the hardwood.

On the other side of the door, Trammel paused to reload his six-shooter as the other men poured lead into the jailhouse. He couldn't see much with all of the gun smoke, but he knew some of the bullets had to be getting through. The old building looked like a good wind might bring it down.

One of the boys cut loose with a shotgun and struck the door.

Trammel quit reloading when he heard the men cheer as the jailhouse door finally swung inside. It was too dark inside to see anything, but he knew no one could have lived through that barrage.

Trammel closed the cylinder and cheered. Mackey had been run off and now his colored deputy was dead. "We done it, boys. We finally cracked that son of a bitch!"

The gunmen were still cheering when a fifty-caliber round from Billy's Sharps turned Trammel's head into powder. His body twitched in the saddle as the panicked horse ran into the others in terror.

Before any of the men could regain their composure, another blast from the jailhouse hit another rider in the side, punching him out of the saddle and into the rider next to him.

The three remaining men fought to get their mounts under control as they tried to escape the carnage.

Harrah was the farthest away and spurred his horse as he broke free and headed in the opposite direction.

The gunman on foot leapt onto the jailhouse

boardwalk and approached the open door in a crouch, his six-shooter in his hand. The Sharps boomed again from the darkness, sending a third horse bucking as its rider screamed. The last horseman wheeled his mount around and got the hell out of there.

The remaining gunman kept moving toward the open door, pistol ready to shoot the bastard who had killed his friends. The man who had taken Trammel's head off.

He was about to fire through the doorway when he was thrown against the wall not once, not twice, but three times. It was not until he fell backward and saw the blood on the jailhouse wall—his blood—did he realize he had not been pushed. He had been shot.

As he lay on his back, he looked up at the sky and saw a man on a black horse speeding by.

He wondered if that was the man who had killed him.

It was the last thought he had before he died.

Mackey caught up to the rider who had cut right, riding back toward the old JT Ranch. He brought Adair to a halt, leveled the Peacemaker at the fleeing rider, and fired. The bullet caught the man in the center of the back. He slumped forward as the horse continued at a full gallop. The motion of the animal dropped the rider from the saddle within a few strides.

Mackey brought Adair around to chase the last rider who'd set out for the hills. He was a good distance away, too far for his Winchester and way too far for his Peacemaker.

He was glad to see Billy appear at the end of Front Street, aiming the Sharps at the fleeing man.

"You think you can get him?" Mackey called out to him.

Billy Sunday grew very still, then squeezed the trigger. The great rifle boomed, and when the gun smoke cleared, Mackey watched a horse, unencumbered by a rider digging spurs into its sides, running off into the distance.

Billy lowered his rifle and looked up at Mackey. "What do you think?"

Mackey flinched when another gunshot came from behind him.

The man he had shot in the back was on the ground just off the trail. He had raised his pistol and fired at them, but missed. The effort appeared to have taken all of his remaining strength, for he lay on the frozen ground panting.

Billy approached cautiously with the Sharps at his shoulder, ready to fire again if necessary.

Mackey brought Adair around and trotted toward the dying man. "Do that again and we'll bring you to the doctor. You can die easy out here or in a couple of weeks after more pain than you can imagine."

The dying man let his pistol drop above his head and pulled his mask down from his face. Mackey recognized this man as one of Trammel's friends. "You're Clarke."

The man coughed and a trickle of blood ran down his cheek. "What difference does that make now?"

"Not much," Mackey admitted. "Neither does the name of the man who paid you to attack us. Tell me and I end this quick."

Clarke lolled his head on the frozen ground. "I'm dead anyway."

"Don't be so hasty," Billy said. "Bullet struck you in the back, went out through the left. Not bleeding as much as you would if the bullet hit your gut." He lowered his rifle and looked up at Mackey. "I can save this man, sheriff, if you want me to."

"Good idea. Let's fetch a wagon for him and run him over to Doc Ridley. He's Hell-and-Jesus with a scalpel. He'll fix this man right up."

"No!" Clarke yelled out. "It was Grant, you bastard. It was Grant who paid us to shoot up the place. The hotel, the jailhouse, and once you were dead, anything else we wanted. Didn't say nothing about that jail being a fortress, though."

Mackey pulled his Peacemaker and held it so Clarke could see it. "How many of you were there? Tell me and this ends here and now."

"Seven of us," Clarke said. "We could only

372

get seven. We wanted more, but no one would go against you after the way you stood up to Underhill and his Regulars."

A cold wind blew down the trail, but Adair held her ground.

Clarke looked up at Mackey. "Damn you, sheriff. I made good on my end. Now it's time for you to do the same!"

The sheriff looked at his deputy. "You think he's telling the truth?"

Billy lowered his rifle. "I believe he is."

So did Mackey. Which was why he raised his Peacemaker and made good on his promise to a dead man.

Chapter 31

A harsh wind blew through the cemetery as Mackey and Billy watched the gravediggers lower the last of the dead men into the ground. The preacher, an old drunk with a Bible who claimed to be a cleric, muttered his final verse from the good book before turning to the sheriff for payment. Mackey gave him the five dollars they had agreed upon and watched him toddle down the hill toward The Tin Horn Saloon.

"Jesus." Billy pulled his hat back on. "That's the first man I've seen go into that place in months."

Mackey pulled on his hat, too. "It's warm and it's close. Besides, he lived up to his end of the bargain."

The two lawmen stood beneath a dirty gray sky as the ditchdiggers began to fill in the graves.

"Glad the company's paying for laborers to do the planting," Billy said. "I'd hate to have to break up frozen ground like this."

"We've done our share of digging," Mackey said. "Company's been good for something, I guess."

Billy gestured back toward town. "Looks like these boys aren't the only company men come to pay us a visit."

Mackey turned to see Walter Underhill riding up toward them on the big brown sorrel of his. The former marshal's blond mane had streaks of gray in it, same as his moustache.

Mackey thought he looked leaner now than he'd been when he'd first ridden into town looking for the Boudreaux boys more than six months before. He looked rested, less haunted than he had back then. He looked like a man at peace with himself and who liked what he saw in the mirror.

Mackey was glad for his friend, and he had come to view Underhill as a friend, but knew, someday soon, he just might have to kill this man who now worked for James Grant.

Underhill tied off his horse at the iron gate surrounding the cemetery and walked up the hill. "Mackey's Garden's more crowded than I remember."

Mackey ignored the comment. "Figured you'd be inside getting yelled at by Grant for losing control of your men."

"I didn't lose control of anyone," Underhill said. "These boys took it upon themselves to attack you on their own. Paid the appropriate price for it, too, I reckon."

Billy said, "You come up to congratulate us on beating your boss's plan to kill us or you want a shovel? Maybe help with the graves, seeing as how they were your men and all."

"Nope," Underhill said. "Came up here to give you boys fair warning about what'll happen tomorrow following the election."

Mackey kept looking at the gravediggers work. "All right."

"You've probably figured out by now that Grant's going to impose some big changes the second after he takes the oath of office. He's going to announce them before the town in his speech tomorrow."

"Let me guess," Mackey said. "You're going to be the chief of the new police department, and he's abolishing the sheriff's office."

Underhill held on to his hat in the face of a hard wind. "Didn't know he told you already."

"He didn't," Mackey said. "Just know how the man thinks. Your boss isn't exactly subtle." He looked down at the fresh graves. "As you can see for yourself."

If Underhill disagreed, he held it well. "That means my office will be the new law in this part of the territory. It's not the way I want it, but I don't have any say in the matter."

"Sure you do," Billy said. "You could refuse the order. You're elected, same as him."

"I thought about that," Underhill admitted. "Thought about it long and hard. He'd just put one of the others in my place, someone who might not be as partial to you boys as I am."

Mackey held no ill will toward Underhill. He

had enjoyed being a lawman in Texas and would be a fool to give up the chance to be one again. That did not make him like it any better. "Just say what you came to say, Walt, and be done with it."

Underhill obliged. "That means anything you do against Mr. Grant or Mr. Van Dorn or any other citizen of this town will be against the law. That'll put you boys up against me and my men. I'd like to avoid that if possible."

"We'd hate for you to be in that position," Mackey said. "We sincerely would."

Underhill looked down at the graves. "I know I'd have to kill you, and I wouldn't want to do that."

"I know you'd try," Mackey said. "And we both know you'd fail."

"One-on-one, maybe. But it wouldn't be one-on-one. It'd be against me and thirty men I have with me. You boys are hard cases, but I've never seen two men take on thirty."

Billy grinned. "That's because you've never seen us work."

Mackey didn't like the direction the conversation was taking. "A lot can change in a day, Walter. Let's see what tomorrow brings."

Underhill toed the ground with his boot. "Damned bad time of year to be up here under any circumstances. Hope it's the last time we have to be here. Any of us."

The Texan pulled off his glove and held out his

hand to Mackey. "I wish you luck, Aaron. I wish you peace."

Mackey looked up at the big man before shaking his hand. "Likewise, Walt."

Then Underhill held out his hand to Billy. "You too proud to shake my hand?"

Billy hesitated, then shook it. "Be seeing you, Walt. Get a good night's rest. Tomorrow's a big day."

Underhill put his glove back on and strode back down the hill at his own pace. Mackey and Billy turned to watch him leave.

Billy hawked and spat. "Be a shame to have to kill that man."

"Yeah. It would."

"But we'd kill him if we had to, wouldn't we?"

A gust of wind buffeted them, but Mackey did not move. "Yeah. We would."

Both men looked up the road when they heard the jangling of a team of horses pulling a stagecoach headed into town.

"Wonder if that's the stage we've been waiting on," Billy asked.

Mackey pulled up the collar on his coat. It seemed to be getting colder by the minute. "Let's hope so. For all our sakes."

Chapter 32

Sheriff Aaron Mackey and Deputy Billy Sunday watched their office slowly die from the jailhouse porch. Mackey rocked slowly back and forth in his rocking chair, despite the cold.

Billy stood against the post, his back to the wind, building a cigarette. "Despite the cold, at least we have company."

Mackey paid no mind to the four riflemen in front of the Municipal Building across the street. The wooden scaffolding had been removed to reveal a red brick and iron structure that bore more than a passing resemblance to a castle. Marble stairs led up to a wide entrance where two large copper lamps stood guard on either side.

The four riflemen had not taken their eyes off the sheriff and his deputy since they'd come out of the jailhouse half an hour before. "At least we're well protected."

Billy had glanced at them once when they had first walked out onto the boardwalk. That had been enough. "Man on the far right's got a lazy eye. Probably can't shoot for shit."

Mackey had noticed that, too. "Let's hope we don't have to find out. Besides, the show's about to start."

The company's carpenters had erected a

makeshift podium in the middle of Front Street, just outside the Tin Horn Saloon. Most of the town had braved the cold wind to see the future of their town being born before their very eyes.

Another canvass banner buffeted against the wind above the podium, declaring:

Congratulations, MAYOR GRANT! *Congratulations,* COMM. UNDERHILL! CONGRATULATIONS, DOVER STATION!

James Grant took the podium to thunderous applause. Men threw their hats into the air and ladies cheered. The future was at hand.

Mackey pulled up his collar against the cold air. "You ready to be unemployed?"

"Already unpinned my star to throw at the son of a bitch when he comes to collect them."

Mackey looked at the spectacle unfolding up the street. Grant motioning for the crowd to be quiet even while he soaked in the applause. "Got the sign ready?"

Billy nodded. "Whenever you are."

Mackey stood up and went inside. "Best pull it out now while we can. I've got a feeling we'll be needing it sooner rather than later."

Together, they dragged the wooden sign wrapped in canvas onto the boardwalk and resumed their spots just as Mayor James Grant began his speech.

"Today is a grand day in the history of Dover Station!" He was wearing a heavy coat with a fur collar, a sash across his chest with "Our Mayor" embroidered upon it and a brand-new silk top hat all the way from San Francisco atop his head. "I am humbled to have been formally sworn in as your mayor."

Another round of cheers and hat tossing followed, but Grant continued. "I know many of you remember the way things used to be. The way Dover once was. The crime. The hardship. The dismay of frontier life. But I am fortunate to only know this town as a place that has stared adversity in the face and refused to look away. A town that is finally coming into its own and embraces the future with open arms. Your faith in me is proof of that belief, and I assure you that your faith is well placed, for I believe the future of this town is brighter than any city on either coast. Why, given our current rate of growth, I see no reason why we can't become as big as Detroit one day or perhaps even Chicago."

Another round of thunderous applause brought another spit from Billy. "Anybody bother telling that son of a bitch both of those cities are on the water?"

Mackey smiled. "What is it that Harrington

always says? Never let the truth get in the way of a good story."

"But I am not blind to some of the troubles we have faced, even since I began working for the Dover Station Company. Like all of you, I have seen what can happen when we allow lawlessness to creep into a place. The slum of Tent City and the crime it has bred. The inability of an overworked and understaffed sheriff's office too small to handle the challenges of a small town on the rise. We admire Sheriff Mackey and Deputy Sunday for their valiant defense of the town when duty called and we will forever be in their debt. But we cannot afford to allow gratitude to take the place of efficiency."

A grumbling went through the crowd as Grant continued. "You've all seen what I'm talking about. The vile Marxist influence that was allowed to breed unchecked and corrupt our workers. The massacre of the Bollard twins and the attempt on the life of Mr. Ross by the coward Eddows were merely symptoms of the lawlessness that has taken our town by the throat. When I saw how powerless the sheriff was to prevent crime in our fair town, I knew I had to act. Not just as an executive of the Dover Station Company, but also as a servant to the people that made this endeavor so successful. We can no longer tolerate the wanton violence we have seen in our streets the last few days where marauding gunmen felt they could attack our people without consequence."

Mackey heard his father's voice cut him off. "The bastards paid for it, didn't they?"

Many in the crowd agreed as Grant recovered quickly. "But I dream of a town where such men would not dare set foot in Dover Station, much less assault our hardworking citizenry. That is why, as my first act as mayor, I am abolishing the office of the sheriff and replacing it with an organization far better suited to address the challenges of a growing town. Today, you elected Walter Underhill as your police commissioner. As of today, he will be in charge of a police force of thirty trained and well-armed men prepared to enforce the laws of our fair town. Our new Municipal Building will be completely finished in a couple of months and will stand as a beacon of justice that will be the envy of the territory."

More grumbling rose from the crowd as Brian Mason handed a book up to Grant, who placed it at the podium. "I am signing the law abolishing the office of the sheriff before all of you now and hope you will join me in thanking Sheriff Mackey and his people for their years of service to Dover Station."

He produced a pen from a shelf in the podium and promptly signed the book, before handing it back to Mason and continuing with his speech.

Billy spat into the street. "Guess that makes it official."

Mackey eyed the riflemen across the street. Now there were ten of them. All in brown dusters and brown hats. All sporting brand-new Winchesters, too. "Yeah, I suppose it does."

When Mayor Grant was done, he ended his speech with a flourish and held both hands up to the crowd. He was met with cheers, though decidedly fewer than when he had first taken the podium.

Mason brought over a horse, a speckled gray, and Grant moved into the saddle without stepping down from the podium.

He brought his mount around and slowly trotted down Front Street. Underhill and twenty riders fell in behind him, leading a grand procession toward the Municipal Building and, Mackey wagered, to formally evict them from the premises.

The sheriff remained seated and his deputy remained against the post as Grant brought his horse to a dead stop in front of the jail. Underhill and the twenty riders fell in at a straight line behind him.

Grant looked like he was about to float right out of the saddle. "Good, you're both here."

Mackey kept rocking. "Morning, Jimmy. Hell of a speech."

"Since you heard it, it saves me the time of explaining it to you. Your services are no longer required, Mr. Mackey. Yours, either, Mr. Sunday. So I demand that you hand over your stars and promptly get the hell off town property." He brought his mount forward and held out a gloved hand. "I want you to hand them to me right now."

The twenty riders tensed as Mackey stopped rocking and slowly stood. The sound of ten Winchesters levering rounds into their chambers echoed across Front Street from the Municipal Building.

Billy eased off the post and placed his star in Grant's hand.

Mackey did the same.

Grant looked down at the symbols of authority and dumped them over his shoulder into the mud of the thoroughfare. "It didn't have to end this way, Aaron. We could have reached an accord, you and me. We could have found a way to end this honorably, but you forced my hand. You bucked me at every turn, and now you'll pay the price for it. You've lost again, just like you always do. Now, get the hell out of here before I have you shot for trespassing, you son of a bitch."

Mackey and Billy looked at each other. Then, Mackey lowered himself back into the rocking chair. Billy went back to leaning against the post, smoking his cigarette.

Grant grinned. "Defiant to the last. Good. I was hoping you'd play it this way. Gives me the satisfaction of ending it once and for all."

He looked to his left. "Commissioner Underhill. Have your men present arms."

Underhill wheeled his sorrel past Grant. "Damn it, Aaron. I warned you about this."

Grant went scarlet. "You have your orders, Underhill. Tell your men to present arms or I'll do it for you."

Mackey kept rocking. "Don't worry about it, Walt. His order isn't legal anyway."

"Not legal?" Grant's eyes bulged. "Not legal? Are you out of your mind? You saw me abolish this office. Of course, my order is legal."

"It'd be legal if we were trespassing," Billy said. "Except we're not. You are."

Grant began to laugh. Eventually, the twenty men behind him began to laugh as well.

But Underhill didn't laugh. He didn't even move. "What do you mean?"

"What I mean," Mackey said, "is that all of you boys are trespassing. But I'm inclined to let it go, given that today is a special day and all."

Mackey slowly pulled aside the lapel of his coat to reveal a silver star. It read: UNITED STATES MARSHAL.

Grant stopped laughing.

Mackey nodded toward Billy. "He's got one, too, only his says 'Deputy U.S. Marshal.' "

Billy moved his lapel, showing his star, and winked at Grant.

The mayor and his horse stepped back like he'd been slapped. "Impossible!"

"Came in on the coach yesterday afternoon." Mackey re-pinned the star onto his lapel. "Brand new, too. Guess I've got you to thank for it. All that talking you did about me being the Hero of Adobe Flats and the Savior of Dover Station impressed the hell out of some folks in Washington. Guess it gave them the idea that they needed to have a better federal presence in this part of the world, what with statehood coming and all. Like you said, mayor, Dover Station's a town on the rise."

Billy pulled the tarp off the sign. It read:

U.S. MARSHAL DISTRICT OFFICE
MONTANA TERRITORY

Grant gripped the reins tightly. "Rice did this, didn't he?"

"He spoke to some people," Mackey admitted, "but the decision came from Washington."

He pitched forward in the rocker and stood up. The twenty riders behind Grant moved their mounts backward.

Mackey looked at Underhill. "Commissioner, I'd like a word in private with the mayor here. I'd appreciate it if you and your men could go about your duties. I'm sure you have plenty to do."

Underhill turned to his men. "Let's get these mounts situated in the livery and get to work. We've got a town to protect now. Move out."

The twenty riders filed to their right and rode in a single file at a lope. The ten riflemen in front of the Municipal Building remained where they were. Underhill said, "If you boys don't have anything to do, I'll find you something."

One by one, they lowered their Winchesters and went back into the Municipal Building.

Underhill faced Grant and touched the brim of his hat. "Mayor Grant." Then he looked at Mackey. "Marshal. Deputy." He wheeled his big sorrel around and rode off behind his men.

Billy took his cue and moved inside the jail.

Mackey stood facing Grant. Only a few feet separated them. He could feel the heat of Grant's hate despite the cold air.

Mackey enjoyed the moment. "Now, before you say anything, you'd best remember that it's illegal to threaten a federal officer."

"That star," Grant spat. "That sign? They don't mean a damned thing. This doesn't end anything, you hear?"

"No, it doesn't. In fact, it's just the beginning, because I'm not done with you yet. I'm here to stay, and I've got the full weight of the federal government and your boss's boss behind me. I know you stirred up trouble in this town. I know you were the one behind those robberies. I know you got three good people killed, and I know you tried to kill me."

Grant leaned forward in the saddle. "Prove it, you bastard."

"Can't yet, but this star gives me all the time I need. I'm not going anywhere, Grant, and neither are you. I'm going to sit right here in this office and wait for you to make a mistake, because you will. Your type always does. And when you do, I'm going to lock you in that cell until they hang you."

Mackey knew Grant would have gone for his gun if he'd had one. But as he was unarmed, his only weapon was his mouth. "Good luck on your appointment, marshal. You're going to need it."

He violently jerked the reins and heeled his horse down Front Street, riding as fast as he could away from the jailhouse and from Mackey.

Mackey smiled as he watched him leave.

He walked back into the jailhouse and Billy handed him a mug of coffee. "You know, he'll probably turn this around in his favor. Take credit for the marshal service putting an office right here in Dover Station."

"I wouldn't put it past him. That's his way."

"Just like staying put is ours."

Mackey clinked mugs with his deputy. "Damned right."

ABOUT THE AUTHOR

Terrence McCauley is an award-winning writer of crime fiction and thrillers. Terrence has had short stories featured in *Thuglit*, *Spintetingler Magazine*, *Shotgun Honey*, *Big Pulp*, and other publications. He is a member of the New York City chapter of the Mystery Writers of America, the International Thriller Writers, and the International Crime Writers Association. A proud native of the Bronx, New York, he is currently writing his next work of fiction. Find him on Twitter or Facebook or visit www.terrencepmccauley.com.

Center Point Large Print
600 Brooks Road / PO Box 1
Thorndike, ME 04986-0001 USA

(207) 568-3717

US & Canada:
1 800 929-9108
www.centerpointlargeprint.com